DRUNK SLUTTY ELF
and
ZOMBIES

Funny Fantasy and Science Fiction

By

D. G. Valdron

FOSSIL COVE PRESS

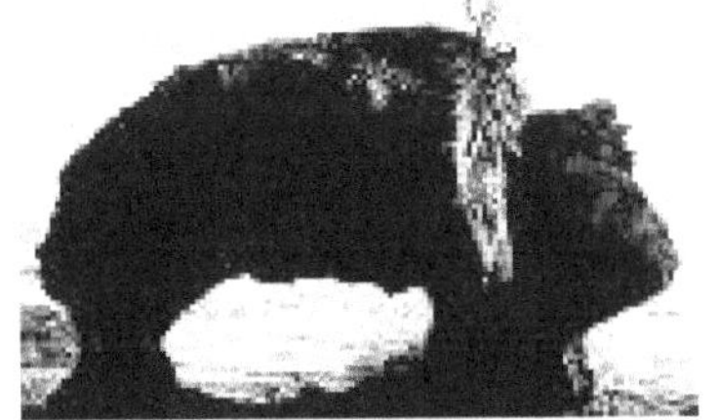

Winnipeg, Manitoba

DRUNK SLUTTY ELF AND ZOMBIES

Fossil Cove Publishing, 1301 - 90 Garry Street, Wpg, Man, Can, R3C 4J4

EBook - ISBN: 978-1-990860-45-4
PrintBook - ISBN: 978-1-990860-89-8 (Ingram Spark)

Cover Art by Jimi Bautista
Copy Editor Paul Carpentier

Published by D.G. Valdron, Fossil Cove Publishing,

Text set in Garamond

DRUNK SLUTTY ELF
and ZOMBIES
Table of Contents

Drunk Slutty Elf and...Zombies!

Two boys sat on a ledge, off the roof of the Royal Apothecary building overlooking the public square. Its elaborate and colourful ledges and balustrades made it easy to climb the four stories, and from its top, you could just see over the city walls, and the hundreds of tiny plumes of smoke waiting outside.

They were watching the screaming man fly through the air, climbing high as his arc cleared the walls, before beginning his inevitable and inevitably fatal descent.

"Lookit the way he waves his arms and legs," the skinny older boy with a gap in his front teeth, laughed. They watched the man tumble end over end, his shrieking rising and falling as he twisted through the air.

Down below on the public square, a few people glanced up, marked the trajectory, concluded that the man wouldn't land anywhere near them, and simply returned to their business. A flying man, after all, was only of concern to the rat-farmers.

"I think he's going to come down near your Ma's place?" the other boy said, he was dark skinned and solidly built. "We should go and see. He might have some money on him, or jewelry."

"Nah," the skinny boy said. "That's stories. They picks em clean before they put them in the catapults."

"You never know! I heard tell of a woman they threw, she was already dead and starting to go, and when she hit, her body exploded and parts went everywhere!"

"Gosh, I wish we'd seen that."

"Yes, and one of her hands ended up in Maid Barley's soup, and it was full of rings. Gold rings, with Jewels. She wasn't wanting for suitors after that. And it improved the soup."

The skinny boy giggled.

"That is until they all turned from eating it and became shambling undead preying upon the living."

The dark boy curled his fingers into claws and moaned gutturally, pulling the slack face of a recent corpse.

"What happened?"

"Oh them rat farmers got em all of course," the dark boy said dismissively.

"What about the gold rings?" the skinny boy insisted. "I bet someone made out, before the sickness took him over."

"I'll just bet! And then there was that live fella, they flung on us. They thought they'd picked him clean, but it turns out he'd hidden his money pouch up his behind. There was a fortune up there. My sister told me all about it. That's why, when you search a dead body, you always need to look up the bum, just in case."

"Your sister is pretty smart."

"Yeah, she'll probably never end up married."

Another screaming man soared through the air, following after the first one. Perhaps he'd done all his screaming when they'd been wedging him into the catapult. The man had apparently run out of breath or something. He'd curled into a ball, to the boy's displeasure.

"Oh that's' no fun," the first boy called out, "give us a show."

But if the man heard, he gave no sign. Instead, he hit a rooftop, bounced off in a clatter of broken shingles, ended up on a lower adjacent rooftop, and then rolled into an alley. The boys assessed the performance critically.

"Seen better."

"Yeah, he just mucked it up towards the end. I like a good screamer. If they're not going to scream, they might as well be throwing dead bodies again."

"I didn't mind the dead bodies," the old boy said reflectively. "Remember when they started out, hurtling cows and horses and things. Some of those were pretty good."

"And fireballs! I loved the fireballs! They were pretty!" the younger boy chimed in. "And all the stones. Good for building. Too bad they run out."

"The horses and cows were best. Good eating then. Now, all we do is eat rats."

"But I like rats," the younger boy commented. "So many great ways to cook them. I like rat better than vegetables…"

"That's true," the older boy conceded.

"And the rat farmers wouldn't have nearly enough rats, if the invaders weren't always throwing the bodies at us."

Momentarily, the boys glanced out beyond the walls of the city. They could just make out the far fringes of the invading host, and of course, the innumerable cook fires that signalled the presence of a besieging army, a forest of tents or banners that stretched out to the horizon. Sometimes, if the winds were just right, and you were up on a rooftop, the breeze would carry the faintest waft of non-rat cuisine.

They stared out over the city walls hopefully, but no more bodies came flying over.

"You think they're done for the day?"

"I dunno," the dark boy scuffed some of the rooftop shingles with his foot, knocking one loose. They watched its clattering skitter as it disappeared off the rooftop into the alleyway below. Diffidently, the skinny boy wandered over to the edge of the roof and looked down.

"Hey look!" he called excitedly. "There's a shambler down there."

"What's it doing?"

"Oh nothing, just wandering around. I think it got trapped in the alley. They're not very smart."

The dark boy carefully picked his way to the edge of the roof, the hints of tantalising cooking from the fires beyond the walls all but forgotten. He looked down. There was indeed an undead corpse stumbling along forlornly.

"Pretty raggedy looking," the dark boy opined. "I bet even the rat farmers wouldn't want this one."

As they watched, a courier trotted through the alley, rudely shoving the animated corpse out of his way. The thing stumbled into a wall and bounced off, but by the time it got turned around, the courier was long gone.

The skinny boy fumbled with his trousers.

"I bet we can hit it."

"From this distance?" the dark boy exclaimed. "No way!"

But he too was fumbling with his trousers. Soon two golden streams were falling on the revenant with uncanny accuracy.

It was the one hundredth and eighty first day of the siege of Ayan-Athor by the forces of Hurndall the Impaler.

* * *

One year before the siege of Ayan-Athor.

The ship tumbled end over end as it slid down the dimensional well. Internal gravity generators compensated, but could only do so much as the crew members were flung this way and that, some of them reduced to smears on bulkheads. But the crew was well trained; they ignored the bodies of their broken comrades and struggled to regain control of their stricken ship.

It was hopeless. Probability had ruptured. The engines, now badly out of synch, were shrieking, going on and off line. Dimensional fracture lines were spreading everywhere, force lattices were unravelling. One of the travellers looked up to see its companion unspool like threads of spaghetti. It took only an instant to register the sight, and then went back to its mission, not even looking up as a fragment of bulkhead twisted, fractured and a metal shard torn from the hull cut it in half.

The ship was irretrievably wounded, out of control and barely holding together as it punched through one dimensional plane after another, spiralling towards certain doom.

But even so, the designers of the ship had been thoroughly cunning. They had anticipated such disasters, and so the fractures and unravellings, the eruptions of dimensional scarring, travelled down pre-directed pathways.

The ship would come apart, yes. But its scattered components could be reassembled.

The last survivor was not aware of its status, methodically working to restore power couplings that were now incandescent junk. Abruptly, it stopped. Its large gray head lifted, the black almond eyes did not blink, as new contingencies were downloaded into its cognitive matrix. It did not question the new imperatives, nor did it spare even a moment on the implications – that the rest of the crew was dead, the ship was lost. It simply accepted its new mission, abandoned its station and its tools, and proceeded to the escape module.

Up in the sky, the Citizens of Ayan-Athor looked up in wonder, as a staggering, flaming saucer appeared tumbling over the horizon, leaving a hole in the sky that quickly closed. They watched, astonished as the wounded craft passed overhead.

A thousand feet above the city, one of the quantum stabilizers blew, showering the city with hundreds of pieces of largely inert, but rather pretty to look at, nanotech shielding components. The shockwave knocked citizens off their feet and tumbled a large section of wall.

Then it was gone, briefly catapulted up into a higher dimension before finally coming apart to spread its components across a continent.

The citizens of Ayan-Athor knew none of that. Climbing to their feet, they dusted themselves off. Whatever it had been, was gone. They had a siege coming up, they got to work rebuilding their wall, now studded with shimmering, mostly harmless, bits of nanomatter.

But there was something more: In the great Courtyard, sitting in a small crater, surrounded by the victims of the impact, was a small golden box with rounded edges, glowing softly. On one side of the box, could be seen an instrument panel with indecipherable writing. Below the panel, a small hatch with an oddly crude latch. Along one edge of the box was a hairline crack from which a luminous liquid light leached.

As the crowd gathered, awed by its radiance, one of the dead sat up and scratched its head. The throng gasped.

Halfway across the world, the last survivor exited its escape pod with a limited suite of tools, only to encounter a group of curious, well-armed humans. As it contemplated the immense task of finding and reassembling the components of its ship, it remembered the primary mission. At least it would be able to collect samples.

It picked up its probe.

* * *

One hundredth and eighty-second day of the siege of Ayan-Athor by the forces of Hurndall the Impaler.

Salvra was still drunk, which made her cheerfully argumentative.

"I'll have you know," she was telling some angry Guards, "I am a 19th level thief, exiled Princess, three quarter elf, and four fifths human, with a dollop of Orc, and I am not publicly intoxicated."

"What's a dollop? Percentage-wise?" one of the Guards demanded.

Scabrous the Malevolent, dark Necromancer, stared pointedly at a squirrel molesting a pigeon on the ledge of a nearby building, and tried not to look like he was with her. Salvra grabbed him by his bony shoulder, and shook him violently, twisting him about so that he was between her and the two burly, rather angry looking Guards.

"Explain it to them," she whispered loudly in his ear, followed by, "while you do, I'll make my getaway. The ignorant brutes will never notice I'm gone."

"We're standing right here," the first Guard said.

"They're simple lummoxes; you'll have no trouble fooling them. Just tell them a story about your Aunt," she whispered even more loudly. A passing scrubwoman glanced over. "Otherwise, just pummel them. They're undoubtedly weaklings and cowards."

Scabrous shivered. Salvra's whisper was so intense, she was literally spitting drunkenly in his ear, and the saliva was pooling out, and trickling down his neck, under his collar.

"We can hear you," the second Guard told her, glowering down at both of them. "Very clearly."

Scabrous whimpered

"So can I," the scrubwoman offered. "What's this about his aunt?"

"Ah," Salvra crowed, "that's a tale for the ages. Let my friend, Scabrous the storyteller, regale you, while I take care of matters… while completely sober."

She turned to whisper again in his ear, even as the wizard cringed away. He'd never imagined a human being could contain that much saliva.

"Just go ahead and pummel them. They're probably so drunk they won't even remember in the morning."

"You're drunk," Scabrous hissed through clenched teeth.

"Oh yeah, I am," she admitted. "They're just stupid."

She shoved him forward, and he stumbled, bounced into an unmoving chest plate, and then stumbled back.

"Avast Craven landlubbers, you face Scabrous the Nologalabal!" she declared.

"Malevolent," he corrected automatically, sounding far more confident than he was.

"Malebolababal," he heard her voice, the sound of it rapidly receding..

"That's not even a word," one of the Guards said, their attention fully on him.

"Malevolent," he squeaked. "Scabrous the Malevolent, Necromancer at large."

From far far distant, he thought he heard a faint call "muddegump."

The two men, filthy, faces blackened with smoke from the many fires around the city, each one a hulking brute, towering over the evil wizard, glared down at him. Scabrous reviewed his preferred options, most of which involved running away, or running away screaming. His own running away, and his screaming.

When he'd begun necromantic studies, he had been assured it would be the other way around. Lots of other people, screaming and running away from him. His teachers had been rhapsodic about it. It was the whole point of necromancy, your victims fleeing in terror of your unholy magics. That had been the whole selling point of becoming a Necromancer.

It hadn't turned out that way.

Throwing himself at their feet and begging piteously was also looking good.

"Well," he said hopefully. He tried a cheerful smile. A smile that he thought was winning and radiant, but more or less came across as 'please don't beat me up too badly.' "Funny thing, I don't think I've ever seen her sober."

"Scabrous," the Guard said suspiciously. "That's a girl's name, isn't it?"

"Not necessarily. It's kind of a gender neutral sort of name," the wizard said.

"My Aunt is named Scabrous," the Guard glowered. "Are you saying my aunt is gender neutral?"

The dark Necromancer thought hard.

"No?"

"I dated a girl named Scabrous," the other Guard said dangerously. "Do you think she was gender neutral? What would that make me, dating gender neutral persons?"

"Enlightened?" Scabrous suggested. He realized it was exactly the wrong thing to say at the exact moment that he was seized by a hand that wrapped completely around his neck. He whimpered.

"Actually," Scabrous choked out, "my father always wanted a girl, and it was the year the plague came round, and Scabrous was a very popular name, Scabby, Scabuleta, Scabbish, Scabert..." he realized he was babbling, but he couldn't help himself. "It was kind of in fashion, also Pustulencai, Pustula, Open Lesions... although that was kind of high class, out on the plains a lot of the long riders named their children Running Sores..."

He couldn't breathe. Desperately, his fingers worked a magical cantrip to break the grip. He stepped back, panting. He reviewed his options again. Running? No. Crying? No. Begging? No.

"Enough of this," he snarled, which would have been convincing, but for the wet smear running down one ear and spreading over his collar and shoulder, and the tears in his eyes, and the snot beginning to stream from his nose, and the obvious terror in his expression. Had he peed himself? He checked. Not yet, but he was sure that was coming.

"I am a terrible Necromancer, so beware my wrath!" he squeaked.

"And you're bragging about it?"

"What?"

"You just said you were a terrible Necromancer," the Guard pointed out, "as in not good at it. Maybe you should apply yourself. I mean, clearly, you dress the part. Or you're trying to. But have some self-respect. Work at it. I'm sure you can become a mediocre Necromancer. Maybe... passable?"

Was the Guard making fun of him? Was that a good thing? Friendly japing, camaraderie, a shared joke that they could have between them. Or was this the sense of humour that involved pulling the limbs off of small animals?

"That's not what I meant," Scabrous began cautiously.

"You're not a Necromancer?" the Guard who had seized him said. His fingertips were smoking, he waved them vaguely, but otherwise it didn't seem to bother him.

"I am!"

"We're not sure we believe you," the other Guard said.

"One, you have some muscle tone. Two, you lack unnatural pallor."

"I've been outdoors a lot," Scabrous said apologetically.

"Three, you are completely free of blisters, burns, boils, blemishes, bites, wounds, suppurating ulcers and other assorted bodily injuries or lesions which come from trafficking in the dark arts."

"That's a common misunderstanding," Scabrous tried to explain, "it's not the dark arts, it's just that traditionally, we fill our homes with various poisons and innumerable traps to deter intruders and…"

Forgetting and stumbling into their own death traps was actually the leading cause of mortality among Necromancers actually, but suddenly, it didn't seem all that relevant to the conversation, so he let his voice trail off. The dubious wisdom of turning one's home into a nightmarish circus of hidden lethal tortures waiting to snare the unwary and bring death to any unguarded moment made picking up the mail or going to the bathroom an often fatal adventure, and any number of injuries and poisonings a daily occurrence, but that could wait for another day.

"In any event," the other Guard said, "we are shielded from most magic arts, so unless you are fifteenth level or greater…"

Scabrous wasn't.

"Then I'm afraid it will not go well for you. Now, about your friend?"

"She's not my friend," Scabrous said quickly, as he backed up. He felt a pang of guilt. "Well, she is my friend. At least, I'm her friend. She doesn't even like me all that much."

The Guard on the left seized his arm. He could feel the bones bending, preparing to snap.

"Whatever she stole," he cried out. "We'll give it back! I'll make sure of it!"

The Guard with smoking fingers grabbed his other arm, pulling hard.

"Hah," the first Guard said, "she couldn't steal a nap, and her fractions make no sense."

Which, if Scabrous had been in mind of it, would have agreed. He'd once added up all the fractions of her claimed ancestry and found thirteen fifths scattered variably among six races. She had enough ancestry for three people.

"It's about the fungus outbreak in the Barracks," the Guard said dangerously. "We've had to do a lot of explaining, to our wives, our girlfriends…"

"Mothers, Sisters…"

Scabrous brow wrinkled at that, but he wisely kept his mouth shut this time.

"The Prostitutes Guild, the Chamber of Commerce."

"Laundry. The Washerwomen were very upset, they charge extra to remove fungus stains and it's blowing a hole in our budget."

"We're very upset. We need you to give her a message. Perhaps you should write it down, so you don't forget?"

"I'd be happy to!"

"Except," one of the Guards said thoughtfully, "how could you write anything down if you don't have arms?"

The other Guard nodded slowly, as if this was indeed a conundrum.

Scabrous said the only thing he could think of, which turned out to be a small strangled "Eep."

"You'll just have to memorise it. Think of this as incentive," the first Guard said amiably.

The pressure on his arms increased, he could feel the bones being pulled out of their sockets, the pressure increasing, the moment of snapping and breaking approaching rapidly…

Then, suddenly, their grip loosened. Scabrous pulled away and stepped back. The Guards didn't move, their expressions didn't change. Their muscled bulged, as if staining tautly. They looked, for all the world, like two squat children about to pull the wings off a fly. He waved a hand in front of their faces. Nothing. He plucked a mirror from a pocket and held it up to their faces. No breath misted.

"What are you doing?" an alien voice sounded in his head.

Scabrous turned around. It was just the Gray alien of course. It's huge bulbous head, black almond eyes, and slender, diminutive, childlike body was unadorned with clothes of any kind. Salvra stood beside it, grinning and swaying.

"Magic?" Scabrous asked.

"Variable stasis field," the voice in his head answered. He had no idea what that meant but he nodded wisely anyway.

"You have no idea what that means," the voice in his head said.

"Something nautical," Salvra commented cheerfully.

"I am not a sailor," the voice in his head said, for what seemed like the infiniteth time.

"Yo ho ho," Salvra said cheerfully, "Arr matey! Pocket of Rum! Jizm the Mizzen mast. I know all the sailor talk."

Once again, for the infiniteth time, he felt the voice in his head give up.

"Hey," Salvra said, "since you've got a valuable cereal peal, can I pick their pockets?"

Scabrous sighed.

"I really wish you would put some clothes on," he told the Gray being.

"I'm not ashamed of my body," the voice in his mind said, the Gray alien shook its head slightly.

"It's not that," he said. "It's just that if you keep it up, she might start…"

He nodded towards Salvra, who was happily rummaging round in the trousers of the first Guard.

There was a long thoughtful silence from the Gray alien. They both glanced at Salvra again as she did unmentionable things with the Guard's nether regions, which seemed to involve braiding. She belched loudly and scratched her bottom.

"I'll think about it," it said finally.

Scabrous nodded. That would have to be good enough.

"I don't think that's where they keep their money," Scabrous told her.

"You never know what you'll find," she called back cheerfully. "Help me bend him over!"

"Seems that the fungus outbreak is continuing to spread across the city," Scabrous commented with careful neutrality.

The Gray alien pondered.

"What now," Scabrous asked. "Sample collection?"

"I just want it understood," Salvra called, pocketing the Guard's money pouches, personal hygiene products, charms, religious sigils, perfumes and contraceptives, "I brought him back to save you. So I get your share."

The Guard's trousers were down around their ankles, and various pieces of their armour and tunics were scattered around the ground. One of the Guards had been wearing lingerie, albeit by Scabrous accounting, it must have been for a particularly formidable woman. He could see the outlines of a radiant bubble around them, and could vaguely discern that somehow, they'd been placed in a frozen pocket of moving time, relative to the world around them, while also exerting an opposite temporal effect on the Guards.

"Sample collection!" she called out. She'd managed to place them in anatomically improbable and obscene poses in respect to one another. Scabrous was impressed at what she'd managed to stuff up one Guard's nostril. "Can I rearrange all their clothes?"

"She wasn't actually. I found her trying to milk a horse," came the voice in his head.

"Well, that's not remarkable," Scabrous said. "It's a siege, people are hungry… horse milk…"

"It was a stallion," the Gray thought at him.

"I've been force feeding that thing the moldiest hay I can find all week," Salvra complained. "How's a girl supposed to get a buzz on in a city under siege where all the breweries and wine cellars are under lock and key?"

"Well, you are a thief," Scabrous said, then thought better of it and shut up.

The alien was taking its samples. By this time, he thought, it must have hundreds of samples. But it never missed an opportunity. Secretly, Scabrous thought it rather enjoyed probing.

"This is purely for science," came the voice in his head.

"Nautical talk," Salvra said. "Can we put their clothes on backwards this time?"

"I have to wonder," said Scabrous the Malevolent, Dark Magister of the unhallowed arts, trafficker with Demonic entities, "are we really doing the right thing? Should we even be here? Is this proper?"

* * *

Gorph the Guard surveyed the plaza. Not many people about. There was a bloodcurdling scream, and a writhing human figure flew through the air, over the wall, towards the tower. Gorph tracked its progress with a practiced eye.

"Hit the wall?" Kevin, the other Guard suggested.

"Moat," Gorph said.

The screaming figure was at the top of its arc.

"Bet?"

"Tuppence."

"Done."

They watched as it slammed into the wall of the castle, leaving a red smear. Gorph grunted and handed over a tuppence.

"Quiet day."

"Yep."

"Nothing happening."

"Nothing."

"Been thinking about my aunt?"

"Pestilenza?"

"No, the other one."

"Pustulia."

"No, the pretty one with the girly name."

"Oh… Scabrous," pause. "She still mad about the fungus?"

Gorph winced.

"Oh yeah!"

Just then, a zombie staggered up and tried to bite Gorph on his shoulder. Its teeth scraped on his leather armour.

"Get off!" Gorph shouted, and pushed the inhuman creature back a few steps. Kevin watched impassively. Cursing, Gorph pulled a rag and rubbed furiously at the hardened boiled leather.

"I don't think he scratched it," Kevin offered.

"No, but sometimes it stains if you let it dry. Miserable stuff," he glared at the Zombie.

The undead revenant had been a middle aged man in life, but now its clothes were visibly rotting, its abdomen swollen with intestinal gases gave it a puffy look. The skin had turned gray and was starting to tear in places, revealing the muscle and bone beneath. It moaned and started forward to attack.

"Stop!" Gorph said, holding his hand up.

The unliving creature halted, as if confused.

"Shoo! Go on! Get out of here!"

The corpse hesitated, as if uncertain.

"SCRAM!"

Almost dejected, the cadaver moaned and stumbled off in another direction, heading towards a washerwoman who cursed and shoved it away. The two Guards watched indifferently as it shambled about the plaza making a nuisance of itself.

"Kind of sad," Kevin remarked. "Reminds me a little of a dog that lived in the alley back where I grew up."

"Ah," Gorph said dismissively. "You can't be nice to them. They'll just follow you home, and keep trying to bite things."

Some children had begun tormenting the zombie.

"Oh oh," Kevin warned, "here it comes."

The angry washerwoman was striding up to them. As they approached, they could see her sleeve was torn, and there was a fresh bite.

"You there!" She yelled unnecessarily. "Guards! You need to do something about those things. See this? This is my fourth bite. A washerwoman can't even be safe in a public square? What's wrong with you?"

Gorph snuck a quick glance at Kevin and rolled his eyes ever so slightly. Nothing to do but let her get it out of her system.

"Citizen Madam," he explained politely, when he judged she'd run out of steam, "you know very well we can't. The Rat Farmers guild has the license; you should report it to them."

She sniffed.

"That scrawny thing?" she snorted, "It's so scrawny, they wouldn't even bother collecting it. Hell, they probably threw it back."

"Nevertheless," Gorph replied.

"Fine, fine," she snapped. But he could tell the fury was gone. "I don't know what we pay you for."

Then she wandered off, muttering. They watched her go.

Further out in the square, the children had the zombie down, and were probably doing something unspeakable to it.

Gorph shrugged. They weren't paid to protect zombies from children. Nothing to do with them.

"Y'know," Kevin began, "I've been wondering something."

"Yeah?"

"How is it that I'm wearing your wife's underwear?"

* * *

"I am unhappy," the Gray Alien announced.

Scabrous the Malevolent looked up sharply. This was the first time that the creature had expressed anything like an emotion. Except for contempt of course, and disgust, and annoyance, loathing, and scorn. But that was sort of a default. Scabrous had the sense that the being regarded them as roughly equivalent to cat droppings on the evolutionary scale.

"Stale cat droppings," the clarification popped into his head. "It's not personal. It's just a neutral assessment of your evolutionary status."

"It seems rather harsh," Scabrous said out loud.

"Not at all. You were designed with a purpose in mind."

That didn't sound bad, Scabrous thought. God guided, god touched, a bit of the divine in each of us. Being a part of some greater cosmic architecture, the notion that life wasn't simply random and meaningless, but there was a plan in mind, a benign celestial design.

"Dietary supplements," came the voice in his mind.

"Excuse me?" Scabrous replied, confused.

""Dietary supplement for large felines," the alien explained, "surveys showed a decline in the leopard population in a certain region. Investigation showed that the animals were suffering a number of vitamin and enzyme deficiencies. The local fauna were surveyed and a species was designated, its biochemistry altered to deliver the proper nutritional elements to the local cat population. To make sure that the leopards would be properly fed, the species was engineered to so it could not climb trees very well, could not run very fast. Easy to catch. No claws, no fangs, no way of

Drunk Slutty Elf and Zombies / Page 17

fighting back. Even the hairlessness, they were trying to reduce hairballs."

Scabrous stared.

"Screaming was engineered in," it continued. "The Leopards really seemed to enjoy the screaming. They wanted to make sure the cats were enthusiastic about their supplements."

Scabrous prided himself on being able to tell when the creature was lying. Not that it ever did. It didn't respect them enough to lie to them, but over time, he'd learned to assess degrees of, for want of a better word, indifferent callousness. This had the ring of truth.

"You were designed to be slow, soft and chewable, with the proper micro-nutritional constituents," it continued. "Basically, you were created to be a multivitamin for leopards. You were never meant to spread. But since you were so good with small cats… you were tolerated."

"I'm not sure I want to believe that," he said carefully.

"If it's any consolation," the Gray thought to the room, "the species that engineered you are very embarrassed by how things turned out."

"Don't mind him. He's just pining for the ocean." Salvra muttered, unwilling to be distracted from what appeared to be a homemade distillery. The odour was rank, smelling of horses and urine. For some reason, she'd become convinced that the alien being was merely some kind of sailor, and nothing could change her mind on the subject… or any other subject for that matter. "Probably misses his parrot. Wants leave this smelly city, go back to the sea."

"We should have left before the siege started," Malowich said glumly.

"We could have left if you'd done your job and found the object," Scabrous snapped.

"Before all the real booze ran out," Salvra complained. "Do you know how hard it is to force moldy hay down a horse's throat, and wait for it to work its way through?"

"It's not that easy," Malowich complained. "We know where it is, but it's inaccessible. Even to… that!" he pointed a finger at the Gray.

He looked around at his companions. Malowich the Procurer was working on his costume, which seemed to be a rather large boned, elderly, overweight, and rather ugly old woman. He fixed a lump of clay to his face.

Malowich was a dealer in arcane objects, and questionable hygienic products, recruited into the group by the Gray over the objections of pretty much everyone. He was a fence, and as the saying went, 'Good fences make good neighbors.'

"Do you think this mole is too much?" he asked. It fell off. Malowich, sometime after the siege had begun, had taken to dressing in women's clothing, on the basis, he explained, that if the invaders broke through, they would murder all the men and rape all the women. And finding penetration preferable to impaling, he'd set about disguising himself as what he considered the surviving gender.

Just then, a walking corpse stumbled into their midst. Scabrous the Shoemaker gently took it by the shoulders, turned it around and guided it on its way. The rest of them barely glanced at the thing.

"Has anyone noticed," Scabrous said thoughtfully, "there seem to be more and more of those things?"

No one paid him any attention of course, except for Salvra, who rolled her eyes and then returned to her brew. She spilled a little, and it ate through the wood of the table.

"WE HAVE BEEN HERE TOO LONG," the Gray alien repeated. Scabrous thought it might be irritable.

"You know," Scabrous said carefully to Salvra, "maybe you could cut back a little on the drinking. Just a little."

Salvra stopped what she was doing, and cast a jaundiced eye his way.

"If I did that," she said flatly, "I might sober up."

Well, he'd tried, he thought miserably.

"I wish Jurgen was here," Malowich complained.

Jurgen was the designated legendary hero of the group, tall, stunningly handsome, muscles everywhere, and not a mark on him anywhere. His catchphrase at the first sign of danger was "I'll go get help!" Jurgen was famous for being the sole survivor of innumerable battles, massacres, slaughters, invasions, attacks, ambushes. Immediately before the siege, with near supernatural acuity, he'd gone for help. That was the last they'd seen of him.

Scabrous the Shoemaker glanced up from his reading. Scabrous the Malevolent bitterly regretted the series of misunderstandings and coincidences that had resulted in the Shoemaker acquiring a price on his head and being forced to join the group.

Everyone liked him better.

"Well, he is more useful and more personable," floated into his mind. "And he has a useful skill."

"How?" Scabrous thought back. He was getting the hang of this mind to mind communication. "He makes shoes. I'm a master of the mystic arts."

"Saw your lips move," Salvra said, she had barely glanced up. "You're a terrible ventriloquist, Bozo."

"Stop calling me that! I was here first." Somehow, the Shoemaker had usurped Scabrous' own name, and everyone had taken to calling him Bozo instead. Bozo the Malevolent didn't have the same ring. But at least it wasn't non-gender specific.

"We all just like him better," Salvra said. Malowich and the other Scabrous nodded. "Well, technically, it's more like nobody likes you. So he wins by default. But if we did like you, we'd like him more."

Once again, Scabrous cursed the day he'd ever unwillingly left his tower to be dragooned along on the alien's miserable quest.

"I'm not sure I believe that we were created to be cat food," he snapped at the Alien. Anything to change the subject. There was a mental shrug from the alien.

"Why would anyone do that?" he asked.

The unblinking eyes of the Gray stared at him.

"Probability Generators."

"What?"

"It is the core of interstellar travel for many civilizations. Put an animal into a box, for some reason, cats work best, they have an affinity for boxes. Introduce a radioactive element with a 50% chance of killing the animal. Its state is not determined until you look, at which point the probability collapses to one state or the other."

"Uhm," Scabrous ventured. "So what? Just look in the box."

"While the cat is in the box, it's in an indeterminate state, both alive and dead. A probability generator harvests that indeterminacy to power a starship."

"You said ship!" Salvra crowed. "You are a sailor, pining for the fjord!"

The Gray ignored her.

"It was a malfunction of the Probability Generator that caused my ship to discorporate."

"Crash?" Scabrous corrected out loud.

"If you put it that way," it thought irritably at him.

"Well," Scabrous replied, "it just means you're human."

"We are not!"

"So your ship, your whole civilization, entire civilizations as a matter of fact, is based on cats in boxes?"

"Yes," the creature seemed to sigh. "This is why we've been here so long. This is where the damaged probability generator fell. But it's leaking, and the city is awash in probability flux. That's why it's been impossible to pinpoint and extract."

Scabrous looked up sharply.

"Wait!" he said. "You said something about indeterminacy, the cat not being alive or dead? And the box leaking uncertainty. Is this why there are so many walking corpses around, neither alive nor dead?"

Malowich, the Shoemaker and Salvra all looked up expectantly.

"Sometimes," the Gray said, "you almost seem intelligent, for cat food."

Salvra shrugged.

"Well, at least they're harmless."

** * **

Day 189 of the Siege. Malowich flounced into their hideout, pulling his skirts up. After adjusting his mole, he announced, "I have it!"

They all looked up blankly.

"The fungus you mean?" Scabrous asked. "It's hard to cure, but there are potions to keep it at bay."

"No," the Procurer said. "The object! Your sailor's Credibility Penetrator!"

"Probability Generator," the words floated in their heads. "And I keep telling you, I'm not a sailor. I don't even own a parrot."

"Whatever," Malowich said breezily. "The point is that we have a chance at it. Up to now, it's been deep in the temple, Guarded by spells, traps, Guards and more spells, and even more Guards. Impossible to reach."

"I still don't understand why you can't just walk in and take it?" Scabrous the Shoemaker asked the Gray. "I've seen you do miraculous things with your magic."

"It's not magic, it's science, and I've told you before: The leaking indeterminacy disrupts my instruments. That's why we have a thief with us."

"S'impregnable," Salvra slurred out from her still. "And I know all about pregnabling, so that's that. No getting in there. Gotta wait for ur chance."

"Ah," Malowich said. "But this is the Festival of the Glabulous Pendant, and so they'll bring it out for a public ceremony at the Palace Chapel tomorrow. It will be exposed, away from the spells and traps, outside its fortress, with only a legion of Guards and a crowd of onlookers. This is the chance we've been waiting for. A Master thief, a nineteenth-"

"Ninetieth," Salvra corrected.

"A ninetieth level Master Thief would have the stealth and cunning to seize it, with no one being the wiser."

Scabrous the Malevolent had a sudden mental image of the group working together. His skills, the other Scabrous's shoes, Malowich's maps and the Gray's gadgets all combining to infiltrate the palace and stealthily lower the thief down from an air duct into a locked room. In his mind, a twisting musical accompaniment started up. After the long period of waiting, they were about to go into action.

Salvra stood up from her still. "I love it!" she announced. "It's time for some Robability Pegnating."

"Probability Generator," a mental voice corrected.

"And I," she announced, "am that pegnator, pregnator, whatever. We're going to do it!"

Then she pitched forward flat on her face and began to snore. Scabrous the Shoemaker stepped over, turned her onto her side, and put a pillow under her head. She snored slightly, as a pool of alcoholic drool formed under her lips. That's why everyone likes him better, thought Scabrous the Malevolent, he thinks of these things first.

Malowich stared at the snoring form.

"Stealth and cunning," he repeated uneasily.

Scabrous's mental image was replaced by a drunken Salvra, spinning from a rope dangling from an air duct, spewing vomit all over the room while above everyone looked down in horror. This would be immediately followed by Guards, more Guards, large Guards, violent Guards, large violent Guards, prison cells, torture chambers, various forms of dismemberment. Yes, that was much more likely.

Or knowing Salvra's idea of stealth, she'd just walk up, smash the casing with a brick, steal it and run away.

* * *

"I'm pregnant!" Salvra announced loudly, stumbling drunkenly through the crowd up onto the dais. She pointed at the High Ecumene. "You! You're the father!"

Everyone froze – dignitaries, nobles, clerics, priests, bishops, influencers, everyone looked aghast and horrified. Only the Royal Gossip seemed excited.

"M- M- M- Me?" the High Ecumene stuttered.

"You!" Salvra slurred. "And it's not the first. Think of our children. Little Toudy, sweet Melch, darling Scabby…"

She raised her hands, counting them off, turning back to the crowd. She threw Scabrous a wink.

"I'm a Eunuch," the High Ecumene protested.

"Pshaw," she said.

"My parents were Eunuchs," he said desperately, sweat beading his brow. "And their parents. And their parents before them. I come from a long line of Eunuchs. No one in my family has ever had sex!"

"A Eunuch, a damned good one," she said. "You got me pregnant right off. That Eunicity worked like a charm, extra potent it makes ya."

"Do you even know what a eunuch is? That's not how it works," he protested.

"It works just fine, as I can attest," she leered at the horrified audience. "All the parts in working order, yessirree! And I'm not the only one. Come give me a kiss."

Drunkenly she smacked her lips in what someone with brain damage might consider coquettish, but really looked more like a large duck trying to spit out peanut butter. As the gathered Ecumenes drew back in horror, she lurched up the steps towards the Altar.

An appalled flurry of whispering ran through the audience as dozens of pairs of eyes tried to look in any direction but the altar, while others pointed fingers. The hushed word 'fungus' cropped up frequently.

Salvra staggered forward. Guards moved to intercept her, but she breathed on them and they crouched back. As she approached, the assembled throng of religious dignitaries cringed back.

Mounting the Altar, Salvra lurched this way and that. "My baby, my baby," she moaned, caressing the fabric of her tunic that covered her bulging stomach. "How will I ever provide for our unborn child? We must raise it together!"

"That's a pillow under there!" the High Ecumene shrilled, his voice tight with panic, as he pointed at the lumpy uneven bulge.

"No it's not!" Salvra responded. "It's motherhood! I am at the peak of my sexual goddessy!"

She thrust her breasts forward, flamboyantly. The pillow dropped out from under her tunic.

"Its come!" she announced, reaching down for the pillow, "just the way the High Ecumene did, suddenly and without warning. I hardly felt it at all. 'Go, Go' I cried out as we made passionate love, but too late, he'd gone already!"

Some in the audience sniggered.

"Still, I treasure or love, the happiest three seconds of my life! I shall call the child of our love Fluffy!. He shall be a Eunuch, just like his father!"

"Guards," the Ecumene shrieked.

"Give him a kiss," Salvra shouted, throwing the pillow at the Guards.

"It's a bomb!" Malowich's shriek from inside the assembled congregation carried over the bedlam. The Guards stopped, falling over each other, scrambling to get out of the way as the pillow tumbled through the air towards them.

Meanwhile, Salvra calmly picked up a golden, jewelled mace, smashed the glass casing containing the glowing box, picked up the holy relic and stuffed it into the pillowcase she'd pulled from her blouse and tossed it to Scabrous the Shoemaker in the front row.

"Stop thief!" she screamed. "He's stealing the sacred relic."

Scabrous the Shoemaker, with every appearance of horror, fumbled thrust the object away from him, throwing it at Malowich.

"Stop them!" Salvra yelled. "They're stealing our child's legacy! To arms! To arms!"

Malowich, also feigning horror and surprise, hurled it away from him, towards Scabrous the Malevolent, standing at the back of the congregation, who caught it automatically, genuinely horrified and surprised.

For a long moment of stunned silence, everyone was paralyzed, as Scabrous stared back wide eyed and uncomprehending, holding the most sacred relic of the city in a stained pillowcase, the entire congregation starring back at him in gaping astonishment and horror at this extreme sacrilege.

"Did you see it!" Salvra yelled. "He just walked up here, smashed the glass and stole the relic! Right in front of me! I saw it all with my own eyes! No respect for motherhood."

She dabbed a tear from her eye. "The High Ecumene was just about to profess his love."

"Was not!" the Ecumene shrieked.

"I saw it too! The brazen blasphemer! After the thief!" Malowich yelled. "Kill him."

Scabrous the Malevolent turned on his heels and ran from the chamber.

A second later, with a mighty roar, led by Malowich, the entire congregation rose up as one in pursuit.

* * *

Clutching the Probability Generator in its pillowcase, Scabrous was blindly running for his life. Somehow, despite his mindless terror, he had enough presence of mind to reflect that this was happening almost constantly since his unwilling association with the Gray alien and the drunken thief had begun.

Behind him, the crowd was rampaging, falling over each other in their eagerness to get to him, baying for his blood.

He could hear Malowich's bellowing voice, shouting out imaginative and anatomically unlikely aspersions as to his birth, ancestry and toilet habits, and suggestions for what they should do when they caught him.

Scabrous put on a burst of speed down the passage, rounded a corner, and almost ran straight into another group of angry Guards. Without hesitation, he right faced, made for an open balcony, and with barely a glance around, climbed over the rail and jumped to a platform just beneath. He then used the Probability Generator to smash a window, climbed through, and continued running.

One floor up, the mob continued its screaming pursuit. Ballroom doors flung open, and angry congregants swarmed towards him, wielding torches and pitchforks.

Scabrous immediately turned in the other direction, found a servants stairwell, and dived down, descending the steps three or four at a time.

Some corner of his mind wondered, "Where had they gotten the torches and pitchforks?"

* * *

"Quiet and stealthy?" Scabrous the Shoemaker was still sitting in the now emptied chamber. From somewhere outside came the sounds of a large angry crowed in pursuit.

The Gray sat beside him. Up on the Altar, Salvra was rooting around, the jeweled mace tucked in her belt, various golden trinkets stashed away or now worn upon her body. A few Guards had remained behind, but were now caught in a stasis field.

"I find being in the company of humans is like being caught in an ever swirling whirlpool of diminishing expectations," the creature said. "Present company excepted."

"Thank you."

The Shoemaker glanced at the frozen Guards.

"Why couldn't you just do that to the congregation?" he asked.

"Far too many for my limited field," the Gray said. "And the Probability Generator disrupts my technology."

"Hey," Salvra called cheerfully from behind the Altar. "I've found the Sacramental Wine! Anyone want some?"

The Shoemaker smiled and shook his head in the negative.

"I find the word 'alcoholic' comes to mind," he whispered, "when it comes to her."

"When it comes to her," the Gray's words formed in his mind, "the word 'alcoholic' is enormously insufficient. I don't think your language is sufficient."

"So where do we collect the Probability Generator?" the Shoemaker asked.

* * *

Scabrous bent over in the darkness, struggling to catch his breath. His blood thundered in his ears, and literally everything ached. His knee throbbed painfully, he was sure he'd smashed it on something at some point.

He felt his scalp; there was a swelling bump but no blood. At some point, one of the Lower Ecumenes had flung a ceramic dildo attached to a complicated series of straps, and it had bounced off his head. But no damage. That was good.

He tried to control his breathing and listen carefully. There were no sounds of an angry mob. That was probably a good thing. He must have lost them somehow, at least temporarily. They'd looked quite angry, and he doubted they'd give up easily.

He conjured a faint light, just enough to see by.

He was in a narrow, winding stone corridor, dank, dusty, cobweb. Crevices along the wall were lined with human bones. There was the sound of small scurrying things moving away from the light.

Catacombs then. He'd heard that the city had been built over an immense necropolis, endless winding catacombs which had never been properly marked. A man could starve to death wandering about down here, never to see the sun again.

He tried to retrace his route in his mind, but it was no use. Everything was a panicked flight of running up and down corridors and hallways, going up and down staircases, diving off of balconies or into dumbwaiters and water closets. It had gotten so confusing that at one point he'd passed his pursuers going the other way.

Well, he was here now; he was relatively safe, time to take stock.

Just then a figure loomed out of the darkness, reaching for him.

Scabrous screamed like a little girl, again.

* * *

But it turned out to be just another walking dead.

"Shoo!" Scabrous hissed, and pushed it away. The corpse backed off a few paces and waited a second. Then it tentatively raised its hands and moaned questioningly, starting towards him.

"No!" Scabrous held up his finger.

The corpse stopped.

"Go away!" he hissed at it. "I mean it."

The corpse's shoulders fell, its head hung.

"Shoo!" he said. "Scram! Get out of here!"

It just stood there, looking forlorn.

The poor thing, Scabrous thought. It must have wandered into the catacombs and gotten lost. It probably couldn't find its way out. The unliving were not very bright, when you came right down to it. It waited on him expectantly, and he felt a pang of pity.

"Look," he said, "I'd like to help. But I'm lost myself."

Gently, he took it by the shoulders and turned it around, giving it a little push, so that it took a few steps forward. It stopped and looked over its shoulder at him.

"Go!" he whispered. It waited. "Look," he told it. "If I find a way out of here, I'll come back and help you. Meanwhile, you're just as likely to get out on your own. All right. Just keep walking."

The thing shambled off. Scabrous sighed. He felt bad about running it off, but he didn't need a zombie following him around like a lost puppy, trying to bite him whenever the thought occurred. He already had enough bite marks, and although they did no real harm, they were annoying. Besides, he told himself, it was probably for the best. Should the revenant make it back to the surface, the rat catchers would almost certainly grab it. The poor thing was probably safer roaming around in the catacombs.

Once he was sure it was gone, Scabrous conjured more light, and sent little firefly sprites to explore. Perhaps with the aid of his magic, he might be able to find his way out.

At least he had his friends. They'd be looking for him.

Or at least, the Gray would be looking for its probability generator. He patted the object in the sack reassuringly.

It would all turn out all right.

* * *

"So where do you think Bozo is," asked Scabrous the Shoemaker. He coughed politely. "I mean the other Scabrous. You've all got me doing it now."

"Who?" asked Salvra distractedly, she was poking through bits and pieces of armour.

"It doesn't matter," said the Gray.

"I'll say one thing," offered the portly fixer, "the man can run! And screaming all the while as he does it! You wouldn't think he had it in him."

"It's a Necromancer thing," Salvra said confidently. "All that running away from angry mobs of villagers out in the country. He probably enjoyed it. That's how Necromancers get their exercise."

"I don't think he enjoyed it," the Shoemaker said doubtfully. "He didn't seem happy at all. Not the way he was screaming."

"Nah," Salvra replied. "I bet he loved it. Total change of scenery. Nice level floors to run on, carpet. Artwork on the walls to admire as he's racing past. Culture! You don't get that out in the countryside."

"Less talk," the Gray projected into their minds. "More work."

Malowich held up a small ceramic object of uncertain proportions, protruding on one side, attached to leather straps. "Where do you think this goes, and on who?"

Salvra glanced at it. "In who," she corrected. "And I have no idea, just stick it in someone."

"You know," Scabrous the Shoemaker said, "I don't really understand sample collection, but I'll go along with it. But really, we need to keep better track of what goes with whom. Maybe make some notes before they're undressed."

Salvra was holding a lopsided bra in her hand, and eyeing the scrotums of several mail Guards.

"Nah," she said. "I like to freehand."

"What about the other Scabrous though?" the Shoemaker persisted.

"Oh he'll turn up," Salvra said, tying a knot. Behind the knot, the tissue was rapidly turning purple. She held up a thumb, siting down it with one eye. They should revive before it explodes, she thought. And if they didn't, she'd just imagine the look on their face. "He always does."

* * *

With a grunt of pure relief, Scabrous flung back the hatch and climbed up into the sunlight. He coughed once or twice and brushed the dust of ancient graves and even more ancient powdered human bones off his clothes. He put up a hand to shield himself from the sunlight, gazing at the vast walls, as he tried to work out where in the city he was.

Vaguely, he wondered if he should go back down and try to rescue the Zombie. The poor thing might never find its way out on its own.

There was something off about the walls though. The perspective, they looked too far away. And the facing, the stonework was too smooth, there was something wrong with that, almost as if…

"Scabrous?" a voice called. "Scabrous the Snot Eater? Is that you? What are you doing here?"

His heart skipped a beat at the sound of a long unheard but still appallingly familiar voice. He turned around slowly, facing the assembled horde of Hurndall, the Impaler.

"Oh!" he squeaked.

He was on the wrong side of the walls.

In fact, he seemed to be in the middle of the enemy camp, judging by the large number of gawping Hurndall soldiers who had watched him clamber out of the Earth, and now encircled him at a respectful distance. Within that circle were four horses draped in crimson, the armoured figures riding them wore red plumage and scarlet banners.

Facing him were the Red Wizards, former classmates from Necromancy College who had made his life there a living hell, for which they're received excellent marks for extracurricular activities, and he'd received years of recurrent nightmares involving being held head first above toilets filled with writhing lampreys.

And apparently, he'd just broken the siege by handing an invading army a route into the city. Everyone was going to die because of him. He was surprised at how badly that made him feel. He'd gotten used to Ayan-Athor, and the citizens not throwing rocks at him. He'd even become fond of the city and its rat based cuisine.

"Terrific," he said.

He swallowed, struggling for his courage. Those nightmarish days of college were a long time ago, he told himself. He was a full-fledged Necromancer now, he had a tower and everything. He'd been published. He wouldn't be bullied this time.

Besides, he thought, he was in possession of a powerful artifact of alien technology. He'd watched the Gray manipulate its tools often enough, surely he could do the same. Whatever it did, the Red Wizards would have no defense against it. He reached into the sack, hoping that it would be useful, or effective, or something.

He took out a chamberpot.

It smelled of fermented horse urine.

Numbly, he stared at it. Of course, he thought suddenly, replaying the sequence of events. Salvra had tossed it to the other Scabrous, who'd tossed it to Malowich, who'd switched it out in the confusion, and tossed him the decoy. He'd fled all over the Palace, running for his life and protecting a stinking chamberpot from Salvra's still. Malowich had probably had it on him the whole time they'd been chasing him, what better opportunity to hide it away, while everyone was focused on him.

He'd been used. He wished that they could have told him. But then, he thought philosophically, lacking a death wish, he'd never have agreed to do it.

All this went through his mind as four of the most dangerous Wizards in the realm, terrifying battle mages whose reputations since college had become legendary, stared down at him.

"Oh damn," he muttered.

* * *

"I still think we should have let him in on the plan," the other Scabrous was saying. They'd managed to exit the Palace in the confusion, Scabrous's exquisite shoemaker credentials had gotten them safe passage out. A few Guards had complimented Malowich on his impassioned pursuit of the blasphemer, but that had been all the attention they had.

Now, as the frenzy and sense of outrage spread across the entire city, the adventurers had a tavern to themselves. The entire city was up in arms over the blasphemy, the siege, the annoyance of the living dead, the price of rat meat, all the day to day concerns of living had been washed away in the face of an all-consuming fury over the desecration. No one wanted to just have a drink. Indeed, hasty effigies of Scabrous were already being burned at various stakes in just about every district. It had been easy to put up a closed sign and bar the door.

Salvra was behind the bar, searching for the secret stash of good stuff that every tavern keeper kept on hand. The others were gathered around the table, staring at the object as it glowed through its covering.

The Gray ignored them as it busily scanned the Probability Generator with its instruments.

"If we had," Salvra said, "he wouldn't have done it."

"As it is," Malowich offered, "I have to say his performance was wonderfully authentic. You had a real sense of mindless terror and headlong panic. He really sold it."

* * *

"Wait," said Scabrous, "what about the people in the city?"

The Red Wizards shrugged.

"Oh they'll probably all be killed," Kemal the Unholy said. "Murdered to the last man, woman and child, in an orgy of rape, pillage and arson. I've seen it before."

"This doesn't bother you at all?" Scabrous demanded.

"Should it?"

"But—but—" Scabrous stammered, "people are going to die."

"Well," Jektar the Red Death replied, philosophically. "That's on you then, isn't it? You just showed us the way in. But don't beat yourself up; it was going to happen one way or the other."

"What are you doing here anyway?" Gorvidal the Loquacious drawled. Of the four Red Wizards on horseback, he was by far the most terrifying. He casually leaned forward on his mount, perfectly at ease. "I thought you were all cloistered with theoretical research. You know, nerd stuff."

Scabrous tried to slow his rapidly beating heart. Each one of the Red Wizards outmatched him, and behind them was

Harndall's entire army. He was a dead man, no matter what. He swallowed and resolved to die bravely.

"I am defending the city," he warbled.

It had sounded so much better in his head. In his mind, his voice had been strong, confident. The Hurndall soldiers were startled, and stepped back. Who was this mighty sorcerer ready to duel no less than four Red wizards?

The Red Wizards burst out laughing.

"I'm serious," he stammered.

Gorvidal the Loquacious wiped at his the corners of his mouth, careful of his lipstick.

"Are you really?" Gorvidal replied. "I suppose you think you are. But really? I'm afraid not. You see, Scabrous, there is an order to the world. There are the people who matter, like me and a few others, and then there are the people who don't matter, you and everyone else, but especially you."

"Scabrous the Malevolent?" Gorvidal sounded the words out. "More like Scabby the Mud-Eater. We certainly saw to your diet back in the day didn't we? Hey remember the toilet full of lampreys? Those were the days."

He tittered at the memory.

"People like you," he said, "are made to be trampled. You are little more than the ground your betters trod upon. The best that can be expected is you might be useful in some way… rather beyond you actually. The best you could ever hope for is to go unnoticed."

Gorvidal leaned forward.

"But here you are… noticed!"

The Red Wizard struck. A dozen multi-coloured bolts of lightning leaped from the ground all around the wizard and his mount. The horse reared up and belched an immense blazing fireball, and serpentine demons flew from the sorcerer's fingertips.

Scabrous felt frozen, as if the world had suddenly fallen to paralysis. His heart surged, his mouth went dry. The first thing he did was flinch, he'd been the victim of Gorvidal's

School tortures to not have the pattern memorized, so when the rambling soliloquy peaked with the surprise attack, it felt exactly like a dozen other occasions. Almost faster than thought, he assessed the sorcerous array of forces racing to obliterate him. Automatically, he flung up a grounding to corral the lightning, turned it back to fry the demons, and then used a completely theoretical abstract conurbation he'd been working on as an academic exercise in creating an invisible portal to view women's bathing areas, to reverse the fireball, popping it through a series of dimensional windows, each passage ramping up its energy exponentially.

Gorvidal had just a second to begin the thought "That's' odd, Pencil-neck—"

And then he was gone, and there was a rather large smoking crater in his place. A very very large smoking crater.

The other Red Wizards were sitting up straight on their horses.

Scabrous blinked and peeked out from between his fingers. Had he done that? He tried to straighten up from his crouch, but his body wouldn't move. He felt rather astonished to be alive right at that moment, and had the vague idea that somehow, at the last instant, Gorvidal had been seized by some suicidal impulse and immolated himself. No, that wasn't right. He had the very powerful sense at that moment, that the universe had gone very awry and that somehow it was his fault.

"Oops?" he offered.

As he glanced from one Red Wizard to the next, he realized that wasn't going to work. He could feel their shields going rigid, the malevolent energies being pulled from the sky, the earth, from the very elemental realms.

Urgently, he took stock of his own magical abilities and quickly sorted through his options: Hide? Run away? Appeal to the old college days? Cry like a baby? Throw himself to the ground and beg for mercy?

One of them was saying something, but Scabrous was too busy searching for a sufficiently pathetic and desperate speech. It didn't matter; they were in no mood to listen. He could feel the hairs on his arms frying as the assembled sorcerous energies built up.

Well, this was the end. A life of being beaten up, overlooked, disrespected, a life that had been an unending succession of failures and humiliations, culminating in being abducted by Salvra and that otherworldly creature for their ludicrous missions.

Why couldn't he have died comfortably, like any normal Necromancer, impaled on the toilet when he'd forgotten to deactivate the spring loaded trap, or devoured down to the bone when he mixed up the jars of insatiable coffee and death mites, or who knows, maybe just exploded into pieces by a moment of carelessness in some esoteric quest for knowledge.

A Necromancer's home contained literally thousands of lethal and poorly catalogued death traps, just waiting to go off. Most times, the stereotypical angry mob never had a chance to exact justice.

It seemed so ironic that he was going to die here, out in the open, literally in perfect safety, nothing more dangerous than a pebble within a hundred yards. Well, a pebble and four red wizards, but they hardly counted.

His last thought, as he was about to be was incinerated, was that he would never be able to deal with that damned fungus.

The ground shook. Scabrous wobbled to keep his balance. Was he incinerated? He'd always imagined it would feel more … flamey. There was another ground tremor, he staggered. He noted that the mounts of the Red Wizards were also struggling to keep their footing, the wizards clinging desperately to their beasts.

* * *

"Oops!" Salvra muttered as the wine spilled across the table from the broken bottle, trickling off the edge of the table. She glanced around quickly. No one was paying attention, perhaps she could lick it up off the floor without anyone noticing. Waste not, want not.

The rest of them were all staring at the golden, glowing probability generator, now badly cracked where Salvra had stumbled and smashed her wine bottle against it. The Shoemaker and Malowich's expressions displayed primordial terror. Even the Gray alien seemed hypnotized, displaying no emotion at all, but focussed absolutely on the artifact in front of it.

Yellow light danced liquidly up and down the crack in the generator, it hummed, ticked several times. Finally, a hatch popped open. The golden glow died away.

Four kittens stumbled out of the hatch, limbs unsteady and awkward, eyes blinking in the light, but still full of innocent feline curiosity.

"Well," the Gray alien thought at them. "Not alive, not dead… Kittens. No wonder the probability fields overloaded."

It picked up one of the kittens and began stroking it.

"Oh look," Salvra said, glancing up from the table's edge. "They have cute little caps."

"Side effect of the Probability Generator," the Alien told her. "Cats in hats in boxes."

The ground shook, and there was a deep rumbling sound emanating from the broken vessel which seemed to pass through each of them and sink into the earth.

"What was that?" Malowich asked nervously.

The alien's huge black eyes blinked, as it tickled the kitten under its chin.

"Oh that?" it replied. "Nothing. Just the probability shockwave."

* * *

When he was sure the ground had stopped shaking, Scabrous climbed carefully to his feet, and looked back towards the city.

The gates to the city were missing, along with a goodly section of the walls for perhaps a hundred yards in each direction. Many of the taller buildings had collapsed, he could see plumes of dust rising. The death toll must be appalling, he thought. Even if, miraculously, everyone survived, the Ayan-Athor was now opened to the Hurndall invaders, who would make short work of the population.

It was the Alien's doing, he could feel it in his bones. What powers did it have access too? It was almost unimaginable.

The Necromancer was overcome with a sense of utter futility. He'd come out here to throw his life away, in a doomed gesture to protect people who he didn't' even know, and who wouldn't have liked him if they had known him. He thought maybe he'd buy an extra moment or two before the wizards dispensed with him and tore down the walls.

But no.

The Alien must have simply vaporized them. The whole charade had been beyond pointless.

And at this point, several things happened very quickly.

* * *

The first was that with the disappearance of the walls, and a considerable portion of the atmosphere around them, there was a sudden inrush of air into the City, carrying with it the flavours and scents of a large mass of living human beings.

The second was that every person everywhere in the city instantly stopped what they were doing, and almost as one, inhaled, tasting for the first time the stray molecules, the cast off skin flakes floating in the air, the traces of bacteria, of dust, the rich, sweet smell of live humans.

Instantly, their brains shut off, and as one, they began running towards the source of that intoxicating scent, the irresistible traces of the living, smashing their way through walls, crawling out windows, leaping off rooftops and over carts, crawling, scraping, fighting their way past every obstacle, but mostly running, running harder and faster towards the living, filled with all-consuming hunger.

From the ruined walls of the city, the undead poured forth.

By this time, of course, they were all undead in the city, and had been so for quite a while.

* * *

Scabrous stared with mounting horror at the screeching, shrieking horde of rampaging undead hurtling towards him. The surviving Red Wizards hadn't waited, the minute they'd seen the horde pouring out, they'd turned their mounts about and fled, not that it would do them any good. The undead were faster and horses would tire, zombies wouldn't.

It had been the Rat Farmers, he'd realized. Feeding human corpses to their rat farms, to sell the rat meat that had sustained the city. And at some point, they'd started feeding the corpses of the living dead, who had gone into the rat meat, and been eaten by just about everyone, infecting everyone in the city to some greater or lesser extent.

That had been why the zombies had been so docile and easily shooed off, they'd just been the dead among the dead. They'd been listless and passive because everyone had been like them. There'd been no living people to eat.

Somehow, he and his companions had been spared, probably the Alien's doing.

But now the walls had been reduced, and an entire shrieking, howling, stampeding horde of ravenous ghouls were racing towards him, racing to fill their stomachs with the first live human they'd find.

Him.

There were, he thought, worse deaths than incineration.

Scabrous screamed like a little girl, covered his face in his arms and curled into a tiny ball, waiting to be torn to pieces as the screaming horde burst over him.

* * *

The Red Wizards did not escape of course. Truth to be told, they made quite a poor showing of it, as they were pulled from their mounts and torn limb from limb. Their instructors at College would have been disappointed; they'd have expected more fight from such relentless sadists.

Hurndall's army never knew what hit it. Truthfully, they'd rather been expecting to indulge in an orgy of rape, murder and looting any day now. That their intended victims turned out to be enthusiastic, unnaturally aggressive, virtually unstoppable, and very very hungry came as a rude surprise, but not for long.

One might hope that Hurndall and his men gave good account of themselves, going down heroically, swinging swords to the last, cursing and fighting as true warriors.

The truth was that mostly it ended with begging and crying, desperate futile attempts to surrender, a certain amount of running away and whatnot.

Hurndall himself tried hiding in an officer's latrine, where his brains were eaten.

* * *

"What are you doing?" a voice sounded in Scabrous's mind.

He was still huddled in a fetal position on his knees. His hands were still clasped in front of his face. He turned his head and spread his fingers just enough to spy the Gray Alien staring down at him.

Fingers?

He still had fingers?

Hastily, he counted them. They were all there. Toes? Yes. In fact, a quick check showed him to be absolutely uneaten. Slightly trampled, he could discern footprints all over him. But definitely not torn to shreds.

"I'm not dead?" he said. "How am I not dead?"

There was no response. The creature before him was not built for existential questions.

"Am I dead?" he asked cautiously. "Or undead? They're not trying to eat me? Does that mean I… we… are like them?"

"No," the voice appeared in his mind. "All my tools are probability shielded. These living/not-living entities will therefore perceive you as the same indeterminate state they exist in."

Scabrous thought about that.

"So… I… we… are tools?"

The Gray didn't bother to reply.

"It turns out," Salvra said cheerfully, "it was just kittens, all along."

"Excuse me?" Scabrous asked pointlessly. But she'd already wandered off, looking for loot, or more likely, booze in Hurndall's Royal stores.

A zombie wandered up to him, staring blankly, and held something out to the dark Wizard.

Scabrous looked at the object it was holding.

It was a human face.

"Oh! My!" Scabrous said. "Thank you, but I'm all right."

The Zombie had no nose, its eyes were sunk into its skull, and one cheek had been torn away, leaving bare teeth exposed. Still, it managed to look skeptical. It held the face out again.

"Really," Scabrous said, "I appreciate that so much. But I'm full. Yum yum. Full up on soldiers. I couldn't eat another bite." For emphasis he rubbed his stomach.

The living corpse shrugged and wandered off, chewing thoughtfully on the face.

Scabrous noted that some of the less torn to pieces enemy soldiers had begun to reanimate. The dead of the city showed them no particular rancor. It seemed that in undeath, everyone was equal.

"I'm glad you're not dead," the Gray alien said.

Scabrous blinked in surprise.

"Really?" he asked.

"No," said the alien. "I don't actually care. But it's a meaningless thing that humans say."

"Oh."

The alien hesitated.

"I find you occasionally useful in small ways," it offered.

"Thanks," said Scabrous. "That means a lot."

There was the mental equivalent of a shrug.

Scabrous glanced around at the undead. There seemed to be more of them. Several of the Hurndall soldiers, the less eaten ones had reanimated.

"Now that you have your Probability Generator sorted out," Scabrous asked, "shouldn't they all be starting to lie down?"

The alien's head swivelled, taking stock of the animated corpses stumbling around.

"Not really," its thoughts rolled in his head. "There's been a massive localized probability adjustment; it should fade away in a decade or so. The effects should be confined to the continent… or the hemisphere… or the planet. Overall, quite limited."

"I see," Scabrous said carefully. In his mind, he imagined an endless horde of the hungry undead, sweeping down on city after city, engulfing nation after nation, entire populations slaughtered only to rise again and become part of the hordes. "Isn't this something to worry about? Maybe was should do something?"

There was the mental equivalent of a shrug.

"It's not my planet," the Alien's thoughts came dismissively.

"I was getting help," a voice announced.

Jurgen the unblemished appeared. The undead seemed to sniff him suspiciously, but paid no more attention. Scabrous stared at the tall, muscular, heroic figure. There wasn't a mark on him. Of course not. Jurgen was unblemished for a reason.

"But alas, I fell in among the Hurndall soldiers, they were hard to avoid, and I was recruited. Not really my choice. I got a very nice signing bonus," the hero concluded.

He paused.

"I figured the best thing to do would be to stick around, just in case. You know how it is."

Malowich and the other Scabrous were approaching on a wagon, the horses nervous, but somehow shielded as well. Jurgen waved.

"I see that our fellowship, long sundered, has been restored," he announced. "What brave new adventure awaits!"

"I have a list," the Gray space alien said.

Scabrous the malevolent sighed, thinking once more about his beloved tower with its endless death traps.

"And a schedule."

Scabrous sighed again. From the wagon, the other Scabrous, the one everyone else liked, reached down to offer him a helping hand into the wagon. The man was just instinctively good, Scabrous thought. After a moment's hesitation, he took it and climbed up and into the back.

"Hey," he said, "what's up with the kittens?"

Pause.

"And why do they have hats?"

The End

HIS PLACE

HE found it halfway through HIS usual rounds. Way back when, HE'd thought the project had been a good idea. Perhaps it had been, but HE had not reckoned on the nearly constant maintenance.

"It" was an infestation. It occupied a little speck circling some mediocre sun, around an obscure galaxy. As HE bent to examine it, the Universe seemed to unfold, every object moving seemingly in an outward sphere, away from HIS point of reference.

That was a constant, no matter where you were, the Universe always seemed to be an expanding shell, with yourself or YOURSELF at the centre. It made a nice impression, just about everyone said so. HE remembered that HE'd had to tinker with the speed of light for hours until HE got the effect just right.

Infestations had occurred before. They weren't a big deal. HE could take care of them. More troublesome were the macro effects, exploding galaxies, stars failing to coalesce, black holes gobbling things up.

Sometimes it looked good. There had been that exploding supernova. HE'd invited all HIS friends over, and carried on as if it was HIS idea.

Mostly though, it was a nuisance. HE found that HE had to regularly go through it with his paraphernalia, tidying and straightening things up. Sometimes, HE regretted making the damned thing. But then, HE would think philosophically, what else would HE have to occupy HIS time.

So there it was: An infestation. As HE bent down to wipe it clean, HE noticed something extra-ordinary.

They were worshipping HIM.

HE paused, just as he was about to clear them off. They were worshipping HIM madly, as if HE needed it, or as if their opinions mattered to HIM.

Fascinated, HE watched them for a while. It was the most appalling display of snivelling HE had ever seen. They exhibited a thoroughly revolting servility, an astounding capacity for self-serving rationalisation, and an attention span even HE found difficult to measure.

Vaguely disgusted, but mildly amused, HE decided to return to them later.

They were still worshipping HIM when HE returned. But now, they had concocted all sorts of outrageous fabrications about HIM and were busily slaughtering each other over obscure points of doctrine. They invented an ADVERSARY to embody all the aspects of HIM they didn't seem to like.

Each time he paused to examine them, there was an unending succession of maniacs who claimed to speak to HIM. To be fair, and HE liked to think HE was fair about this sort of thing, perhaps they did. But HE certainly wasn't speaking to them. Certainly not on terms that familiar, anyway.

It didn't stop the various madmen from making all sorts of promises in HIS name. HE noted the cleverer ones made a point of postponing the promises to the afterlife.

It became a regular point on his rounds. HE would check them out, to see what they were up to. There was the time they decided HE was terribly concerned with whether or not they masturbated. In their minds, HE was supposed to be fascinated by where they put their genitals. It was hilarious, in a queasy sort of way.

They seemed to continually create long lists of activities that they thought were offensive to HIM. Some of these were rational proscriptions for dealing with each other, some of them made no sense whatsoever, in either case, HE had bigger things to do, and didn't give a whit about whether or not they masturbated or ate bananas on a Thursday.

But then, incredulously HE would watch them proceed to violate all his supposed edicts and laws with great gusto. Then they would go back to worshipping HIM. HE was speechless.

Often, HE promised HIMSELF to stop being lazy and clean them out. But his few attempts were half-hearted, and they always crawled back, snivelling like never before. By their persistence, he might have mistaken them for some sort of fungus, but fungus never whined that much.

Sometimes, HE would actually speak to them, but it seemed to have no more effect than stirring a boiling pot. Most of the time, HE simply watched, astounded by their capacity to make the simplest things difficult.

They entered, what was for them, a rational phase: They declared HE was dead, this amused HIM. Then they decided HE depended on them. And then announced that THEY were HIM in some philosophical fashion. HE laughed openly so that mountains shattered and stars winked out.

They declared themselves evolved from apes.

Personally, HE thought weasels were more likely.

But as always, their staggering capacity for self-deception left HIM breathless.

Then one day, HE was startled to return and find them gone. Their little speck of a world had been reduced to even tinier specks.

Had they done that, HE wondered?

It wasn't HE told HIMSELF, as if HE missed them. One could no more miss them, than miss the lint in their navel, or pine for a belly rash, or develop a fond affection for an open sore. All things considered, HE thought, HE was glad that they'd done away with themselves. It saved HIM the trouble.

As HE packed up his tools, pausing only to set things back to the way they'd been at the beginning, HE took one last look around the neighbourhood.

HE stopped, profoundly disturbed.
They seemed to have spread...

The End

King Kong Meets Dracula

SCENE - NIGHT, ON THE DECK OF THE TRAMP STEAMER, THE WANDERER, FOG AND MIST. TWO MEN, STAND, LEANING ON THE RAILINGS, LOOKING OUT. ONE IS A YOUNG HANDSOME SAILOR, THE FIRST MATE, JACK DRISCOLL. THE OTHER IS OLDER, A BUSINESSMAN, CARL DENHAM.

DENHAM - This fog shows no sign of breaking.

DRISCOLL - It's a pea soup, all right. Captain's reduced to quarter speed.

DENHAM - Is that necessary?

DRISCOLL - Uncharted waters, Mr. Denham, we're getting close to this island of yours. Shame if we hit a reef and sink before we get to it.

TWO MORE FIGURES ARRIVE ON DECK, ARRIVING FROM THE RIGHT. THESE ARE A YOUNG BLONDE WOMAN, ANNE, AND A TALL DISTINGUISHED MAN IN A CLOAK, THE DOCTOR.

DENHAM - Doctor, Miss Darrow, pleased to see you up on deck. Even (waves) in this.

ANNE - Hello Mister Denham, (beaming) Hello Jack.

JACK TAKES OFF HIS HAT AND BOWS SLIGHTLY.

DRISCOLL - Miss Darrow..... Doctor.

DOCTOR - Good evening.

DENHAM - How are your patients?

DOCTOR - Resting comfortably for now. I predict a speedy recovery for some.

DRISCOLL - That's good news!

DENHAM - Until someone else gets sick. This is a damnable contagion. We just can't shake it. Have you seen the like, Jack?

DRISCOLL - Never. But I know the Doctor is going to lick it. He hasn't lost one of us yet!

DENHAM - The only ones who seem immune are the four of us, strangely enough.

DOCTOR - None of us are truly immune, Mr. Denham, contagions of this sort are merely... unpredictable. You may find yourself ill before you know it. Perhaps even you, Mr. Driscoll.

DRISCOLL - I count myself lucky so far, Doctor. But I'll say this, I'm sure glad we had you along on this voyage. Without a real Doctor, I'm sure we would have had burials at sea by now.

DOCTOR - I am very pleased to keep your crew alive, Mister Driscoll. Rest assured, this contagion... has my complete attention.

DRISCOLL - Where are you from, Doctor? I can't say I've ever heard your accent.

DOCTOR - Transylvania. Sadly, a land beset by violence and revolution, so that I have been forced to flee, and make my way in this world.

ANNE - The Doctor was royalty back in his country.

DENHAM - You don't say? I never knew that. Keeping secrets, Doc?

DOCTOR - Royalty (chuckles) my ancestors were Kings and Princes, but now, in my native country, I would merely be a Count. Sadly, my home is a long way off, we have been driven out. So now, I am a simple Doctor.

DRISCOLL - How about that. A Count? That's impressive. Count Carfax.

DOCTOR - Count Dracula. It is an old family name, very distinguished, it means 'son of the dragon.'

DENHAM (hint of bitterness) - I heard it as 'son of the devil.'

DOCTOR (charming, but with an edge) - Our enemies had it that way.

DRISCOLL - Miss Anne, would you like to take a stroll along the decks?

ANNE - I'd be delighted, Mister Driscoll. Is that all right, Doctor?

DOCTOR (smiles) - But of course dear girl. But just please watch your step, the decks are slippery. And please, don't stay too long, this fog is not good for your lungs.

DRISCOLL - I'll keep her safe, Doc, have her right back to you.

DRISCOLL AND ANNE DEPART TO THE LEFT. DENHAM AND THE DOCTOR WAVE. ONCE THEY ARE GONE...

DOCTOR - They are too close, those two. You should be careful to keep them apart.

DENHAM - You're very protective of her.

DOCTOR - I have watched over her for years, since she was a child. Her blood is very special. I have great plans for her.

DENHAM - We'll make her a star.

DOCTOR - Something like that. But she must remain pure.

DENHAM - I'll do what I can. (Pauses) Are you sure that island is out there?

DOCTOR - Have I ever mislead you?

DENHAM - No... It's just that if this doesn't pan out, I'm busted. I've put all my money into this, and a good deal of yours. I'll never be able to pay you back.

DOCTOR (sardonically) - That worries you... Money?

DENHAM - Money makes the world go round, Doctor.

DOCTOR - It... has its uses, I will admit. But what truly matters is what you can achieve.

DENHAM (with growing excitement) - An island full of monsters? Collect them, crate them, put them on display. There's a fortune to be made there. And not just sideshow attractions, moving pictures. That's the future.

DOCTOR - (disinterested) Indeed.

DENHAM - I don't get you, Doctor.

DOCTOR - Indeed?

DENHAM - I've had investors before, silent partners. This is the first one that insisted on coming along.

DOCTOR - Just watching over my investment.

DENHAM - You don't want anyone to know, though?

DOCTOR - That is the point of being a silent partner. Best that they think I am a simple Doctor. I would not want anyone to become... excited.

* * *

Drunk Slutty Elf and Zombies / Page 52

COUNT DRACULA STANDS ON THE BOWSPRIT OF THE VENTURE, STARING OUT INTO THE NIGHT. HIS CAPE FLAPS IN THE WIND. ABRUPTLY HE VANISHES, AND A BAT APPEARS, FLYING AWAY FROM THE SHIP.

* * *

NATIVE VILLAGE. A TRIBAL CEREMONY IS GOING ON. NATIVES DRESSED AS APES, DANCING. DRUMS BEATING.

COUNT DRACULA ENTERS. UPON NOTICING, THE CEREMONY COMES TO A STOP. THE DRUMS GO SILENT. DRACULA ADVANCES SILENTLY UPON THE NATIVE CHIEF.

CLOSE UP OF COUNT DRACULA'S FACE, ILLUMINATED BY LIGHT, THE EYES STARING HYPNOTICALLY.

AS DRACULA ADVANCES, THE NATIVE CHIEF AND WITCH DOCTOR RETREAT, FINALLY COWERING. AS DRACULA STARES AT THEM, THE REST OF THE NATIVES FALL TO THEIR KNEES.

DRACULA - You will do as I command. Men will be coming from the ship...

* * *

SCENE - SHORE OF SKULL ISLAND. TWO ROWBOATS PULL UP ON SKULL ISLAND. ONE OF THE BOATS CONTAINS DRACULA, ANNE, DENHAM AND DRISCOLL. DRISCOLL MOVES TO HELP ANNE CLIMB OFF THE ROWBOAT. BUT DRACULA DELIBERATELY GETS IN HIS WAY, ASSISTING HER INSTEAD, MAKING A SHOW OF GRACIOUSNESS.

AS THEY DEPART THE ROWBOAT, THEY ARE UNDER OBSERVATION FROM THE NATIVES.

ARRIVING AT THE VILLAGE, THEY ARE MET BY THE CHIEF AND WITCH DOCTOR, WHO DEMANDS THE WOMAN, ANNE.

DRACULA OFFERS TO NEGOTIATE, BUT ONE OF THE NATIVES GRABS ANNE. DRISCOLL PULLS A GUN AND SHOOTS. THE OTHER CREW MEMBERS BRING OUT THEIR GUNS, MASSACRING THE NATIVES. DRISCOLL CALLS A RETREAT. DRACULA RELUCTANTLY FOLLOWING WITH THE GROUP.

***

SCENE - THE CAPTAIN'S CABIN. DRISCOLL, DENHAM, ENGLEHORN (THE CAPTAIN), DRACULA AND ANNE, ARE ARGUING ABOUT THE DISASTROUS ENCOUNTER WITH THE NATIVES. ENGLEHORN AND DRISCOLL ARGUE THAT IF ANOTHER SHORE CANNOT BE FOUND, THEN THE VENTURE SHOULD ABANDON THE WATERS. DENHAM AND DRACULA FOR THEIR OWN REASONS ARGUE TO MEET THE NATIVES AGAIN. ANNE, FEELING ILL AND DISTRACTED, EXCUSES HERSELF.

ANNE GOES OUT ONTO THE DECK, FOR THE NIGHT AIR. DRISCOLL TRIES TO FOLLOW HER, BUT DRACULA HOLDS HIM BACK, DRAWING HIM INTO THE ARGUMENT.

***

ON DECK, NATIVES SNEAK ABOARD AND ABDUCT ANNE. THE ABDUCTION IS DISCOVERED. THERE IS NO CHOICE, BUT TO GO BACK TO RESCUE THE GIRL, DRACULA ANNOUNCES THAT HE WILL LEAD THE EXPEDITION. BUT ENGLEHORN ORDERS THAT THE CIVILIANS, DENHAM AND DRACULA, REMAIN ON THE SHIP WHILE THE RESCUE IS UNDER WAY.

***

SCENE - AS THE VENTURE'S CREW ROW BACK TO SHORE, ARMED FOR RESCUE, A BAT FLIES OVERHEAD….

***

SCENE - ANNE IS TIED TO THE ALTAR. ABOVE HER, ON THE TEMPLE ON THE WALL, DRACULA STANDS AMONG THE NATIVES, HANDS UPRAISED, CHANTING AN UNHOLY SPELL, GLARING DOWN AT THE FORBIDDING JUNGLE.

THE TREES AND BRUSH AHEAD BEGINS TO TWIST AND SURGE AS OF A MIGHTY SHAPE FORCING ITS WAY THROUGH THE FOREST.

AS DRACULA'S CHANT REACHES A CRESCENDO, A MIGHTY APE BURSTS OUT. ANNE SCREAMS AND SWOONS.

SOUNDS OF GUNFIRE AND SCREAMING. DRACULA'S ATTENTION IS BROKEN. HE LOOKS BACK. THE RESCUE PARTY HAS ARRIVED AND IS FIRING UPON THE NATIVES.

THE APE STEALS ANNE AND VANISHES INTO THE JUNGLE.

DRACULA CURSES.

***

SCENE - DRISCOLL CONFRONTS DRACULA IN THE NATIVE VILLAGE. THE GREAT DOORWAY HAS BEEN OPENED. THE ALTAR IS EMPTY.

DRISCOLL - Doctor! How did you get here? What are you doing here?

DRACULA – You think I would let my ward be abducted and do nothing? I took a small rowboat. I thought I could

Drunk Slutty Elf and Zombies / Page 55

communicate with these savages, and persuade them to let her go.

DRISCOLL - The Captain said to remain on the ship!

DRACULA - I could not stand leave poor Anne in danger, in danger and call myself a man. And you know what they say; sometimes one man can accomplish what an army cannot.

DRISCOLL - Did you see what took her?

DRACULA - I did.

DRISCOLL - What was it?

DRACULA - A great beast. A monster from the depths of time itself. One of many on this forsaken island.

DRISCOLL - We'll have to rescue her. You should get back to the ship.

DRACULA - No. I will go with you. She will need all of us.

* * *

THE APE, KING KONG, RETREATS INTO THE JUNGLE. THERE IT ENCOUNTERS AND FIGHTS A TYRANNOSAUR. ANNE IS PERCHED IN A TREE.

ELSEWHERE, THE VENTURE'S RESCUE CREW, LEAD BY DRACULA AND DRISCOLL MAKE THEIR WAY THROUGH THE JUNGLE, AND ARE PURSUED ATTACKED BY DINOSAURS, FIRST A BRONTOSAUR AND THEN A STYRACOSAUR.

KONG, CARRYING ANNE, CROSSES A GIANT LOG OVER A CHASM. KONG LOOKS BACK AND ROARS, JUST AS THE MEN APPEAR IN PURSUIT ON THE OPPOSITE SIDE. THEY OPEN FIRE, BUT DRACULA HOLDS THEM BACK, LEST THEY HIT ANNE.

STUNG, THE APE VANISHES INTO THE JUNGLE.

THE MEN, LEAD BY DRACULA AND DRISCOLL, BEGIN TO CROSS THE LOG. DRACULA IS THE FIRST TO CROSS. HE LEAPS OFF AND TURNS BACK....

* * *

SCENE - SKULL ISLAND, THE CHASM WITH THE LOG UPON IT. DRACULA STANDS ON ONE SIDE OF THE CHASM, DRISCOLL AND THE REST OF THE MEN ARE ON THE LOG.

DRACULA - I am afraid, Mister Driscoll, your adventure ends here. This is as far as you go.

DRISCOLL - What are you talking about, Doctor? Anne is still out there.

DRACULA - My name is Dracula, Mister Driscoll. And Anne is no longer your concern. I have business to take care of. I cannot permit you to go further.

DRISCOLL - You were working with the savages! I knew from the start there was something wrong with you. We should never have trusted you. You were probably making us sick.

DRACULA (laughs) - Wisdom comes too late, Mister Driscoll.

DRISCOLL PULLS PISTOL, AND WAVES TO HIS MEN.

DRISCOLL - We're coming over. And you can't stop us, Doctor Carfax, or Dracula, whatever your name is. You're just one man, and we have the guns.

DRISCOLL ADVANCES ACROSS THE LOG, FOLLOWED BY SEVERAL OF THE CREW OF THE VENTURE.

DRACULA - I am not a man, Mister Driscoll, and your guns are nothing to me.

DRACULA SEIZES THE ROOTS OF THE GIANT FALLEN LOG ACROSS THE CHASM, AND TWISTS. THE ENTIRE LOG ROCKS BACK AND FORTH. SOME OF THE MEN FALL OFF. DRISCOLL AND THE OTHERS FALL PRONE, HANGING ONTO THE LOG FOR ALL THEY ARE WORTH.

CUT TO DRACULA'S FACE, SHOWING UNEARTHLY STRAIN AT THESE EXERTIONS.

DRACULA HEAVES THE LOG BACK AND FORTH SHAKING IT MORE AND MORE VIOLENTLY, MORE MEN FALL OFF, BUT A FEW REMAIN CLINGING.

DRACULA - You are persistent, Mister Driscoll, but it will not help you.

WITH A MIGHTY HEAVE, DRACULA COMPLETELY LIFTS ONE END OF THE LOG INTO THE AIR, RAISING IT ABOVE HIS HEAD, AND HURLS IT INTO THE CHASM, THE LOG FALLS, TAKING THE REMAINING MEN WITH IT. AS IT FALLS, DRISCOLL DESPERATELY SEIZES A VINE, SWINGING TO PERILOUS SAFETY.

DRACULA GAZES INTO THE CHASM, A SMILE ON HIS FACE. HE LOOKS DOWN, AND FROWNS.

LONG SHOT, WE SEE DIRECTLY BELOW DRACULA, THAT DRISCOLL HAS LANDED ON A HIDDEN LEDGE. DRACULA PEERS DOWN, PLAINLY SUSPICIOUS. A TWO LEGGED LIZARD IS CLIMBING UP THE CHASM. DRACULA STARES AT THE LIZARD. AS IT IS ABOUT TO REACH THE HIDDEN DRISCOLL, DRACULA CONTEMPTUOUSLY SWINGS HIS ARM, CAUSING THE CREATURE TO FALL BACK

INTO THE CHASM, AND UNKNOWINGLY SAVING HIS ADVERSARY.

AT THAT MOMENT, GUNFIRE ERUPTS. DRACULA LOOKS UP ANGRILY. THE REMAINDER OF THE VENTURE'S MEN ARE ON THE OTHER SIDE OF THE CHASM.

DRACULA - Your guns mean no more to me than the creatures of this hellish place.

DRACULA TURNS AND STALKS OFF, ON THE TRAIL OF KING KONG.

* * *

SCENE - SKULL ISLAND, KING KONG'S MOUNTAIN. KONG, CARRYING ANNE WALKS INTO THE RUINS OF A LONG ABANDONED TEMPLE. THE GREAT APE SITS, AND BEGINS TO PLAY WITH ANNE, SETTING HER DOWN. SHE ATTEMPTS TO FLEE AGAIN AND AGAIN, BUT HE CATCHES HER EACH TIME. BORED WITH THE GAME, HE PICKS HER UP AND BEGINS TO PLUCK OFF HER CLOTHES.

DRACULA - STOP!!!

DRACULA APPEARS ON THE PLATFORM OF THE TEMPLE, JUST ABOVE KONG, HIS ARMS OUTSTRETCHED.

KONG GROWLS ANGRILY, LEAPING TO HIS FEET.

DRACULA - Obey me!

KONG PACES BACK AND FORTH, BEATING HIS CHEST AND ROARING.

DRACULA - Obey!

KONG COWERS AND SKULKS.

DRACULA - Bring me the girl.

KONG TURNS AWAY, ATTEMPTING TO SHIELD ANNE PROTECTIVELY AGAINST HIS BODY.

DRACULA - Obey!

SEETHING WITH RESENTMENT AND FRUSTRATION, THE GREAT APE PLACES ANNE ON THE ALTAR AT DRACULA'S FEET, AND THEN PACES BELOW.

ANNE LOOKS UP AT DRACULA, WHO STARES DOWN AT HER, FACE CONTORTED IN EVIL LUST.

ANNE - Oh Doctor, I feel like I'm in a nightmare.

DRACULA - Be at ease child, this dream is coming to an end.

ANNE - Doctor, I don't want to be here.

DRACULA - You are meant to be here, child. It is my will that you are here. This place is your destiny.

ANNE (gasping) - What do you mean?

DRACULA - Do you see that creature before you, child? Once there was a race of them, and a mighty civilization was built upon sacrifices to them, built upon the power of joining beast to human. Now it is the last of its kind.

ANNE - What do you mean, Doctor? That sounds like black magic?

DRACULA SHRUGS

DRACULA - Magic... or Science? There is little difference. That crude beast is the gateway to power beyond even that which I possess; power to defy the sun, to defy God himself.

ANNE - Doctor, what are you saying? You're frightening me.

ANNE TRIES TO FLEE. DRACULA GESTURES HYPNOTICALLY, AND SHE FREEZES IN PLACE.

DRACULA - You shall play your part, child. Wait, I have preparations to make. When the time is right, I shall give you to the beast, and your sacrifice shall give me the power I seek.

* * *

SCENE - SKULL ISLAND, APPROACH TO THE CAVE. DRISCOLL IS CLIMBING UP TOWARDS THE TEMPLE. UNKNOWN TO HIM, HE IS FOLLOWED BY A HUNGRY SERPENT-LIKE CREATURE.

* * *

SCENE - SKULL ISLAND, KONG'S MOUNTAIN, THE TEMPLE. ANNE STANDS AT THE EDGE OF THE ALTAR, UNDER A SPELL. KONG IS PACING BACK AND FORTH BENEATH THEM. BEHIND AND ABOVE, DRACULA IS CHANTING AGAIN, HIS VOICE STEADILY RISING IN PITCH AND TENOR. FROM NOWHERE COMES THE SOUND OF DRUMS, PUNCTUATED BY THE GROWLS AND ROARS OF KONG.

DRISCOLL APPEARS AT THE EDGE OF THE TEMPLE WATCHING FROM CONCEALMENT.

DRACULA STRETCHES OUT HIS ARMS, RAISING HIS CAPE, LIKE TWO GREAT BLACK WINGS, PRONOUNCING...

A PTERODACTYL ATTACKS DRACULA FROM BEHIND. THE VAMPIRE LORD CRIES OUT IN ANGER AND ALARM. THE SPELL BROKEN, ANNE COMES TO HERSELF AND LETS OUT A PIERCING SCREAM.

BUT BEFORE SHE CAN RUN, KONG, NO LONGER UNDER DRACULA'S CONTROL, STEALTHILY SWIPES HER WITH ONE PAW, AND CRADLING HER IN HIS ARM, TRIES TO SCAMPER OFF.

KONG STUMBLES INTO THE SERPENT-CREATURE
THAT HAS BEEN STALKING DRISCOLL. ANGRILY,
THE CREATURE COILS ABOUT THE GIANT APE.
KONG RELEASES ANNE TO DEAL WITH IT.

DRISCOLL APPEARS TO RESCUE ANNE, AND THE
TWO OF THEM FLEE TO SAFETY....

KONG KILLS THE SERPENT CREATURE. UNABLE
TO FIND ANNE, HE GOES OFF IN SEARCH OF HER.

* * *

DELETED SCENE - DRACULA, IN A MIXTURE OF
STOP MOTION AND LIVE ACTION FIGHTS OFF
THE PTERODACTYL AND FINALLY KILLS IT BY
IMPALING IT ON A LOG.

* * *

ANNE AND DRISCOLL FLEE THROUGH THE
JUNGLE, ESCAPING KONG. THEY MAKE IT BACK
TO THE VILLAGE, WHERE THEY MEET DENHAM
AND ENGLEHORN. IN COMBINATION, THE
NATIVES AND SAILORS PREPARE A DEFENCE.
KONG BREAKS THROUGH AND RAMPAGES
AMONG THE NATIVES BEFORE BEING RENDERED
UNCONSCIOUS BY GAS BOMBS.

* * *

KONG IS THEN BROUGHT TO NEW YORK, WHERE
DENHAM PROMISES TO EXHIBIT HIM AS THE
NINTH WONDER OF THE WORLD.

* * *

SCENE - NEW YORK CITY, MADISON SQUARE
GARDEN, BACKSTAGE, FOR THE UNVEILING OF
KONG. KONG IS NOT VISIBLE, BUT HIS GROWLS
AND MOANS CAN BE HEARD.

DENHAM, DRISCOLL AND ANNE ARE TALKING.
ANNE IS IN AN EVENING GOWN. DRISCOLL AND
DENHAM ARE IN TUXEDOS.

DRISCOLL (tugging at his collar) - I don't like this monkey
suit.

DENHAM - Monkey suit? Hah! Good one kid. Get used to
it, you're in show business now, and you're both going to be
stars... along with our big friend there.

KONG'S RUMBLE IS HEARD.

ANNE - I don't feel safe.

DENHAM - Oh don't worry my girl. Those chains are
unbreakable. Trust me; everything is going to go fine. Now
you two go off and rehearse your lines. I have a few things to
take care of.

ANNE AND DRISCOLL DEPART STAGE LEFT.
AFTER THEY ARE GONE, DRACULA ENTERS
STAGE RIGHT. DENHAM JUMPS, HIS EXPRESSION
SHEER TERROR.

DRACULA - Good evening Mister Denham.

DENHAM - Oh my god! Count Dracula! We thought you
were dead! How did you escape that island?

DRACULA - No need to concern yourself. I have returned
to see how my silent partner has done. Vulgar and tawdry as I
expected.

DENHAM - We're not partners. You're a fiend. A monster.
Jack and Anne told us all what you'd done.

DRACULA - And yet, I had not done enough.

DENHAM (pulls a gun) - Get out of here, damn you! Before
I call the police!

DRACULA - I do not fear your toy, and soon I will be beyond even your police.

DENHAM - I know you Devil! I know what you do fear!

DENHAM REACHES INTO HIS COAT. DRACULA SPRINGS UPON DENHAM AND BEARS HIM TO THE GROUND, BREAKING HIS NECK.

* * *

SCENE - NEW YORK CITY, MADISON SQUARE GARDEN. THE AUDIENCE HAS CROWDED IN. KONG IS CONCEALED BY A CURTAIN. DRISCOLL AND ANNE WAIT IN THE WINGS, ON STAGE LEFT.

ANNE - It's late. It's late. Where is Denham? He should have been on stage twenty minutes ago. People are getting restless.

DRISCOLL - He's just drawing it out, building up tension for the big reveal.

ANNE - I'm getting worried.

DRISCOLL - No worries. Tell you what, I'll go have a look for him, make sure he hasn't gotten stuck in a closet or something.

DRISCOLL KISSES ANNE, AND THEN DEPARTS.

AFTER DRISCOLL IS GONE, ANNE LOOKS OUT TO THE OTHER SIDE OF THE STAGE AND GASPS, AS DRACULA APPEARS OPPOSITE HER.

DRACULA STRIDES OVER TO THE CENTER OF THE STAGE, WHERE HE MOUNTS A SMALL PLATFORM, A RE-CREATION OF THE ALTAR OUTSIDE THE NATIVE VILLAGE.

DRACULA - Good evening. I am Count Dracula. My friend and partner, Mister Denham, is suddenly indisposed, and I have agreed to take his place for this momentous.... shall I say.... monstrous... occasion?

ON THE OTHER SIDE OF THE STAGE, ANNE CLASPS HER HAND'S TO HER MOUTH IN TERROR.

DRACULA - But first, before I introduce the star of our pageant, an appetiser as it were. The young woman who stole the monster's heart, and inspired the desire that has led him to this hall tonight... Miss Anne Darrow.

DRACULA GESTURES HYPNOTICALLY. ANNE FALLS BACK UNDER THE SPELL, AND WALKS STIFFLY ONTO STAGE. DRACULA, SMILING, LAYS ONE ARM OVER HER SHOULDER AND WAVES TO THE CROWD AS IT APPLAUDS. ANNE STARES OUT BLANKLY, WITHOUT EXPRESSION.

DRACULA (whispers) - Soon, child, your purpose will be fulfilled.

DRACULA - My partner, Mister Denham, would have told you a rousing tale of adventures, I have no doubt. But that adventure is the past, it is dusty pages. I, Count Dracula, bring you the here and now. I bring you glory. I will show you the future. On this stage tonight, my long quest is fulfilled, my plans will come to fruition, and it shall be before your eyes. I give you... King Kong, the Eighth Wonder of the World!

DRACULA GESTURES, THE CURTAIN PULLS BACK AND KING KONG, IN CHAINS IS EXPOSED.

KONG ROARS. THE AUDIENCE GASPS.

DRACULA - An awesome beast. But still merely a beast. But abide my children, for tonight; I shall bring you a ninth wonder, a sight that you shall, each of you carry to your graves.

DRISCOLL (shouting) - Dracula!

DRISCOLL AND SEVERAL POLICEMEN RUN ONTO THE STAGE, ACCOMPANIED, ODDLY ENOUGH, BY

A PRIEST. DRISCOLL AND THE POLICEMEN HAVE GUNS DRAWN. THE POLICE ARE VISIBLY INTIMIDATED BY THE GIANT PRIMATE NEXT TO THEM.

DRISCOLL - Dracula! You are under arrest.

DRACULA (sneering) - Mister Driscoll, good of you and your... friends, to join us. But you are too late.

DRISCOLL - Not by half. Move away from Anne, or we'll shoot. (Calling to Anne) Anne! He murdered Denham.

AUDIENCE GASPS

DRACULA (imperiously) - Your guns mean nothing to me.

DRISCOLL - But this will!

DRISCOLL PULLS OUT A CRUCIFIX. DRACULA HISSES AND COWERS, SHIELDING HIMSELF WITH HIS CAPE. ANNE'S SPELL IS BROKEN, AND SHE SCREAMS AND JUMPS AWAY, FLEEING INTO DRISCOLL'S ARMS. DRISCOLL AND THE POLICEMEN ADVANCE.

DRISCOLL - It's over, Dracula, you are finished.

DRACULA - You foolish man!

DRACULA GESTURES AT THE GREAT APE. KING KONG ROARS AND BEGINS TO STRUGGLE. THE POLICEMEN SLOW IN THEIR ADVANCE TOWARDS DRACULA, TERRIFIED BY THE GIANT FIGURE. ONE OF THE MANACLES SNAPS. A POLICEMAN SCREAMS AND SHOOTS AT KONG, BUT THIS ONLY MADDENS THE GREAT APE.

KONG BREAKS FREE, SWEEPING UP POLICEMEN AND TEARING THEM TO PIECES. THE AUDIENCE ERUPTS IN PANDEMONIUM AS THE GREAT APE

RAGES AMONG THEM WILDLY, TO DRACULA'S LAUGHTER.

DRISCOLL FLEES WITH ANNE.

* * *

DRACULA CLIMBS UP ON KONG'S BACK. AFFIXING HIMSELF AT THE BACK OF KONG'S NECK. FOR A MOMENT, THE APE RESISTS, BUT THEN FALLS TO THE VAMPIRE'S SPELL.

KONG GOES ON A RAMPAGE THROUGH NEW YORK, MAIMING AND SMASHING, WITH DRACULA'S CAPE FLYING VISIBLY BEHIND HIM, AND DRACULA'S SHOUTED EXHORTATIONS TO DESTROY EVERYTHING HE TOUCHES.

DRACULA - The blood! The blood of the ape is exhilarating. More blood! I will drown this city in blood!

* * *

ANNE AND DRISCOLL FLEE THROUGH THE CITY. JACK PUSHING THROUGH THE CROWDS WITH ANNE IN TOW.

ANNE - This nightmare will never end. He's hunting us. I can feel it. I can feel him in my mind, searching for me. Oh Jack, what are we going to do?

DRISCOLL - The police will take care of those horrors. Or the army will. Come on, babe. I'll take you somewhere safe.

* * *

DRISCOLL TAKES ANNE TO A HOTEL. SHE LIES ON THE BED.

ANNE - Oh Jack, I can feel him. It's as if he's looking at me. My head hurts.

DRISCOLL - Wait here, babe. I'll get you some ice.

DRISCOLL LEAVES ROOM.

A MOMENT LATER, KING KONG'S ARM BURSTS THROUGH THE ROOM AND SEIZES ANNE. HER SCREAMS BRING DRISCOLL BACK. HE OPENS THE DOOR TO SEE THE ARM WITHDRAWING AND LEAPS UPON THE FIST, BUT A FLICK OF THE FINGER SENDS HIM FLYING.

* * *

NOW WITH ANNE IN KONG'S POSSESSION, THE APE RAMPAGES ACROSS NEW YORK, WRECKING A CROWDED ELEVATED TRAIN AS DRACULA LAUGHS MANIACALLY, ALMOST DRUNK ON THE APE'S BLOOD.

DRACULA SPIES THE EMPIRE STATE BUILDING.

DRACULA - There, go there. Atop that building we will be out of range of accursed policemen and guns. There we can finish the sacrifice.

KONG HEADS FOR THE EMPIRE STATE BUILDING.

IN HIS WAKE, DRISCOLL FOLLOWS.

* * *

DISTANT SHOT OF KONG CLIMBING THE EMPIRE STATE BUILDING, DRACULA'S CAPE FLYING FROM HIS NECK AS THE VAMPIRE CLINGS, HOLDING A SCREAMING ANNE IN HIS HAND.

* * *

SCENE. ATOP THE EMPIRE STATE BUILDING. KONG, DRACULA AND ANNE.

ANNE - Why are you doing this to me? Why? I thought you cared for me. You looked after me. How could you be like this?

DRACULA - All these years, child. I have prepared you for this moment.

ANNE - Why? What moment? What do you want?

DRACULA - Why? Power. To walk in the sun again. To be truly immortal. To raise up legions. To live as a Prince. What else is there?

ANNE - I don't understand. How?

DRACULA - An ancient rite. A pure sacrifice to a godly beast... Come, it is time for you to fulfill your destiny.

DRACULA SEIZES ANNE, AND BEGINS CHANTING....

DRACULA - To the dark spirits and the things that dwell beyond the walls of night, I give to thee....

DRACULA'S BROW WRINKLES, HE LOOKS CONFUSED.

DRACULA - What is this? Something is wrong?

DRACULA'S FACE ERUPTS IN RAGE.

DRACULA - Impure! You are impure! (Raging) How could you do this to me! You worthless slut!

DRACULA HURLS HER AGAINST THE DOME; SHE CLINGS TO THE LEDGE OF THE EMPIRE STATE BUILDING, AS THE APE LOOKS DOWN AT THEM FROM ABOVE. THE APE GROWLS MENACINGLY, CLEARLY PREFERRING ANNE.

DRISCOLL - Get your hands off her!

DRISCOLL HAS APPEARED AROUND THE EDGE OF THE DOME. ANNE IS PRONE BETWEEN THEM. DRACULA SNARLS IN FURY.

DRACULA - Driscoll! Accursed mortal, I should have snapped your neck and thrown you overboard that first night on the ship. I will remedy that mistake.

DRACULA STEPS FORWARD, BUT AS HE DOES, HIS BODY SHAKES SUDDENLY, AS BULLETS FROM A BIPLANE STITCH THROUGH HIS CHEST. BUT THOUGH SHOT SEVERAL TIMES, DRACULA DOES NOT FALL. KING KONG ROARS AND SHAKES HIS FIST AT THE BIPLANES NOW FLYING AROUND.

DRACULA SMILES HUMOURLESSLY.

DRACULA - I told you, Driscoll, bullets mean nothing to me.

DRISCOLL, PULLING ANNE TO HER FEET, AND HOLDING HER IN HIS ARMS, PULLS OUT A CRUCIFIX. BOTH DRISCOLL AND ANNE HOLD IT TOGETHER, STARING THE VAMPIRE DOWN. DRACULA SHRINKS FROM IT, COWERING BEHIND HIS CLOAK.

DRISCOLL - Not so tough now!

DRACULA - You forget, I control the beast!

KING KONG REACHES DOWN FROM ABOVE, SLAPPING BOTH DRISCOLL AND ANNE. DRISCOLL ALMOST FALLS OFF THE LEDGE. DRACULA CATCHES ANNE.

DRACULA - Now slut, die!

ANNE SCREAMS

SUDDENLY, KONG'S HAND REACHES DOWN AND SEIZES DRACULA, LIFTING THE VAMPIRE HIGH IN THE AIR. THE VAMPIRE'S ARMS AND LEGS KICK, AND DRACULA SHOUTS WITH RAGE, BUT THE GIANT APE REFUSES TO OBEY. INSTEAD, HE WAVES THE STRUGGLING VAMPIRE IN THE AIR

ABOVE HIS HEAD, AS IF THREATENING THE BIPLANES.

CLOSE UP OF DRACULA'S FACE SCREAMING IN IMPOTENT RAGE AND FURY.

KING KONG IMPALES DRACULA ON THE ON THE EMPIRE STATE BUILDING RADIO MAST.

AS THE VAMPIRE BREATHES HIS LAST, THE BIPLANES, KNOWING ONLY THAT KONG HAS KILLED ONE OF THE PEOPLE UP THERE WITH HIM, UNLEASH THEIR FURY, STITCHING HIM FULL OF BULLETS.

ANNE AND DRISCOLL TAKE THE OPPORTUNITY TO ESCAPE INTO THE HATCH, LEAVING KONG TO HIS FATE.

THE BIPLANES STITCH THE GIANT APE WITH BULLETS AGAIN AND AGAIN, UNTIL HE FALLS.

* * *

ON THE STREET FAR BELOW, THE GREAT APE FINALLY BREATHES HIS LAST.

ANNE AND DRISCOLL ARE IN THE CROWD GAZING AT THE MIGHTY CORPSE.

ANNE - I don't know which was the greater monster. At the end, he destroyed Dracula, and the planes destroyed him.

DRISCOLL - No. It was beauty that killed the beasts.

FADE TO BLACK

* * *

FADE IN. IT IS THE NEXT EVENING. NEWSPAPER BOYS ARE STILL HAWKING THE STORY OF THE GIANT APE.

A FLATBED TRUCK HAS LOADED KONG'S BODY, AND IS DRIVING HIM OUT OF THE CITY.

KONG'S EYES SNAP OPEN.

THEY ARE BRIGHT RED.

＊＊

BACKGROUND

In 1932, David O. Selznick was suddenly and unceremoniously fired from RKO Studios, by studio head David Sarnoff. Ostensibly this was a cost cutting measure, as Sarnoff resented the young impresario.

Concurrent with this a number of projects in development were cancelled. Among these were Merian C. Cooper's, King Kong, a project that Sarnoff found excessively technical and obscure, seeing no real audience. Cooper had been brought to RKO by Selznick and the men were close. When Selznick found a new posting at Universal Studios, he sought to bring over Cooper and his project.

At this time, under studio head Carl Laemmle Jr., Universal Studios had found a niche in horror and was developing its pantheon of monsters, Dracula and Frankenstein had appeared in 1931, the Mummy in 1932.

Bela Lugosi in particular, was a major star, moving from Dracula in 1931, to Murder in the Rue Morgue and White Zombie in 1932. However, neither of these movies had been as popular as Dracula, and Laemmle Jr., was casting about for a vehicle to bring back Lugosi and his most famous character.

Initially, King Kong appeared to be a perfect fit, an addition to Universal's horror pantheon. But despite Selznick and Cooper's enthusiasm, Laemmle Jr. had reservations. Laemmle Jr., like Sarnoff before him, found himself intimidated by the ambition and technical requirements of King Kong.

In an effort to guarantee bankability, in an early case of studio meddling, Laemmle Jr. insisted on the addition of Bela

Lugosi to the cast and Dracula to the script. After considerable argument, Cooper relented. King Kong became King Kong Meets Dracula. Thereafter, Laemmle Jr. largely left the production alone, although the final shot of Kong's red eyes, hand painted onto each print, was a Laemmle inspiration, albeit one which has never been followed up on.

The decisions were not without controversy. For different reasons, both Cooper and Lugosi were unhappy with the result. Despite acquiescence, Cooper bitterly resented Laemmle Jr's meddling. For his part, Lugosi immediately objected to second billing in the title, Dracula following after the Ape. He resented the portrait of Dracula in the script, finding it a radical departure from the previous portrayals, and was heard to comment that the part deserved a stunt man rather than an actor. It would be over twenty years before Lugosi would agree to return to the role.

The two monsters would immediately part ways. Dracula was absent in the comedic sequel, Son of Kong, released six months later. Subsequent iterations of Dracula would be played by Lon Chaney Jr. and John Carradine, and would encounter Frankenstein, the Wolfman and even the Mummy, but would never again encounter the great ape. Universal Studios followed up with another monster duo, Bride of Frankenstein, and avidly crossed over its monster franchises, but Kong, due to the difficulties and expense of stop motion, was the odd man out.

Cooper parted ways with Universal, and over the next decades, attempted to produce a remake, invariably without Dracula due to rights issues, but usually with a replacement character, typically a witch doctor or a mad scientist. The 1970's Dino De Laurentis remake for instance, featured Gene Hackman as a renegade biologist filling the Dracula role. The Peter Jackson remake adapts and reduces the role to a maddened sailor, a prior visitor to Skull Island broken by his experience.

While it is settled movie lore that Dracula wasn't originally part of the story, the myth persists that the original drafts and outlines with RKO had no equivalent character. Dracula and his entire subplot was a complete interpolation. Proof of this is in a succession of drafts under RKO and even early in the Universal period which depict a straightforward adventure with no subplots.

For generations, film historians have speculated about what King Kong would have been without Laemmle's meddling, nevertheless King Kong Meets Dracula remains revered as a landmark of Cinema.

The End

The Headless Horseman

I remember once walking along in a country rode in Connecticut, late in the evening, and suddenly hearing the clip clop of horse's hooves.

At first I tried to ignore the sound, but as night fell, the sound of hooves grew closer and closer. I darted onto a hiker's path to avoid it, but the noise followed me down the path.

I'd heard stories of a headless horseman who prowled these roads at night, accosting unwary pedestrians for his unnatural purposes. My imagination ran away from me, and I imagined that I was pursued by this same demonic entity.

The moon came out; an owl startled me with its hoot. The sound grew closer. It was practically upon me.

I started to run, my heart pounding, my breath coming in ragged sheets. I coursed down the path, heedless of obstacles. Behind me, my mysterious pursuer broke into a gallop.

I burst into a clearing. Ahead of me lay shelter, a light standard, a small public building. Already winded, I gathered my remaining energy for a sprint. I could almost feel the demon horse's breath upon my neck.

"Excuse me," a sepulchral voice boomed behind me, "is this yours?"

I stopped, frozen in place by that unearthly voice. Slowly I turned.

My heart froze in my chest. For there before me was a horse with glowing red eyes, sparks flew from its hooves as it stamped the ground. Smoke billowed from its mouth and nostrils. The beast conveyed a sense of mass beyond the bulk of its huge frame, as if it was made of something more fearsome than flesh and bone.

But fearsome as the horse was, the rider was even more terrifying. Dressed in ragged black leather, the patches of flesh, the bulging muscle and sinew, that shone through had an unnatural sheen, an oily quality that did not resemble wholesome sweat, but rather a corpse like slickness. The frame of he who sat upon the horse was massive, the wrists and hands heavy and powerful, the thighs thick as tree trunks, the barrel shaped chest giving it a bearlike aspect.

But the worst part was that the figure had no head! Where the head should have been, was the merest wisp of steam issuing, and the hints of an unearthly glow.

"Is this yours?"

And the figure held out the grisly trophy it had carried as it pursued me.

It was my own head!

"Oh shit," I swore. Quickly, I reached up to feel my neck.

"I found it on a picnic table a ways back," the headless horseman said.

"Yes," I said taking it from his hands, "it's mine. Thank you for returning it."

"Not a problem. Glad to be of service."

I checked my head. None the worse for the wear. I shined a spot on the forehead with a bit of spit and rubbed it against my elbow for luck.

"I really do appreciate this," I said. "Most people wouldn't even bother. They'd just drop it off at the lost and found, or they'd toss it in the trash."

"Does this happen a lot?" the horseman asked.

"Oh gosh," I said, snapping my head back on and making sure the clasps were tight. "This is so embarrassing. People are always telling me that I'd forget it if it wasn't screwed on tight. I'm chronically absent minded."

"Think nothing of it," the horseman said. "Happens to the best of us. I could tell you stories…"

"I'm sure you could," I replied. "This happens all too often. All the time with me. Wallets, car keys, heads..."

"I know what you mean."

"Well... thanks."

"You're welcome."

"Uh... if there's ever anything I can do..." my voice trailed off, as I realized it was not wise to make such offers to supernatural beings, even if they had been kind enough to return your head to you from wherever you'd forgotten it.

There was an awkward silence.

"I notice that we're near a public men's room," the Horseman observed suddenly.

"So we are," I replied.

The horsemen casually adjusted his pants, and I noticed that his fly was unzipped. From the shape pressing against the fabric of his trousers, I realized that truly this was a horse man.

"So..." the horseman said, "do you come here often?"

Well, I'm not that kind of person. So even though I appreciated his kindness, I wasn't inclined to reciprocate as he might have hoped. There's a limit to gratitude.

He remained a headless horseman.

The End

The Matter of the Goat

"Hey Dennis," came my brother's cheerful voice on the phone, "you want to make a few dollars?"

I suppose that was where it all went wrong.

It was summer in the 79 or the early 80s, I was down working late at Dad's Garage. Neither of us were twenty, back then. We were kids out in the Maritimes, living on the edge of this little pulp and paper town.

"What's up?" I asked.

"Old Man McCurdy's goat got loose again. Someone spotted it running around the cemetery. We go get it, bring it back to him; he'll give us twenty bucks. We'll split it."

I thought about that. Old McCurdy was a frequent customer at the garage; he drove around in a four door Maverick that had apparently been painted with a roller. God knows where he got that car from. But it was Dad's mission to keep that car alive. We never made much money off him, but as Dad would say, that wasn't the point. Old guys like that out in the countryside, being able to drive was essential.

He had a goat as a pet. I have no idea why. I don't think he ever let it in the house. I sure as hell don't think he walked it. Mostly it was tied up in his yard, either the back of the front.

Once in a while it would get out, and the trouble was, if the cops or animal control got it, it ended up at the pound, and he'd have to pay Fifty dollars to get it out. So you know, if someone was nice enough to catch it and bring back before then, he'd find a few dollars.

So it made sense.

Usually, on these sorts of things, John would call his friend Bobby. They hung out a lot. John, and I though, we weren't enemies or anything. We were okay with each other. We were just very different, and we didn't do a lot together.

Once in while we'd go camping, or work on something together. One time he got a flat out in Atholville, so I brought him a spare tire and a jack. Stuff like that. I kind of liked those occasions. Maybe we didn't have a lot in common, but he was always my brother, and there's something to that.

Like I said, usually he'd do this stuff with Bobby. But I guess Bobby wasn't around. So I was next on the list.

"Sounds good," I said.

"Be there in five."

I shut down the garage and cleaned up. There wasn't really anything important I was doing, Just some body work and puttering around. I found some old cords and some rope. I figured that would do.

True to his word, John showed up with his 1967 navy blue convertible, a Fury. That was a hell of a car, huge engine, big as a boat. Relic of a bygone era of flash and ambition, when everything was bit and shiny.

When you're the son of a mechanic, growing up at a garage, sometimes you get to drive a sharp car. We'd found it in junkyard, it had been in fairly good shape, and restored it. We had project like that.

We'd restored Dad's original 57 Ford Convertible, black and white, with tail fins. When I was a kid, I used to think it was the Batmobile. He'd put it away in the back years ago, so long that a tree had actually grown up through it. But when we were teens, we cut through the tree, and spent a year rebuilding it.

My car was a 73 Comet. Actually it was a challenge, a rusted out piece of junk that I'd painstakingly put back together, cutting away rust, welding plates, buffing, smoothing and filling, replacing just about every part of it, including the engine, transmission, breaks, shocks and steering.

Dad remained a mechanic right up until his death at 79, kept his license to the end. He had his garage for sixty years.

John went into the family trade, he's got his own garage now, it's a pretty good outfit. I'm proud of him.

But anyway, we're talking the goat.

Honest to god, we thought it was going to be simple, go out to the cemetery, snatch the critter, bring it to Old Man McCurdy. He'd be grateful, we'd each make ten. Yay. What could go wrong?

Wrong cemetery. We went, we looked, nothing. We drove around the neighbourhood a little bit. No goat. I was ready to call it quits. But John could get stubborn. If the goat wasn't there, maybe we were at the wrong place.

There were a bunch of little cemeteries, so we drove around. Second graveyard, still no goat.

It was getting dark. I was kind of doubtful about the whole notion of chasing a goat around a cemetery at night. There are some things that just don't seem like good ideas when you say them out loud.

But John didn't want to quit.

So we decided to try one more cemetery, the Catholic one by the river. That was a ways out; god knows what the goat would have been doing out there. But why not?

Third time was the charm; there was McCurdy's goat, minding its own business, eating the flowers, and thinking whatever it is that goats think about. We pulled up to the cemetery gate. It took a look at us, decided not to be concerned, and went back to dismantling someone's memorial wreath.

That, by the way, is why I put plastic flowers on graves. Real flowers, the first time, when it's fresh. But afterwards, plastic flowers. They last longer, and you never know when a goat is going to come round.

Anyway, it was dark by that time, but everything seemed
to be going well. I had the cords, John had the rope. We
weren't displaying them, didn't want to put the critter off.

The plan was we were just going to walk up very casually,
and then lead it back to the car, and head over to McCurdy.
John had laid a tarp down so it could sit in the back seat. I
wasn't thrilled with that. I'd have to be in the back seat with
it, to keep it from doing anything stupid, like jumping out, or
eating the leather seats. But it didn't seem like a big deal.

We walked up to the goat, and the goat casually walked the
other direction. Like it wasn't even paying attention to us, it
just happened to see something over there, so it went that
way.

So we just followed along, and it kept ambling in the
wrong direction. Very casually.

John was going, "Here kitty kitty." Which didn't make a
lot of sense to me. But it wasn't working.

The goat kept ambling. John and I split up, coming at it in
two directions, and it just moseyed in a third direction.

It was deliberately avoiding us. The bastard.

I've seen that with some critters. Most animals, when they
want to avoid humans, they just make tracks and keep on
going. But every now and then, you'll run across something,
cats, dogs, Canada geese, raccoon, even a deer. They're not
that worried about humans, they're casual about it, as you
approach, they just happen to act like they're casually going
somewhere else, keeping that distance.

We started speeding up. The goat started speeding up.
Next thing you know, we were chasing the damned thing all
over the cemetery, being disrespectful to fresh graves.
Accidentally knocked over a tombstone. We'd have it
trapped, and it would just slip away. We got it, and it
squirmed free.

Finally, we caught the thing.

Now, I suppose if you're a cowboy, or a farm boy, the
thing to do would be to truss it up and hog tie it like a

Christmas turkey. We were a couple of mechanic's sons, and this was a furiously struggling creature. So what I'm saying is that our rope skills were sort of random and free form.

I'm still amazed that we didn't end up accidentally tying one of us to the goat.

I remember the goat struggling and bleating as we worked, and I swear to god, there was something insulting about the 'Bahhh.' Like it was mocking us.

Anyway, we got the goat tied up, and carried bodily over to the car. That whole thing about the back seat? Forget it. That shaggy little bastard had used up all its goodwill. The spare tire went in the back seat; the goat went in the trunk.

Then we put the tombstone back that we knocked over. Mostly. It's not as easy as it sounds. Those things are heavy. You'd think that they'd be anchored better. Maybe it was just that one. But we got it like mostly upright. Leaning about sixty or seventy degrees.

"Do you think anyone will notice?" John asked.

"It looks fine," I said. "Whoever looks after these places can finish up."

It was pretty late, but mission accomplished. We had the goat!

We were looking forward to dripping in on Old McCurdy, dropping off the goat, he'd be happy as a clam, the critter would be back where it belonged, and we'd each have a little money.

McCurdy lived in a place in the hills called Dundee. Going by the main roads, we'd have to go all the way round, but John figured he knew some short cuts on the old country roads. Fine with me. John liked to drive around. Me, I was a point A to point B sort. So I figured he knew what he was doing.

And he did, sort of.

The thing was country dirt roads, middle of the night, no streetlights, no signs... We got a little lost. Easy to happen. Not horribly lost. It's not like we didn't know where we were, approximately. It's just easy to kind of miss a turn, or take the wrong turn, or overshoot the mark. So all we needed to do was retrace our steps, and then retrace them again.

That's what we were doing when the police car that had been quietly following us for a mile, turned on its flashing lights and siren, right behind us.

We just about jumped out of our skins. We slammed on the brakes; they must have expected us to run, because they almost plowed right into us. We could hear the police car's breaks locking, spray of gravel behind us. My heart was just pounding out of my chest.

We were looking at each other. What the hell did we do? What did they want? What are we going to do?

John said, "Don't tell them about the goat!"

You're a couple of teenagers, it's the middle of the night, you're driving around on dirt roads with a goat in your trunk. That made perfect sense.

"They'll take our goat, Dennis, they'll take our goat!" John was whispering urgently. "They'll just bring it to the pound. McCurdy'll have to pay fifty bucks to get it back again. He's an old man. He doesn't have that kind of money."

I don't know why it was so important to him to convince me with the 'poor old Mr. McCurdy' shtick. I was already convinced. I had not had a good relationship with the cops. There had been certain misunderstandings. I didn't like them. I didn't trust them. As far as I was concerned, I minded my own business, and they could all just piss off.

We'd been at this all night. That goat owed me ten dollars, goddammit. I wasn't going to give it up.

Besides, they'd probably accuse us of stealing it. Like who the hell steals goats? You ever hear about that? Have you read headlines about goat-stealing rings? You read brochures and television specials about how to protect your goat? Goat theft prevention?

Yeah, maybe in the 8th Century, goat-stealing was a thing.

No! It's fucking goat! No one wants to steal a goat. I'm surprised that people didn't pay not to have goats returned.

"Mr. Jones, we've taken your goat, and if you don't pay the ransom…. We'll bring him back!"

"No, no, not that, I'll pay anything. Don't bring her back!"

But the point is that my relationship with the police was so poor that I wouldn't put it past them to accuse me of goat stealing. I was feeling righteously angry at the thought.

So the point is, as the officers approached on either side, and as we waited, that we were decided on one single thing, with the absolute certainty come from a lifetime as brother.

We were not going to mention the goat!

Which made it difficult to explain what we were doing driving around in a convertible on backwoods dirt roads in the middle of the night. One of them walked up. John got a flashlight in the face.

"What are you doing?" the officer asked.

"Nothing."

"Where are you going?"

"Nowhere."

"Just driving around," I said.

The thing was, they'd run across the Caldron Boys, driving slowly around dirt roads in the middle of the night. We each had our separate encounters and our distinct reputations with the law. So they'd probably concluded that we weren't up to anything good.

I have no idea what they thought we were doing. Bootlegging? Drug running? Looking for a connection? Who the hell knows?

"In the middle of the night?"

"Is that illegal?" I snapped.

The flashlight was on me.

"Where were you coming from?"

I looked away from the flashlight.

"Home. We're out for a drive. We'd like to get going," I snapped. "I'm not saying anything else."

"Is that a spare tire in the back seat?"

"Yeah," John said. "The trunk is full. We had to put it in the back."

I could have kicked him. Because I knew what was next.

"What's in the trunk?"

"Nothing."

Ouch. He did it again.

"It's just full of junk," I said quickly. "It's nothing."

"Can I take a look?"

"No!"

Well, that got us pulled out of the car, standing on the side of the road with flashlights in our faces.

Well that was it, if they weren't suspicious then, they were over the top. At that point, they figured they had a major criminal bust on their hands. And whatever it was, it was in that trunk.

They were absolutely sure; they had like a big time crime. I'm sure they were thinking headlines, commendations, whatever it is that juices cops up. They knew they had us, and it all came down to whatever it was that was in that trunk.

And me and John, we were going to eat broken glass before we told them about the goat. To hell with that. We didn't see any good outcome to that. I wasn't about to have cops steal my goat. Or arrest me on a totally fake charge of goat theft. It just wasn't on. We were both stubborn as hell, that's the one big thing we had in common.

Which left us at a stalemate, because they weren't going to let us go without seeing what was in that trunk.

The conversation went something like this.

"Open the trunk."

"No."

"That's an order."

"I don't care. No."

"We'll make you open it."

"No."

"Open it or we'll arrest you."

"Go ahead. We didn't do anything. We'll sue you."

"Fine, we'll get a warrant. Then we'll arrest you."

"Get a warrant then."

"We have a right to look in that trunk. Probable cause."

"Forget it."

"Boys, come on, it's late. We're all tired. Just open the thing and we can all leave."

"No."

"What are you hiding?"

"Nothing."

"So open it."

"No."

"That's suspicious."

"No it's not."

Okay, that doesn't sound so bad. But repeat that about a hundred times, in the middle of the night, over what felt like an hour and a half, standing out there in the middle of nowhere with flashlights in our faces. I guarantee, you will want to peel your own face off in frustration at the sheer inanity of the thing. It was like hell, and I just kept getting more and more frustrated.

There was a knock from the trunk. The goat had been quiet, but it must have woken up, or gotten loose or something. We all heard it.

"What's that?" one of the officers asked, startled.

"Nothing," John said.

Then it kicked up a racket.

And my god, you never saw two officers pull guns so fast. It was amazing; it was like they'd been practising their quick draw all night. One moment, they're standing there. Next moment, the goat is kicking away at the inside of the trunk, and zap the guns are in their hands.

Both pointing them at me, I noticed. One was covering John, but they were both actually pointing at me. I thought that was pretty unfair. I thought about saying something. But then decided not to.

I settled for glowering at them, and trying to telepathically convey the words "you arseholes."

I decided that this had gone far enough.

"It's a goat," I said.

Of course, they didn't believe me.

John chipped in. We tried to explain the whole McCurdy thing. The damned thing was that the more we told the truth, the less they believed. We kept saying it's a goat. Listen. But the damned thing wasn't bleating, or not bleating loud enough. Instead, it was making sounds that I'd never heard out of a goat in my entire life. The cops were shouting at the trunk, and every time they did, the thing would kick again, and wail like a thirteen year old girl.

"You're both under arrest, don't move, hands up, move away from the car. Open up the trunk!"

I've noticed this about cops. Quite often, when they're giving instructions in tense situations, they contradict themselves. It's always 'don't move' and 'get down on the floor.' 'Give me your papers' 'Wait! Don't move!' 'Show me your hands!' It's like they don't even listen. God help you if you point out that its contradictory orders or ask which ones to comply with. Because then, apparently, you're resisting!

"How can we open the trunk if we have to move away from the car?" I asked.

"Shut the hell up, you're under arrest!"

"You already said that," I pointed out.

"Shut the hell up!"

"Shut up, Dennis," John whispered. I was disappointed. You expect back up from your own brother, but no, suddenly he was on their side.

So we moved away from the car, until we were standing in the headlights of the police car, with our hands on our heads. I felt like a goof.

One of the cops kept us covered, just like in a movie, while the other went and got the keys. They weren't there, of course.

"Where are the keys?" the cop asks.

"In my pocket," John says.

"Give them to me," the cop says.

"No," John says.

"That's an order."

"I don't care."

I could feel my eyeballs rolling up in my head, because it was clear that we were about to embark on another idiotically circular conversation for another hour and a half.

"Just give him the keys," I said sourly, still stinging over that 'shut up, Dennis,' thing.

"I'm not giving him my keys," John said.

"Fine," I snapped. "Give me the keys. I'll open up the trunk. They can see the goat, and then we can get out of here."

For some reason, everyone thought that was a good plan. Which, in hindsight it really wasn't.

So, I got the keys, and one cop stayed with John, and the other went with me to the back of John's car. I got the twitchy short one with the mustache and the attitude. That's terrific.

"It's just a goat," I said. But they just weren't having it.

"Open the trunk," the cop said, mean and nasty, like he was in a Clint Eastwood movie. His gun was still on me, which just annoyed me because there was no need. I was going to open the trunk.

I put the key in and popped the lock, and the minute the trunk cracked open an inch, the goddamned goat came boiling out, like he was spring loaded. You'd have thought there was a catapult in there, the way he came out. I stepped away. And the goat just blasted straight into the cop.

He went back on his ass, all the air going out of him, and he gave this red faced "Woof!"

John burst out laughing. I don't remember what the other cop was doing. I remember he shouted and jumped like a little girl as the goat ran past. I remember having this fleeting thought, like Jesus, he couldn't even be a little bit useful and grab it. But no, grabbing goats was apparently not in cop job description.

If this was a proper story, the damned goat would have hit the officer right in the nuts. I really wish that would have happened.

But from what I recollect, it was like the goat hit the cop in the midsection, knocking the wind out of him, and then tried to climb him like a ladder, so for a second, the two of them were tangled up, while the officer staggered back, and then landed on his ass. The goat disentangled and ran away.

John was literally bent over laughing, he thought it was hysterical, the greatest thing ever. All I could think was, just one damned thing after another.

The cop, to give him credit, bounced back to his feet. It was like a cartoon, and his ass was made of rubber. Boom, goat knocks him back on his butt, and POW, he just bounces right back up. He's freaked out. He's totally red in the face. He's just totally over the top.

"What was that! What was that! What did you do!"

"I told you..."

He was poking me in the chest with his gun.

"What the hell was that? What the hell was that?" he was screaming at me.

I just kept staring at him.

"I told you, it was a goat," I said.

Of course, John is no help, doubled over laughing like it's the funniest thing ever. The other cop seems to have no idea what to do. I think he wants to laugh, but he's afraid his partner will shoot him for it.

I'm thinking if I get shot because of this asshole, I'm going to punch him. If he shoots me, I'm going to punch him right in the face. You're not supposed to punch police officers, but he was working up to it.

His partner calmed him down, and they put the guns away. Then we had to tell the story all over again, the same story that we'd already told them three times. But I don't know, maybe the shock of seeing an actual goat had made them forget it. What a waste of time.

At least this time they believed us. Sort of.

Of course, now that the trunk was open, they had to have a look, because you know, maybe we were smuggling goats and heroin. Because everyone knows goats and heroin go together.

Actually, they don't. I mean, I don't think so. I'm pretty sure that they don't. If I was a drug trafficker, I'd never smuggle goats and heroin together. What if the goat ate the heroin? Not that I have any direct knowledge of these matters, for the record. It just seems reasonable.

So anyway, we had to explain the whole thing over, and they had to look in the trunk. I was so bored and frustrated by the whole thing. I was pissed off. We were all just standing around, using tinier and tinier words to try and get through Officers Dudley and DoRights tiny pea brains, and meanwhile, the goat was fucking off to wherever.

So finally, I said, "John, you deal with these arseholes. I'm going to go find the goat."

I didn't say 'arseholes.' I said 'Officers.' But I was thinking it.

"Where are you going?" The red face officer screamed. "I didn't tell you that you could leave."

It's the middle of the night, middle of nowhere, on a dirt road. Where did he think I was going? Was this some stealthy escape plan? Was I up to something? Were they going to shoot me? What the hell were they thinking?

"I'm just going to get the goat," I said patiently, and stared at them.

After about a minute, it got through.

"Okay, go get it."

Seriously, what were they going to do? Shoot me for >goat-finding?' Is >goat-searching' in the Criminal Code? They all looked at each other and said fine. John was better at dealing with them than I was. They liked him better. Around me, they always acted like I was going to pull out a lead pipe and start beating them to death, when all I was doing was returning library books.

So off I went, down the road and into the woods.

I couldn't see a goddamned thing. It was all just black. I was pretty good in the dark back then, my night vision was pretty good. But this was black; it was all I could do not to stumble into trees. There wasn't much of a chance I was going to find the goat, I was pretty sure of that. But I was stubborn. And I didn't want to go back to the car while the cops were there. So I figured I'd give it a try.

I did my best to move quietly. The thing was, I didn't figure the goat could see any better than I could, and he was a noisy little bastard. So I had a small chance that maybe I could sneak up on him.

Then, I got lucky. There was a shape, not too far from me. I held still. It held still. Then it moved. I rushed it. I mean, I put everything I had into it. He took off, but I was rocket. I caught up and tackled the little bastard to the ground. He put up a fight; he was kicking and thrashing for all he was worth. But I was angry, he'd messed with me for the last time. So I got one arm around his legs, and one arm around his body, and had it in a bear hug so he couldn't move.

He wouldn't give up. He just kept thrashing as I was trying to carry him, so I was barely keeping my balance. I kept stumbling into trees and bushes hitting my head on branches, struggling to keep my balance. All the time, all I could think was, >I really hate goats.' Finally I spied the lights of John's fury off through the bush, and headed in that direction.

I stepped out onto the road. John was waiting for me.

And, as it turned out, I was holding a deer.

Not a goat.

A fucking deer. Not big, not full sized. I think a little bigger than a faun. I don't remember if it had spots, honestly I don't.

For a moment, John is absolutely speechless. He's just dumbfounded with astonishment.

Then he bursts into laughter.

And here I am holding this stupid deer, which has finally decided to stop struggling in my arms. I turn my head, and I'm looking it in the eye. And I give it this look of utter betrayal. Like the whole thing is its fault. Like it's done this to me deliberately. I genuinely feel hurt and betrayed, like somehow, the goat and the deer have conspired to pull this on me. And of course, John just can't stop laughing. He's having the greatest time.

I put the deer down gently, all four legs touching the ground, and I back away.

But the deer doesn't move. It just stands there, looking at me illuminated in the car lights.

It's like its going 'What the hell was all that about?' It was as if, after all this bother and struggle, it was expecting something more dramatic to happen. Beats me.

Or like maybe it's waiting for an apology.

Well screw that, I'm not apologising to a frigging deer.

And honestly, now it decides to be peaceful? Why couldn't it do that when I was trying to carry it, instead of making my life seven kinds of hell?

"Shoo!" I finally say.

It scampers off.

In hindsight, I shouldn't have made that mistake. Looking back, the shape was different, the fur was finer, not as coarse. I don't know. I really thought I had the damned goat. If it ever happens again, I'll know better. Won't make that mistake twice. Not that it's likely to ever happen again.

John finally stops laughing. He doesn't actually stop, he just sort of runs out of breath to laugh. He pants for a while, catches his breath, and then starts up again. I wait patiently.

I've decided that I have no brother. That's it. We're done. I'm not saying another word to him for the rest of our lives.

People will come up and say, "Hey, I saw your brother…"

And I'll just say "Sorry, no relation."

Generations from now, when we're both old men, our grandchildren will come to me, and try and get us to patch things up. But I'll just hold my head high, and tell them >ask him about the goat.'

I get in the passenger seat. He gets in the driver's.

"What do you want to do now?" he asks.

"Let's just go," I say.

I'm done. We both know that it's gone. After all this time, there's not a chance that the goat's around. It's gone into the bush, and we'll never find it. Maybe it'll get eaten by a coyote or bear or something. Hope springs eternal. I'm just so fed up.

We drive maybe two hundred yards down, when we see the goat in our headlights.

The bastard. The complete goat bastard.

The complete goat rat sneaky bastard.

It felt like he was screwing with us.

Normally, I'm not down with punching animals. But I so wanted to punch this goat. Not kick. Not slap. Just, punch him in his goat face.

And just like in the cemetery, he does the same damned thing. He just looks up, like he's going, >oh hi, guys.' And then goes back to whatever he's eating on the side of the road, as if it's the most casual thing in the world.

We got as close as we could in the car, until he started moving away.

Then we stopped.

The goat stopped, pretending to nibble on some roadside fern. But we all knew he was just screwing with us.

John put the car in park, let it idle. We looked at each other. We didn't even have to say anything. I know that sounds like High Noon, or something by Sergio Leone. I suppose we said something. But it didn't feel like that. Because really, we'd both decided that we weren't going to let that bastard get away. We didn't need to talk about it.

We crept out on both sides of the car. We shut the doors quietly. The headlights were in its eyes, we figured that gave us an advantage. Then.... we leapt.

And it went. It wasn't quite like chasing the goat around the cemetery. This time, we knew what to expect, and we were a lot better at it. It felt a lot less like the goat was laughing at us, and a lot more like it was desperately struggling to keep out of our way. The bah's were less 'What a couple of maroons!' And more 'Oh shit, that was close, they almost got me.'

On the other hand, there was a lot more falling down on our part, because... Woods and bush. A lot more stumbling into things, going headlong into trees and branches, or stepping into pits and soft spots and just going tumbling. A lot more scratching and bruising.

Also, the goat didn't seem to particularly like the bush. I thought his night vision was no better than ours, and he wasn't much for stumbling around either, he kept working his way back to the road, which is how we got him. He must have known where he was going, because he put up a hell of a fight. This time we didn't even bother to try and tie him up, just got the rope around his neck

Of course, when he realizes he's going into the trunk, he puts up a new fight all over again, and he's screaming and basically making a fuss.

But we get him in.

I remember, just before John shut the trunk, he pointed his finger at the goat and said, very firmly, "Stay!"

It worked! The damned thing shut up for a second. He slammed the trunk. Immediately, it started kicking and screaming.

We got back in, and we looked at each other. The sky was starting to get light. Dawn was coming.

"What do you want to do?" I asked.

"These old guys," John said, "they get up pretty early. I say we should go over."

Drunk Slutty Elf and Zombies / Page 17

I thought about that. The goat was kicking and butting around in the trunk, making its non-goat noises.

"Or," he said, "we can just take it back to the garage and bring it over later."

I thought about that.

"Fuck that. Let's go."

We drove over to old man McCurdy's. I'd never been out there, but I recognised his car in the yard. He had a nice house. Smaller than I expected, a little fenced garden on the side. John went and knocked on the door while I got the goat out of the trunk.

Of course he tried to blast out, but I grabbed him by the horn, and shoved him right back in. Then we wrangled him out and over.

Old McCurdy takes a look and goes.

"That's not my goat."

We were both speechless.

"Are you sure?" John asked.

I didn't even want to say anything. I wanted to just walk away. He was asking if McCurdy was sure? Like maybe he's mistaken? Like he doesn't know his own goat? Like maybe he's decided to play a joke on us and pretend it's not his goat? Jesus Christ!

"My goat's over there," he points, over at the apple tree. And sure enough, tied under the apple tree is McCurdy's goat, he's just lying there, with his legs folded up under him, eating fallen apples.

They don't even look alike. Now that they were both in the same place. No resemblance.

"Oh," John said. "What do you want us to do with this one?"

I have no idea what he was thinking. Maybe McCurdy would give us money for delivering a strange goat? Maybe buy it from us? Maybe tell us who really owned it, because possibly goat owners are all in it together and know each other. I don't know. Maybe he didn't know either. We were

both just tired, exhausted, bruised and scratched, and
probably smelled like goat.

"I don't know," McCurdy said. "Maybe put him back
where you found him?"

Which, really, was the only thing to do, I suppose.

Glumly, we drove back to the Cemetery. He must have
tired out, because he stopped making a fuss after a while. I
don't think we said ten words to each other. We got there,
John gave me the keys, I opened the trunk. Why was I always
the one to have to open the trunk? I braced for the goat-
splosion, but no, when I opened the trunk, he just laid there
and looked up at me. I had to reach in and pull him out.

I noticed that he'd peed all over the trunk. Not my
problem. I slammed it shut. I figured that John could
discover it later.

We set the goat down on its feet in the cemetery, it
scooted off a few feet from us, then it stopped. We looked at
it. It looked at us. Then it went off and started pulling at
some weeds near a tombstone.

That's about it. John dropped me off at the garage and
went home. It was still a couple of hours before opening, so I
managed to catch a little sleep before it was time to go to
work.

I have no idea what happened to the goat. I hope it
exploded.

But apparently, they don't do that. Still, the image makes
me happy. One moment, there it is being a goat, and then
>boom!'

In hindsight, you know, kidnapping a goat from a
cemetery at night... We were probably doomed from the start.

Anyway, this is a story from when I was young and stupid,
and the time I almost got shot to death by police, in the
middle the night, on a dirt road in the middle of nowhere,
over a stupid goat. It was the second time I almost got shot

by cops. I didn't think about it much back then, but in hindsight, it kind of bothers me.

So that's why I hate goats.

* * *

The goat nibbled at an arrangement of flowers placed in front of a black marble tombstone. It couldn't read the names on the tombstone, but it found itself attracted to the polished finish. As it nibbled, it kept a wary eye on the two youths, watching as they drove off.

When it was sure that they were gone, it picked its way to the center of the cemetery, to the great gray sepulchre that lay at the center.

There was a stench of sulphur, wisps of smoke rose from the ground in front of the sepulchre, and rapidly congealed into a dark and formless cloud hanging in the air. At the center, a lambent red glow came, faint at first, but slowly intensifying, growing more distinct until it have the impression of two malevolent red eyes.

"You're late!"

"You'll never believe what happened," said the goat. "It was the damnedest thing."

The burning eyes did not blink as the story unfolded.

Finally, it spoke.

"So what the hell was that about?"

"Beats me," said the goat.

The glowing red eyes blinked thoughtfully, contemplating the fate of the universe.

"Try again in another thousand years?"

"Yeah, sure," said the goat.

The End

Friend Life

The tiger crept stealthily into the clearing.

Amend looked up from where she was taking soil samples. She smiled.

"Oh hello," she said. "Look at you, with those yellow and black stripes. You're beautiful!"

The tiger paused.

"Oh don't be shy," Amend told it.

It stared at her, as if considering.

"Come, come," she coaxed it. "I won't hurt you."

As if it understood her words, perhaps reassured by the tone of her voice, it seemed to decide, padding forward softly, its eyes fixed on her. She took a couple of careful steps toward it, careful not to frighten the creature.

"Yes," she smiled. "Oh your fur is so lovely. I bet you just love to be petted, don't you?"

It was only a couple of feet away. She stretched out her arm towards it.

"That's it," she whispered, "come a little closer."

Her fingertips were bare inches away. The tiger stretched out its neck, its nostrils twitching curiously.

Then its jaws snapped.

"Oops!"

Amend didn't feel pain, not at first. She had a sense of a blur of motion, and then a sharp yank on her arm. And then suddenly, her fingers were missing, and part of her hand. She stared at it, distracted from the tiger.

"What?" she wondered out loud. "What's this? What happened?"

The tiger seized this inopportune moment to leap on her.

"Wait! Wait!" she cried out, as the big cat's weight bore her down. "I can't play right now. I ... something's wrong with my hand. Give me a moment."

But the big cat ignored her requests. Instead, its jaws clamped down on her arm as she tried to gently push it aside.

"Ouch!" she cried out, as its fangs sank into her flesh. "Ouch! Ouch! That hurts. Stop that!"

But it ignored her request, seizing her body with its paws, claws tearing across her skin.

"Ow!" she said. "I said that hurts. Are you listening? Stop it right now."

She batted its nose gently with her free hand, trying to get it to pay attention. It just snarled, biting down again and again.

"I do not consent to this!" she cried out. "I do not consent. I find this unpleasant!"

Blood was spurting all over now, as her flesh was mauled. She was horrified; blood was all over her uniform.

"I'm responsible for cleaning this," she screamed, but somehow, she couldn't make the cat notice her distress.

After that, she only screamed and gasped.

And then panted.

Finally, there was no noise at all in the clearing, except the sound of the wind, and the noises of flesh tearing and bones crunching as the tiger fed.

* * *

The robotic probe dropped out of Overspace somewhere out in the Oort Cloud, in a region so cold and empty that the vacuum itself ached.

It had no name, and barely an identity. It was known simply by its catalogue designation, and hosted a complex of dumbed down artificial intelligences, narrowly focussed on their individual missions. Firing off its Ion drive it began a long thirty year fall into the solar system accelerating steadily, nearly reaching the orbit of Mercury before slingshotting again into the cold darkness. During its time it meticulously mapped the orbits and characteristics of every mass in the system, from gas giants to slags of rock few hundred meters across.

Then, when it finally ascended to the vast empty darkness beyond any world, it leaped up into Overspace, to its next destination, to catalogue another star.

Its data eventually found its way, a few centuries later, to the Great Archive.

Another fifteen hundred years later that data was retrieved, weighted, measured, evaluated and analysed and quantified. The judgement summarised: No particular interest.

Over the next ten thousand years, the summary evaluation was reviewed a few times, turned up by artificial intelligence search engines pursuant to various inquiries. Each time sifted, weighted and then abandoned.

Finally, one particular set of search parameters, sorting through billions of worlds, narrowing the search to a bare hundred thousand candidates, turned up the summary evaluation. The packet triggered secondary search criteria, and the entire data package was requisitioned.

Five hundred years later, the survey ship, Fomalhaut, dropped out of Overspace, in the orbit of Jupiter on the far side of the solar system from that gas giant, its shields and engines buffeted by the soup of stray atoms and charged particles that permeated the inner solar system.

* * *

"Status," Quilin asked.

Y'hain leaned back in her seat, studying the displays. She yawned, chloroplasts under her skin darkening.

"It's another Mausoleum system," she replied. "Another bust."

"Y'hain's right," Shafe said. "I'm cross referencing orbital data against the base, so far no anomalies. There's nothing floating around out there that's moved off a predicted orbit in over ten thousand years. No one has moved a meaningful amount of mass here in all that time."

"Thiral," Quilin asked. They were from the same base culture, so he tended to default to her judgments.

No radio, no emissions, no signals," Thiral said. "Not ten thousand years ago, not now. Y'hain's right, the system is a mausoleum."

"There's plenty of evidence of habitation. Planets two and four show terraforming processes."

Quilin grunted. Terraforming processes meant little. From time to time in human history, kingdoms, empires, confederations and coalitions, high on their own grandeur would go on some forsaken binge to remake their corners of the universe, envisioning some far future of endless garden worlds.

But no matter how vast the ambitions were, a planet, any planet, was enormous and clung tenaciously to its own homeostasis.

You didn't change a planet overnight with superconducting magnetospheres, orbital reflectors, or selected algae and lichens. Not even by dropping Oort cloud comets to gift oceans and atmospheres with their frozen volatiles. Whatever you did, or hoped to do, it would take hundreds of thousands of years to work itself out, for new equilibriums to evolve and for a world to hopefully stabilize. Very few civilizations that indulged in terraforming lived long enough to see their work fulfilled.

All this assuming that a planet didn't ultimately reject human meddling and return to its original homeostatic regime, or some other equally inhospitable plateau. Planets lived on geologic time scales. Humans didn't. Whoever had decided to meddle with these two planets had been so long ago, that even their civilisation was forgotten.

"There are signs of installations all over, and I've got thousands of profiles that suggest asteroids converted to floating habitats. But..."

Habitats had usually been built for a life span of a thousand or ten thousand years or so, which someone, somewhere had apparently thought was a long time. It wasn't. Slowly, steadily the vacuum leached away the habitats volatiles, thermal distortions did the rest, inside inbreeding and entropy worked away in the ultrasimplified habitat ecologies, toxins accumulated. After a while, whatever was living in the habitats could only be called human out of some form of politeness. After a longer while, nothing was left but desiccated mummies. They'd been another of humanities dead ends.

"Mausoleum system," Quilin.

There was no shortage of them. Over the hundreds of thousands of years of the human spread, space was rife with Mausoleum systems where humanity had come, bloomed and occasionally withered away for one reason or another.

"Cascade collapse?"

"Probably. Third planet seems to have life; I'm reading stable methane, oxygen, carbon dioxide, a water cycle. So the system wasn't sterilized by a solar hiccup."

"Or it crept back," Y'hain said. "At this distance there's no telling what's down there. Could just be slime molds and algae."

Life was relatively common in the Universe. One in every thousand systems had managed to evolve something resembling protozoan life. Complex life was rather more rare. One in a million systems managed some form of that, typically microscopic and crude.

"Shall we call it now?" Shafe asked. "Is this the home world of the human race?"

"No," Y'hain said. "It's another bust."

"Maybe," Thiral said.

"I'll reserve Judgment," Quilin said. "Let's take her in and check it out."

* * *

"It's not Earth," Y'hain said. "It's early. Sixth Age maybe? Possibly as far back as third or fourth, judging by the biota."

The landing module had found a flat table land bisected by a meandering river. The underlying soil was soft; the module's pads had sunk into the soft soil, but had stabilized.

The ground was spongy under Quilin's feet. He had the urge to take off his boots and walk barefoot on the grass. He gazed at the trees, the brown waters of the river, the animals coming to drink. Nothing unusual about them, there were hundreds of worlds with similar scenes, all life and species transplanted from the fabled home world. Or that was the theory, at least.

All over the planet, landing modules had descended, releasing swarms of drones, surveying the biology and geology of each continent, harvesting immense amounts of information, which would eventually be assembled and collated in order to fit this world into the long lost history of the human dispersal.

Some sort of insect landed on his forearm. He gazed at it. After a moment, it flew off. The insects were very friendly on this world. This was the dozenth such visitor. But they seemed to do no harm, so he ignored them.

"The insects here are friendly," he said conversationally.

Y'hain's brow furrowed.

"What?" she asked, clearly perplexed.

Y'hain had no experience of friendly insects, little experience of any insects at all. Barely any had made it to the simplified ecology of her Homeworld so it was difficult for her to even notice them. He'd noticed them landing on Y'hain and departing literally all day. They appeared to be beyond her threshold of perception.

Quilin rubbed at a painful stinging sensation on the back of his neck, but didn't connect that to the insects flying around. He decided not to pursue the conversation.

* * *

"It's Earth," Shafe said. "No doubt at all."

Quilin scratched at the red bumps on his forearm and tried to focus on the debate raging around him.

Drunk Slutty Elf and Zombies / Page 26

"Nonsense," Y'hain snapped.

"A series of holographic images snapped up onto screen, depicting the animal life of the world. Elephants, cattle, antelope, bats, birds, lizards, frogs and fish. For each, a luminous skeleton appeared, separating itself from the body, hanging suspended in the air. A human skeleton would appear beside each, matching bones glowing red.

"Every single animal on this world," Shafe said, "has a human skeleton. The mammals are all perfect structural matches. They have the same organs, the organs have the same functions, they're even positioned identically."

"That's because it's a torture garden!" Y'hain replied.

An involuntary shudder ran through the chamber.

Torture gardens were the product of regimes which had sought to tailor the human genome, twisting and warping the human form into a thousands of variants, each more bizarre than the last, sometimes fitting them into social or economic niches, sometimes trying to create warped ecologies, or sometimes simple exercises in sadism and perversion. Torture gardens seldom thrived, their inhabitants being confined to decaying societies on niche worlds.

Quilin had once visited a torture garden, an ancient floating habitat, far past its engineered live span, whose inhabitants had twisted themselves again and again for survival, until their society had finally collapsed. They had left a diminishing population of pallid eyeless worms, crawling painfully about on truncated limbs, toothless rubbery mouths sucking up the algal blooms that grew in the excrement they left behind. The worst thing was that they still harboured the flickers of sentience, they'd been aware of their suffering.

He'd had nightmares about it for years.

"No," Shafe said. "There's organic divergence from human. Go past mammals, you have birds, less overlap, reptiles, amphibians, fish. This isn't a torture garden. There are no signs of genetic tampering with a human template. This is a natural world, it's an evolved world."

"There are dozens of cases of evolved worlds," Y'hain said. She was scratching as well. To Quilin she seemed unusually irritated, or irritable, as if in discomfort. Y'hain wiped her running nose and sniffled.

Quilin was bored of the debate. Neither would give an inch, both delved into increasingly abstruse arcana, peculiarities of molecular biology, species counts, biological diversities. The only thing that they agreed on was that the planet was a biological mess, which you could expect from sixth era. It had been a time of wild genetic manipulation, an explosion of engineered life forms, mostly inefficient, until the final ecological suites had been established.

He tuned out, leaving an avatar in his place, and requisitioned ship status. He was disturbed to see that the medical situation hadn't improved. He tagged the Chief Medical Officer, a Breen who consented to suffer under the identity designation "Fortu."

"We have six per cent of crew reporting symptoms," he told Fortu. "I thought I told you to clear it up."

"I'm sorry," Fortu replied, the man's eyes were red and watery, like Y'hain he seemed to be sniffling; his mucosal membranes were definitely inflamed. "We're having trouble tracing the contaminant."

Was he going into a sexual phase? Quilin hadn't seen any reference to that in the updates, and regs required the intermittently gendered to report their activity periods. He pinned a note to check into that. Fortu was a good crew member, and so it was surprising they'd overlook it.

Still, Quilin had no desire to have Breen sexual fluids splashed all over his ship. A reprimand might be in order.

"That's not an adequate answer," Quilin told them.

Fortu fluttered his hands in frustration. Definitely in a sexual phase, Quilin thought.

"It's hard," Fortu said. "At first we thought it was a planetary contamination. Some exotic molecule in the environment."

That's what Quilin expected, the air had smelled funny down there.

"But... We've had cases on ship board, so now we're thinking that there might be some kind of system defect in the Landing Modules. We're running system diagnostics, and conducting manual evaluations on sections of the Landers... But..."

"But?"

"Nothing."

Quilin noticed that one of the friendly insects had landed on his arm. The world was full of friendly insects of every kind. Had someone reciprocated the affection and brought it on board? There was a protocol about crew acquiring pets. Not strictly forbidden, but there were forms to fill, permissions to obtain. At the very least, they should keep track of them. He made a notation to follow up, then forgot about it, he had pressing matters to discuss.

"It's obviously not nothing," Quilin insisted.

"No..." Fortu agreed, he leaned forward conspiratorially. "I've been searching the archives. I think it might be a ... disease."

"A what?" Quilin's brow furrowed.

"A disease."

"Dis... ease," Quilin sounded it out. "Some sort of emotional discomfort? Is someone... a number of people upset about something."

"No," Fortu said. "It's a kind of transmissible contaminant, carried by active propagating agents, bacteria or virus."

Now he was lapsing into Breen gibberish, soon there'd be sexual fluids squirted all over the place. It would be all over the ship, dripping from things, there'd be puddles of it, they'd have to upgrade the scrubbers.

"Look," Quilin said angrily, "I don't care about your sex life. Just find the contaminant and purge it. That's all."

Fortu sneezed, expelling sexual fluids. Quilin rolled his eyes; the Breen wasn't even trying to hide his overtures. He thought about telling the Breen he wasn't interested, but ... maybe later.

Just then an emergency notice broke in.

"Captain," the voice sounded panicked. Quilin recognized Onage, one of the Landing Module commanders. A steady reliable hand. His first thought was: Why was she not following protocol? But her next breath ended all questions.

"Someone's been killed," she cried. "Eaten!"

* * *

All the pieces of Amend had been gathered together, and placed in rough order, on a table in the large biological specimen's evaluation chamber.

Quilin absent mindedly waved away one of the friendly insects as he starred down at the mutilated form.

"This is Amend," he said. "Her specialty was floral specimens."

Everyone nodded.

The smell was pretty rank. He gathered that she was in process of decomposition. That or the smell was perforation of internal organs, gastro-intestinal tract. He wasn't sure. This wasn't his department.

It was definitely a solemn occasions. He should say something. He scratched absently at the welts on his skin. Others in the room shifted, trying to scratch unobtrusively

"So," he said finally. "Where's the rest of her?"

"She was eaten," Onage told him.

Quilin nodded. He sighed. Botanist jargon. What a day. Horny Breens squirting body fluids, an unknown contaminant oozing off the Landing Module systems, and now botanists unable to speak plainly.

"You mean some kind of allergic reaction?" he asked doubtfully. What kind of reaction could do this?

"No, she was eaten," Onage repeated.

Quilin's brow furrowed.

"Was there an accident? On planet? Did she fall down?"

"No, she was eaten."

"So no accident on planet?"

"Eaten."

"I see," he said. "Something happened to the body when it was being shipped back?"

He'd have to write the retrieval crew up for sloppiness. Imagine misplacing entire body parts. Quite a lot of it, from the looks.

"Eaten."

"Would you stop saying that!" Quilin snapped. "Just tell me what happened to her!"

"She was eaten..."

Quilin flushed with irritation. He understood the tendency of experts to resort to technical terminology, and he was well experienced with how colloquial terms could be distorted into jargon. But this was a serious occasion,

"What does that even mean?" he snapped.

"There was a predator, and it ate her. She was eaten."

Quilin was beyond frustrated.

"So there was a predator involved, and..."

"It ate her."

Quilin controlled his anger. Shafe sneezed. Fortu glanced at him. He favoured them both with a dark look.

"Predators don't eat humans," he told them. "Everyone knows that."

It was certainly true. Quilin was well aware of the biological curiosity that predators represented. They were native only to evolved worlds, however, where their local biochemistries made them incompatible with human life.

Predators never ate humans, most were incapable of even registering the presence of humans. In the worst cases, a predator might briefly show some curiosity before rapidly losing interest. In hundreds of thousands of years, there was no record of any predator anywhere ever injuring a human.

"This one did," Shafe said. "It ate her."

Quilin thought it over.

"So you're saying that a predator came along, and it ate her."

"Yes."

He thought about that. He could just about get his head around it. But there was still the other problem.

"All right. Well then, where's the rest of her?"

"Eaten."

"Eaten?" Quilin's brow furrowed. "By what? Some sort of acid? Do we have a contamination issue?"

Whatever contaminant could do that to a human body represented a potential danger to the entire ship.

"By the Predator, it ate her."

Quilin's brow felt hot. His temple was throbbing. He balled his hands into fists, and closed his eyes, muscles stiffening as he ran numerical sequences to calm down.

"All right," he swore. "I have had enough of this nonsense. I'm calling a staff meeting for quarter shift. In the meantime, want a full investigation, immediately. I want to know exactly what happened, and how. And I want that report presented at staff."

He sneezed. His eyes met Fortu's.

"Business before pleasure," he snarled at the Breen, and stalked off.

* * *

Luckily there was a video record of the encounter with the tiger. It played at the staff meeting. The officers watched it carefully, freeze framing and going back and forth. But no one could find fault with any of Amend's actions.

The behaviour of the tiger was simply inexplicable.

Quilin felt terrible. He felt feverish and sweaty, but somehow, he found himself shivering. His sinuses were congested, his nose ran constantly. He attributed it to grief over Amend.

Or possibly Fortu's sexual phase. That was the trouble with humans who had intermittent sexual seasons, most of the time they were fine, but when they went into heat, they pumped out an overwhelming cocktail of pheromones that affected everyone.

Quilin wasn't a racist, but this was the last time he was going to have a Breen on board.

A couple of friendly insects buzzed around, their wings a high pitched hum. Quilin thought their affectionate presence was inappropriate at such a solemn occasions. But apparently, dignity had just fallen completely off the table. Some people, he groused, were on the edge of a reprimand. Who would be irresponsible enough to bring pets aboard and not keep track of them?

Whatever it was, almost all the staff officers were affected. Many seemed listless, flushed or clammy; they exuded sexual fluids, coughed or sneezed. Even Y'hain's chloroplasts had a yellowish tinge.

"Report please," Quilin ordered.

Shafe stood up.

"The tiger attack..."

Quilin grunted. Here we go again, he thought. Shafe was starting with impenetrable technical jargon like 'attack.' He was sure biologists garnered a lot of amusement to describing predator actions and motivations in terms of human behaviour, but to the lay person, it was utterly misleading.

Shafe stopped for a moment, looking to Quilin. He waved, "Go on."

Shafe cleared his throat a couple of times.

"The tiger attack," he began again, "was the final piece of the puzzle. It proves conclusively that this world is Earth, the original home of the human race. Y'hain?"

Y'hain sat there looking sour.

"Concur," she finally said grudgingly. "This is earth."

Quilin didn't know what to think. He didn't see the connection himself. It made no sense.

And if the planet was Earth, shouldn't that be a cause for celebration? Why were they so dour? What had they been searching for through all these years? What had people been searching for, for millennia?

"Would you like to explain yourself," Quilin said.

"It's simple," Y'hain said, "it's painfully simple. Predators only exist on evolved worlds. Not human worlds. They're a product of naturally evolved alien biology, filling a niche in alien ecosystems. That's why predators never bother humans; they're biologically incompatible on a molecular level."

"So this isn't Earth?" Quilin didn't see it. There was something here, something he should be grasping, but it was hard to get his mind to work correctly.

Y'hain and Shafe glanced at each other.

"Predators only exist on evolved worlds, not seeded ones," Shafe explained patiently. "This is an evolved world, and so it has predators. But these predators are different. They're biologically compatible with humans. They've evolved to eat humans."

"And other animals, obviously," Y'hain offered.

"Yes of course. But us too. Which means," Y'hain said glumly. "This is where we evolved. We evolved as lunch."

"Oh," Quilin said. "Wow."

He thought for a moment.

"That's a... disturbing thought. But we've finally found Earth. That's good right."

"It's an entire planet full of species that have evolved to eat us," Shafe said flatly.

Quilin was speechless.

"That's insane. Where did they come from? How did they evolve? We don't have these things in the human realm."

"We didn't take them with us when we left Earth," Shafe said. "We went out into space; we left all the things that liked to eat us behind. We left the predators behind, the parasites, fungi, bacteria, viruses. We left most of our ecology behind; we took a simplified suite of species into the stars with us."

"We left it all behind," Y'hain said sourly, "but it's all still here."

"There are ambiguous references in deep antiquity to tales of creatures that might be identified as Earth predators. Maybe in some of the early expeditions, we took some, perhaps mostly harmless forms. But the dangerous ones, they got winnowed out. Left behind, slowly phased out."

"Huh," said Quilin. He could see from the rest of the staff that they shared his astonishment. He'd never thought of the possibility of alien predators on earth. It just seemed weird. The whole idea of predators just seemed so embedded in alien ecosystems.

"It gets worse," Y'hain offered, "predators are manageable I suppose. We would just need protocols to deal with them. With Tigers for instance, don't try to pet them. Maybe... Sticks to push them away. We could work it out. But there are predators..."

"And then there are predators," Shafe picked it up. "Micro-predators. Parasites. Just about every mammal, every substantial life form we examined was crawling with parasites, tapeworms, ringworms, worms, lice, ticks, fleas, flukes, things that eat, things that burrow in skin, that lay eggs in hosts, that infest lungs, organs, intestinal tracts. Entire hierarchies of creatures, taxonomies, diversities, smaller and smaller, down to resolutions below the human eye, below cellular levels. This whole planet is literally predators and parasites, preying on top of each other, practically down to molecules. Literally thousands, tens of thousands of them, of all kinds, many undetectable. We could spend years cataloguing all the things that eat us."

"Do you know those friendly insects we keep seeing?" Y'hain asked.

Quilin glanced down, there was one perched on his shoulder, as if attentive.

"It's not being friendly," Y'hain said. "It's not being affectionate. It's drinking your blood. We've decided to call it a mosquito, after the old sampling probe."

Horrified, Quilin jumped to his feet, brushing the creature off his shoulder, images of the tiger attacking Amend filling his mind. They'd been drinking his blood all this time! How much blood did he have left? He barely stopped himself from racing to the medibay for a transfusion. Suddenly, the air seemed to be full of their high pitched whines. How long had they been on the ship? He just stopped short of declaring an immediate emergency.

"We think it might be responsible for all those welts…" Y'hain said. "And the itching. It gets worse. We think some of them may be carrying and transmitting human-targeting bacteria, malaria, fevers."

"The Mosquitos aren't just predators, they have predators and parasites feeding on them," Y'hain concluded. "And it turns out, their predators and parasites like us just as much."

"At least," Quilin said desperately, "they like us. Maybe we could form an alliance against the … mosquitos?"

"They like us," Shafe explained, "as in, they eat us too."

"The thing," Shafe said, "is that all those thousands and thousands of varieties of predators and parasites that are infesting the animals here… they're all evolved to eat us. They're designed to eat us, everything, from insects down to bacteria and virus. Even protozoans, there are amoeba in the water, if it gets into your intestinal tract…" He drew a finger across his throat.

"It's nightmarish," Y'hain said. "This is a hell world. Everything is designed to eat us. It's like some military war crimes testing site, but magnified by a millionfold."

Quilin shivered, remembering the holograph images of gambolling animals, herds of thousands of migrating cattle, creatures hopping through the grass, nestling in dens. He had an image of all of them literally being devoured to skeletons in midstrides.

"That can't…" he said, he couldn't finish. He started again. "That's insane, how does any life, how do the animals survive. They all look healthy. Why aren't they dying en masse."

"They're adapted, I suppose," Shafe said. "They're used to it."

"And we aren't," Fortu broke in. "It's been hundreds of thousands of years since our species has had to deal with these things. We went into the universe, leaving behind all our predators and parasites. They weren't wanted on our brave new worlds. We have absolutely no resistance."

Fortu sneezed, spewing sexual fluids, and then laughed bitterly.

"I'm not horny, you racists! I'm sick!" the Breen announced. "This planet is filthy with bacteria and viruses. Not all of them target our species, but there are enough that do, or that aren't picky about us. We've barely encountered a fraction of them. We've stumbled across a snowflake sample from an iceberg, and look at us."

They coughed.

"And you know what? I have no idea what to do? Through most recorded history, medicine has been a matter of identifying, tracing and treating contaminations. Now we've got targeted self-replicating pathogens with multiple strategies and pathways for moving from one host to the next, including... mosquitos. The techniques to even detect that were lost aeons ago, much less the techniques to control or combat them. I don't even know how to treat symptoms."

"It would be a nightmare. Multiply that over and over, thousands of times, for each parasite, each micro predator, each insect, arthropod, isopod, worm, fluke, fungus, protozoan, bacteria, virus, combinations, adaptations."

"We've done simulations and casualty projections," Shafe said. "Several versions, all of us, checked and vetted. Would you like..."

"I think I'd better see them," Quilin said shakily.

He switched out of the staff meeting, and downloaded the files. A map of human space appeared, with cascading columns of numbers. To his horror, red, pink and yellow glows erupted successively from Earth, contamination spreading along pathways across the universe entire sections of space turning red. Columns of numbers showed contamination rates, impacts, mortality.

"Worst case?" Quilin's whisper was strangled. "Is that the worst case?"

"Probably best case scenario," Fortu said dryly.

Quilin paused to absorb that.

"Recommendations?"

"Leave," Shafe said. "Leave, don't come back. Report this as a Mausoleum system of no interest whatsoever to anyone, and hope no one else ever comes here."

Quilin looked around. Thiral, Fortu, Y'hain all nodded. One by one, the rest of senior staff signalled their agreement.

"It's... uh," Quilin began, "it's heartbreaking. How many centuries, how many thousands of yours, how many hundreds of expeditions have searched for Earth, searched for our birthplace, our common legacy? That's a hard thing to turn your back on..."

He fell silent. He heard a whine.

A friendly insect landed on him. What did they call it? A mosquito? With some guilt, he slapped it.

"But I agree," he said finally, "let Earth return to legends and mythology. Let's forget this world."

He examined his palm. There, nestled was the crushed remains of the friendly insect, even crushed it was beautiful, a thing delicacy and symmetry, almost a work of art.

And around it a red drop of his own blood.

He felt queasy.

"And let's do something about these damned mosquitos! Immediately!"

* * *

Eventually, the Great Archive uploaded a file update on an obscure Mausoleum system on the galactic arm. Unfortunately, the update was empty, a formatting error that erased existing data on the system, and somehow even eliminated its location.

In the larger scheme of things, it meant little. The universe was vast; data was always being updated, deleted, or lost.

Elsewhere, the search for Earth went on.

* * *

On board the Fomalhaut, hidden in its water recirculation systems, mosquito larvae had found congenial habitat and were rapidly growing successive generations to maturity.

Mysteriously affectionate insects had already managed to find new homes on space stations, worlds and floating habitats, and begun their spread through the universe.

Aeons ago, humanity had battled to leave them behind. But now that battle was finally lost.

The End

Daddy's Girl

"Spare some change, Missy?" the grimy bum mumbled at them, a block from the movie theatre. His grin exposed cracked and yellowing teeth. Even from a few feet away they could smell booze and solvents on him.

Jennifer halted in indecision, almost twitching like a frightened rabbit, her hand darted into her pocket. Sally grabbed Jennifer's arm and pulled her, stepping away from the wino.

"Sorry," Sally told him, "not today."

He turned to watch them as they passed.

"Spare a blow job then," he snapped at them.

"Get bent," Sally snarled.

The bum exploded. "Fucking sluts," he screamed, leaping forward. His hand caught Jennifer's hair, twisting her blond curls in his wrists.

Jennifer shrieked as he jerked her head back.

Pain flashed across the bum's eyes, like two bright arcs.

He realized his nose had been broken. He blinked tears out of his eyes and shook his head.

"Let her go," Sally screamed.

Again shooting pain on the inside of his knee.

She'd kicked him again, he realized, outraged.

"Bitch," he gritted out, as his leg gave way. He wanted to drag the blond down but somehow her hair had slipped out of his fingers.

"Sluts," he grunted, as he rolled to his hands and knees, trying to climb back up. "I'll show you."

Sally kicked him in the left kidney twice, leaving him writhing on the ground in pain.

"Sally!" Jennifer screamed, drawing the name out.

"Just a minute," Sally said, and kicked him again.

Then they were running breathlessly down the street.

* * *

They ran all the way to Gein's Sundaes. "No running in the premises," Mae Gein warned them as they swung into a booth.

Jennifer was gasping for breath, but laughing at the same time, with a combination of hysteria and elation, as they ordered cherry sundaes.

"That was so cool," she told Sally.

Sally was flushed, but not breathing nearly as heavily.

"Shit happens," Sally said.

"Christ! You're my hero," Jennifer said, "here I am wandering through life, wondering if my breasts are too big or too small, not having any idea what's going to come next. But you, you know. You handle everything."

Sally blushed. "Not everything," she said, "just assholes. My dad says you have to know how to deal with assholes."

"I'm so glad you guys moved here. I wish I had a dad like yours."

"Your folks are pretty cool," Sally shrugged.

"They're all right. I mean, it's not great or anything. But it's not like they beat me."

Abruptly, Jennifer bent across the table and lowered her voice.

"You know what I heard?"

"What?"

"My mother was talking to Miss Henshaw, you know, the lady who works down at the liquor market..."

"And?"

"And she says that Miss Symington, Ruth Anne's mother buys a lot of rye."

"A lot?"

"A lot."

"She's got a problem."

"No wonder Ruth Anne's so moody all the time."

Drunk Slutty Elf and Zombies / Page 2

"Did you hear about how she got into a fight with the teacher the other day? She punched her!"

"No!"

"Got expelled from school for a whole week."

"Wow! My Dad would kill me if I ever got expelled."

Jennifer laughed. "No he wouldn't, your Dad's an old softy. I've talked to him; he'd give you the moon."

"When did you see my Dad?" Sally asked cautiously.

"Oops," Jennifer giggled, "he made me promise not to tell."

"Secret's out," Sally teased, leaning forward. "Was it in your romantic hideaway?"

"No way, he's old!" Jennifer made a face, "Last weekend at the supermarket. He was picking up a few things and he pushed a cart around for me and mom."

Sally leaned back.

"You don't like your friends knowing your Dad," Jennifer guessed.

"Who does?" Sally replied. "Friends are friends, dads are dads, never the two should meet."

"Yeah," Jennifer said, "I guess I'm a little like that myself. But I'm not as psycho about it as you are."

Sally shrugged.

"I love my Dad," she said defensively, "I just like to keep things...separate."

The doors to the shop swung open. A lanky middle aged police officer with a pot belly strolled inside.

He surveyed the place, nodding casually to the girls and strolled over.

"Hello girls," he said.

"Hello Officer Gacy," Sally replied.

He pulled out a picture.

"You know this young man?"

They both nodded.

"Of course we know him, that's Tommy. We're all in the same class together with your son," Sally told him. "I have a date with him next Thursday."

"You didn't tell me that," Jennifer giggled.

"I don't tell you all my secrets," Sally said smugly.

"Not till afterwards," Jennifer replied.

They both giggled.

"When was the last time either of you saw him?" the Officer asked.

"At school," Jennifer said.

"Yeah, school," Sally confirmed. "Is he in trouble?"

"No, no," Officer Gacy said quickly. "He's just missing is all. Probably nothing, but his folks worry."

"They're right to worry," Sally said soberly, "people disappear all the time. I saw it on TV."

"Not around here they don't," Officer Gacy reassured her. "So what have you girls been up to?"

"We just got back from the afternoon movie," Sally said.

"Yeah, and some creep tried to assault us," Jennifer said, "but Sally stopped him."

The Officer glanced at Sally. "Maybe we'd better look into that. Can you give me the details?"

He pulled out his notebook and jotted down the girl's story and the description of the thug.

"Do you think there's a connection between that creep and Tommy going missing?" Jennifer asked.

Officer Gacy scratched his ear with the pencil.

"I doubt it. Tommy's probably just out on a tear, he'll show up presently. This bum, you told me about, sounds like a mean drunk is all. A night in the tank should straighten him out."

"Well, he scared us," Jennifer said.

The Officer nodded, "don't worry; we'll be on the lookout for the creep too. Supper time's coming up; you girls should be getting home. If you're still scared, we could give you a lift home, to your parents' homes."

"That's all right," Sally said, "we'll be fine."

Officer Gacy looked from one to the other, then shrugged.

"Jeffrey is waiting in the car, so I'll be getting along; we've still got some donut shops to check out."

"All right, Officer Gacy," Jennifer said, as they waved him goodbye.

Then she turned back to Sally, "so, about the movie...wasn't Tom Cruise just great...."

* * *

It wasn't until Sally was walking home alone that her thoughts turned to Tommy.

She really liked Tommy. She liked his easy grin and his ready wit. They'd gone out a few times, but it was just kid's stuff. Nothing serious, nothing to be tied down over.

Sally hoped Tommy was all right.

How long had he been missing? She wondered.

Officer Gacy to the contrary, she didn't think he was the type to disappear off on his own.

Maybe he'd dropped by to visit at friends?

Maybe at her place?

Maybe he'd met Dad?

Fuelled by a horrible certainty, she began to run home. Arriving at the house, she sprinted up the steps and through the door.

Quickly, she checked the carport. The car was there. She ran back into the house. The kitchen was empty.

"Daddy," she called.

There was no answer.

She ran into the living room, ducked her head into the dining room and the hall closet. Nothing.

She raced to the stairs.

"Daddy," she yelled.

No answer. He probably wasn't up there, but she had to look anyway. She leaped up the steps, taking them two at a time, calling out again as she poked her head into the bedrooms and the bathroom.

Damn!

She hurdled down the stairs and dashed to the basement door she'd consciously avoided. It was locked.

She swore and rushed back into the kitchen. She grabbed the coffee percolator on top of the fridge and shook it twice. The keys to the basement fell out.

Sally stalked back to the basement door.

Grimly she remembered her father's warning never to go into the basement.

She set the key into the lock and twisted it. The creak of metal twisting was only loud to her. Then the second lock, it slid back quietly.

Slowly, the doorway yawned black before her. From the outside, it seemed like a regular basement door, made from cheap panelled wood, with light coat of green paint, peeling here and there.

It was only when you opened it that you realized it wasn't. That the cheap wood backing hid a heavy oak slab reinforced by a steel plate, hanging on cast iron three inch hinges.

You couldn't see it, but she knew that the frame was countersunk and reinforced into the concrete of the basement walls itself.

They moved from one town to another every few years. But in every house, Daddy always liked to have the basement armoured and reinforced the same way. When she'd been young, she'd sat on the basement steps, watching him.

It was for a bomb shelter, he would tell her, when she was just a little girl.

Nothing could get in through that door. Nothing was getting out past it. Not even screams.

She wasn't supposed to, but once in a while, growing up, she'd sneaked in.

She hesitated a second, biting her lip, there were no sounds from below. Sally stepped over the threshold.

The steps were covered with plastic. She felt it twist under her runners.

Her heart began to pound.

I could go back up, Sally thought. He's probably out for a walk, or down at the corner store renting a movie or picking up a slurpee. Maybe he's visiting.

The cars in the garage, and he isn't in the house.

No reason he had to be in the basement. Lots of places he could be. I'll just go back and lock the door and watch television. He'll come back from his walk, and we'll have a nice family dinner.

She reached the bottom of the steps.

There was a second door here. She tried it.

It wasn't locked.

She stepped into Daddy's Den.

She stood there blinking in the soft light. There were three or four lamps around; all of them on, casting diffuse light through pink or brown lampshades. In one corner of the den was his sewing bench, with its collection of needles and threads and the little singer sewing machine.

When she was young, he used to make beautiful gowns for her. It made her feel like a princess.

On the other side of the room was the big screen colour TV. There was no cable in the basement, and no signals could penetrate. Instead it was hooked to the VCR. In a little cabinet beside the TV were Daddy's special tapes.

Facing the TV was a handmade sofa and a couple of chairs, covered with layers of supple worked leather. She knew what the furniture was made of.

On a shelf above the sofa was a row of human skulls. She resisted the urge to count them.

Sally walked straight through the den to the cavernous workroom.

The odour of drying blood and urine assaulted her senses. Grey concrete walls were lined with hooks and braces, power drills, and flensing knives.

Tommy was chained spread eagled to the rack in the corner.

Daddy liked to play and play.

She approached the boy with horrified fascination.

"Tommy," she whispered.

He moaned softly, his chest rising and falling. He didn't seem aware of her. At first she'd thought he had been wearing shorts. But now, as she approached she could see that skin and flesh had been removed, exposing textured muscle and fat below.

"Oh no," she whispered to herself, shreds of denial slipping away. It was true. Damnably, horribly true.

A toilet flushed behind her. The bathroom door swung open.

A long dark shadow from the harsh bathroom light crept past her feet.

"Daddy?" she whispered.

She turned slowly.

There he was, silhouetted against the naked glare of the single bathroom bulb, wearing nothing but his bloodstained leather apron.

He looked at her.

"Dammit Daddy," she screamed angrily, "how many times have I told you not to eat my friends."

The End

Gift of Night

Payr Gilar, Project Director, was wearing his James Dean sunglasses and leather jacket, looking cool and vaguely rebellious, when the comm beeped.

Or at least, he liked to think that the sunglasses and jacket, made him look like James Dean. What they made him look like was a cross between an otter and a parrot in dark glasses and a vinyl windbreaker, which is what he was, more or less.

"Yes." He keyed the intercom with a stubby webbed finger ending in a pair of claws.

"We've found a live human being," the comm warbled excitedly. Payr recognised the voice of his friend Trett, babbling with excitement.

"On my way." Payr hit the locator and grabbed his Philip Marlowe Trenchcoat as he waddled out.

The discovery of a live human was an event of astounding importance. The human race, by this time, had been a collection of popsicles for forty-five thousand years.

The locator took him to the Biological Structure divisions. Also known as Autopsyville. There was a small crowd already gathered, and more arriving. Payr shouldered his way through. Trett was already there.

At their feet was a corpse. This shouldn't have been unusual. Biological Structure division processed up to 800 corpses a day.

But this one wasn't human.

"His name was Chik Ho," Trett told him, "A second grade pathologist."

Chik looked like a large otter with glossy button eyes and a parrot's beak. He was wearing a loud Hawaiian shirt with an Elvis Lives button. The part of his body that lead to his head, the human equivalent would be a throat, was torn out. Chik lay in a pool of yellow blood; small chunks of his own flesh were spread around him.

"What happened?" Payr demanded.

"He called in a report that his subject was alive and moving. When the first people arrived they found this."

"Hallucination?" Payr wondered, "A lab accident perhaps."

Some of these humans had indulged in potent chemicals. A few of these chemicals, if not handled properly could severely disorient the Gerven mind. Payr briefly constructed a scene where the Pathologist accidentally triggered some possession of the corpse, mace or hairspray or something, and then hallucinating, had inadvertently killed himself.

Trett was examining the lab equipment for yellow blood.

"Whatever made those wounds isn't in this lab."

He indicated the examining table.

"Registration shows that there should be a body on this table. It's gone too."

"Someone killed him, and stole the human body as a red herring." Payr recognised Ludoc from Cultural in the crowd. Ludoc had gotten far too immersed in the more violent aspects of human culture, thought Payr. Although, on second thought, it was kind of hard to avoid.

Still, something had happened here.

"Payr," someone else called, "a report just in from sector nine. Someone's found a puddle of Gerven flesh and blood."

Not another disaster, thought Payr.

"How much?" he asked.

"Enough that whoever lost it isn't going to make it. They are looking for the body."

"Terrific." snarled Payr, "Seal off the areas, send in a multidisciplinary team. I want a complete workdown. Trett, supervise."

With that said, the station director waddled off.

* * *

Earth had been a dead planet, far beyond the orbit of Pluto, when the Gerven had found it. Its life a memory, its oceans huge fields of ice, even much of its atmosphere had frozen out, falling in flakes and drops to cover the surface of the dead world with a Cryonic blanket. It had been pulled from its orbit forty-five thousand years before by a rogue black dwarf that had veered through the solar system. Out into the cold dark, where its life had gone out like a candle flame.

The Gerven might have missed it altogether. Their first probes showed no habitable worlds whatsoever. No place that might have given birth to life. The Gerven had been searching ten thousand years for life other than their own. They had never found it.

A routine exploratory ship, stopping on the way to another star, had decided to examine the ice world which had been coincidentally near. A degree or two of arc farther out, and they would have ignored it.

The first scans had shown obvious signs of intelligent life. The news hit Gerven society like a lightning bolt. It was followed, shortly after, by the sad roll of thunder.

Forty-five thousand years isn't much time as the universe weighs these things. Geologically, it isn't even a heartbeat. From any objective viewpoint, the Humans and the Gerven were literal contemporaries.

The news went out.

We have found our brothers.

They are dead.

Something like a collective howl of mourning rose from the Gerven race. The universe was a lonely desolate place. It seemed infinitely tragic to finally find someone else, and find that they had passed on.

But even the remnant of other lives was of staggering importance. The Gerven feverishly organised a major research effort to journey to the ice-world and discover the secrets of this lost race.

* * *

Toucin thought of himself as a fairly typical Gerven. True, his beak was bigger and brighter than most, but in most other respects he felt quite ordinary.

His most distinctive quality was his fascination with the extraordinary. It had been that way since his yearling days, and his bond parents had encouraged it. He had a boundless quest to explore that had lead him to the stars.

His specialty on the base was Phonetic reconstruction, slowly assembling bits of ancient tape and disc until his comrades could once again listen to the breath of a living world. It gave him great pleasure. Sometimes, when he was alone, he would just unfocus his eye membranes and listen to the world of long ago that he had formed in his head.

That was why it took him a moment to recognize the sound. That was why he was one of the few who could recognize the sound.

Sobbing, he realized with a shock. It was human sobbing coming from a maintenance chute. A sound no one had heard for forty-five thousand years.

This must be it, he thought. This must be the live human that they found.

Excitement surged through him. He had worked among the ruins of humanity for years. But to actually meet one? To come face to face with another intelligent being.

He recalled the strange death of Chik, but dismissed it from his mind. It's had a chance to calm down, he thought. It will be rational.

He tried to remember the fragments and meanings of human speech that he had encountered. He wished that he understood enough of the grammar to actually construct messages. Still...

"Hey Bro," he chirped, "be cool. Be cool now. Everything's going to be fine. Chill out. We is hot. My man. What's your sign baby."

There was a break in the sobbing, and then what he interpreted as soft questioning noises.

"That's right, my man." Toucin encouraged, "We're doing good. Aren't you fine girl."

Slowly, he made his way into the maintenance chute.

* * *

"The flesh was gripped between two irregular surfaces, which contained at least a few piercing instruments, and simply torn out with lateral motions. Comparatively little flesh was actually torn out, the severity of the wound is the result of widening or pulling apart, not removal." Pathologist first Grade Stac was concluding his report. He wore a mustache and goatee on his beak, inspired by Colonel Sanders.

"I know of no instrument in Pathology section with matching configurations."

"As well, I must point out substantial bruising on upper limbs as well as on head and forebody. Bruising is consistent with great pressure applied, possibly to immobilize the subject. Finally, I would note minor tearing in the muscle groups which would suggest the victim struggled."

"Not an accidental death then." said Trett.

"No, Assistant Director." replied Stac, "All indications are that death was protracted, that subject struggled to avoid it, and that subject was opposed."

This was profoundly disturbing news. The last murder in Gerven society had been well over three thousand years ago. These few thousand volunteers to the ice world had been the cream of the crop; it was almost obscenely inconceivable that any of them could have committed such an act.

"Suppose," Trett speculated, "that Chik had a companion. In the course of examining the body they release a psychosis

Drunk Slutty Elf and Zombies / Page 13

producing compound. Chik hallucinates and announces that the human is alive, his companion kills him and runs off with the body."

Early on in the project, in the course of handling lower strata corpses, Trett had accidentally maced himself. He had never quite gotten over it.

"Records indicate no companion. Chik worked alone." said Totruc, the head of Environmental Maintenance.

The alternative was even more inconceivable.

"What about the tissue in the corridors?" Payr asked, "Have we found a body yet."

"None," replied Totruc from Environmental Maintenance, "All extant persons have been confirmed as alive and well at the time."

There was the equivalent of a throat clearing from Stort, the senior molecular analyst.

"Something very strange there, Gentlefellows. When we learned that all extant persons were accounted for, we speculated that the blood might have been a mixture of bloods from various persons, or might be supplemented with synth. It was mostly blood, many of the flesh chunks turned out to be coagulation. So we did a manifold tissue patch on it."

"Yes," prompted Payr.

There was a noticeable pause.

"It's Chik's. All of it. We did a volume comparison on the death site, the two numbers matched Chik's estimated body fluid volume."

The news was too stunning. It defied reason that whatever agent had killed Chik had then somehow transported a substantial portion of his body's elements and then abandoned it.

"Perhaps this is meant to confuse us." Trett speculated.

"Something more. Tissues of both sites showed substantial traces of a foreign virus. An uncatalogued virus which showed no affinity for Gerven biology." He left the conclusion there to hang.

This was almost welcome. A virus was just a lump of complex molecules. Not truly alive or dead. It might conceivably survive a forty-five thousand year freeze. But....

"Are you suggesting the Virus killed him?" Payr boggled, "How? Did it explode his throat and teleport his blood away?"

As he said it, it seemed a more acceptable proposition than any of the possibilities so far.

"Just to be safe," Trett said, "I think we should time review everyone in Pathology. And Cultural Studies too, they are too inured to violence."

Suddenly the Portal unlocked. Benyd, a low level records tech swept into the room with an armload of equipment. Carelessly elbowing senior personnel out of the way, he began setting up a display matrix on the window.

"Begging your pardon, honoured ones, I think you must see this for yourselves."

Trett was about to object, but Payr silenced him with a gesture.

The display flickered into life. It showed a human being, dressed in casual clothes, on a table. Chik Ro's disembodied voice supplied commentary.

"Anomalous body found in upper strata..."

"That's ridiculous," interjected Stac, "Upper Strata were the last to succumb; they were heavily insulated and bore mechanical heating and respiration. Dressed like that it has to originate in lower strata, probably a victim of the first few big freezes."

The arm of the body on the display twitched. A murmur rose from the audience. Strangely the voice of Chik continued with its physical description.

"It isn't unusual," Stac told them, "We get movement in a lot of bodies; usually it's a symptom of differential thaw within the body structures."

It twitched again, the eyes flicked open and the arms seemed to sweep together.

"Odd movement," said Stac, "Almost co-ordinated. But that's just an illusion. We see it from time to time."

The body turned and got off the table. Their beaks clacked in shock as the body left the view frame and they heard Chik's excited voice.

"It`s alive! It's alive! Open comm, all channels. Attention: I've found a live human, repeat a live..."

Then the voice abruptly cut off. The display continued to show an empty examination table.

The technician cut the display.

They sat there in silence.

"So there is a live human." someone said.

"I wonder how it survived." All thought of Chik had temporarily left their minds.

"I heard that someone in Cultural was collaborating with Molecular on a human style fiction where one of the frozen bodies is resuscitated. We can track that down, it may give us some insights."

"How long between Chik's last recorded words and the arrival of other persons on the scene?" Trett asked.

"A minute or less," came the answer.

"Then we have to assume that we have a live human, and that its first act was to kill one of our people," said Payr. It seemed an infinitely tragic thought. Everyone had fantasized about finding a live human, some rogue pocket of survivors. No one had imagined that the first contact would be like this.

"I don't know if we can assume it's automatically hostile," Stac mused, "When it woke, it woke on an autopsy table, surrounded by a number of very intimidating instruments, and faced by a being outside its previous existence. Add to this the obvious disorientation produced by millennia of hibernation. It may have been employing reflexive behaviour in an apparently hostile situation."

Payr remembered the display view and how, shortly after the first twitch, the body had seemed to galvanize into frighteningly focused movement. He had read no hesitation there whatsoever. Still, he could not claim to read human movements. No one could, anymore.

"Then violence may not be its main response?" Trett asked.

"It's alone and disoriented in a completely alien environment, obviously devoted to the dissection of its people and its culture. I suggest that we handle this carefully. We must try and make it understand that we are its friends."

They considered this. Payr thought about sitting down and having a conversation with a real, live, human being. Maybe even James Dean. It was worth the risk.

"Assignment for Cultural services then: Formulate messages of peace and goodwill, both visual and auditory, designed to placate the human and convince it of our intentions. Environmental will distribute and broadcast these messages. Cultural and Environmental will co-operate on a contact protocol for the human, which shall be standard training for all personnel, that should save future lives."

The comm rang.

"Senior Gentlepersons," the voice blurted, "we have evidence of another attack. No body, but a substantial pool of blood and flesh."

They looked at each other.

"Work on that protocol." Payr said grimly.

****

The Gerven were not especially interested in human technology. A star spanning culture, they had exceeded most human science. There were, of course, fascinating accomplishments like the pencil, or certain data encryption methods, as well as such morbid achievements as a truly staggering variety of weapons.

But for the most part, the Gerven were fascinated by humans as people and cultures. Who they were, how they lived, their food, their clothes, their language.

Such reconstruction was not easy. After forty-five thousand years magnetic patterns on discs and tapes had faded, chemicals had reacted on strips of film; even paper and inks had lost much to time. The pyramids had been built for eternity; but it seemed that most human communications had been built to stretch no farther than next week. The job of restoring even partial coherence to the long lost materials was a painstaking one. The task of wringing meaning out of the fragmentary relics of an alien culture, even more so. It was further hindered by the immense variety of cultures and subcultures and the contradictory opinions they had all held of themselves and others.

* * *

Cirit was an engineer. No ifs, ands or buts there. Cirit was an engineer. To him, engineering was simple and straightforward. There was a fundamental honesty to his craft that he loved. You knew exactly where you stood, and what you were doing, or why be an engineer in the first place?

He liked his work.

He didn't like this particular job. Go through the service corridors with a crew and find the human before it harmed itself or anyone or anything else.

It sounded simple. But to Cirit and his three companions it was anything but.

In the first place, where were you supposed to find the human? It could be anywhere. His team, and other teams had been trudging corridors for days. Suppose it didn't want to be found? That didn't make any sense to Cirit. But who could figure these aliens?

Then, supposing that you did find it, then what? Would it come along quietly? Would they have to restrain it? How do you restrain a crazed alien? What if they injured it? Who would get the blame for that?

What if it injured them? Cirit, like everyone else, had heard of the bodies that had been found.

No one had thought this out properly, he felt. They'd been given some nets and safety poles culled from old human designs (A black mark against the race, he thought, if they needed artifacts like this regularly.), a handful of reassuring alien phrases, and the physical layouts for the base.

Could he really call it an alien, he wondered, after all, this was its world. But then, if they had all been dead, could they really claim ownership.

He wished that he was back with the fascinating problems of hydroponic maintenance.

He did not see, so much as hear, the human coming out of a side chute. Geri, the closest one to the human, threw his net over it.

The human simply pulled it off. Cirit cursed, they could have used some training. He and his companions surged towards the human, it was already on top of Geri.

"We come in peace!" he squawked as he threw himself on the creature.

It buckled and heaved under them. Another of his companions Kerk was pulled down by the human. Cirit's blood froze as he heard the sickening sound of bones breaking. He was losing his hold, raw alien strength was tearing the net open.

"We come in peace." he wailed as the human shook free and attacked his last companion.

"We come in peace." he shrieked. The alien turned toward him. He chuttered with fear, and ran, calling out the human phrase over and over again.

Suddenly he faced a blank wall. He turned to face the human bearing down on him.

"We come in peace." he said desperately, "We come. We come. We come."

The human paused, its face twisted. Was that a good sign? Cirit wasn't sure. He was just an engineer.

"Welcome." it said.

***

As they walked, they passed a sign that read in English:

"Friends Friends Peace Surrender. Phone Home. We are your Friends. We mean you no harm. Can we talk? Let's take lunch."

"How many so far?" Payr asked his friend, Trett.

"We've just had report of an eighth disappearance. Five bodies have been recovered. All in the same condition as Chik."

"Hmm," mused Payr, "Patterns?"

"The attacks seem to be occurring at twelve hour intervals, give or take three hours. They are invariably accompanied by blood dumping at another site within a few hours of the attacks. It suggests highly ritualised behaviour."

"Interesting. Is it using tools in its attacks?"

"Possibly. Our best guess, however, is that it's using hands and teeth, which are significantly at odds with otherwise complex actions. It is very good at recognising and evading our sensors."

"Any luck communicating with it?"

"None. Search parties are unable to locate it. It does not respond to any of our messages. We have even moved into a third phase: providing communication aids, blackboards, pencils and paper, telephones, even computers. It hasn't utilized anything. Most disturbing, the last two disappearances were versed in the contact protocol."

"It doesn't seem interested in communicating."

To change the subject, Payr asked.

"Have you heard the news from the beamship yet?"

"No."

"They found the death star." The great dark body that had murdered the human race.

"They tracked its path backwards. Two million years ago it passed within a light year of the home system." Payr went on.

Trett gasped. Into his mind came the vision of a malevolent deity, guiding the death star from system to system to cleanse the universe of intelligent life.

"There is speculation that it was partially responsible for the cometary bombardments that disrupted the environment and spurred the evolution of our own race."

"Ironic," was all Trett could think to say. Visions of a malevolent deity warred in his mind with the concept of an arbitrary one. He could not say which he preferred.

They were silent as they walked into the conference together.

* * *

With perfunctory clacks of his beak, Payr greeted the assembled sages from Cultural Reconstruction section, who had been added to the study list.

"So far we have lost nine of our people," he addressed them.

"The human shows no signs of moderating its behaviour. We have been unable to capture it. We have been unable to consistently track it. The situation has moved beyond the extreme, it is becoming intolerable."

He sat there, letting an embarrassed silence grow.

Ridak from Environmental systems mumbled.

"It appears to be confined to main base, which suggests that it cannot survive well in the outside environment."

Trett clacked his beak angrily. That much was obvious. The human had been frozen on the outside for forty-five thousand years.

"There are many sections of the base which are only intermittently occupied. This is partly due to our social structure, which encourages dense clustering for social and residential purposes, and partly due to the fact that the base is constructed for much larger research populations which we anticipate in the future."

Another member from Environmental took up the slack.

"We have estimated that during periods of peak concentrations approximately 80% of the base is largely unoccupied. Even during periods of peak activity, about 30% at any specific time is only lightly occupied. This makes it difficult to track the Human."

"It doesn't leave normal traces which would allow us to track people. It isn't using the communications nets, accessing information, or tapping food and water systems..."

Payr briefly wondered, if the creature wasn't tapping into the food distribution systems, what it could possibly be eating. He pushed the thought away. There were missing Gerven.

"In short, it is outside our normal tracking system." the Engineer finished.

"It is killing people. How do we stop it?" Trett asked bluntly.

The Environmental chiefs clacked their beaks.

"Until we can properly model its behaviour, we have no way of knowing where or why it will kill. It's a cultural problem."

Payr turned to Cultural section.

"As you recall, you'd asked for a behavioral profile on the human to analyze and predict its actions," Edler, the head of Cultural Reconstruction addressed him.

Payr nodded.

"We've amassed a great deal of data on human cultures, much of which is fragmentary, and which we understand only imperfectly..."

"Yes," Payr prompted.

"You must understand that this Humans situation is unique. There is nothing similar in any of our records. We have a number of instances of lone or isolated humans in hostile territories waging guerilla warfare, or living out a scavenging existence. But as to explaining or predicting the behaviour we have witnessed so far..."

"You have nothing," Payr finished for her.

She clacked her beak and ducked her head apologetically.
"Nothing."

"I think it's a Vampire."

All heads swivelled to look at the one who had spoke. It
was a diminutive Reconstructive Literature Technician. It
chutted apologetically, and pressed its blunt fingers to its
plastic velcro slide rule pocket protector. It wore a thin
necktie and coke bottle glasses.

"A what?" asked Trett.

"A predatory human variation. It consumes body fluids."

The head of Cultural Reconstruction stood to shudder
with exasperation.

"I got the idea from the Humans behaviour. It attacks its
victims, consumes large amounts of body fluids, and then
apparently voids them later elsewhere."

It seemed to Payr, that the technician had summarised the
Humans behaviour perfectly. A predator.

"Obviously, it voids our blood because it cannot
metabolize our biochemistry. Why does it keep attacking?
Why doesn't it learn?" asked Payr.

"This is nonsense," the head of Cultural Reconstruction
argued, "Vampires have been classified as part of
representational culture, they are not real. They are in the
same class as Serial Killers, Mimes, Kennedys and whatnot.
Besides, humans weren't a dominant species long enough for
human specific predators to evolve."

"We have some evidence that Mimes really existed. I don't
know that we should rule out the existence of Vampires.
Especially when we might have one preying on us," the
Technician defended.

"What else can you tell us about vampires?" Trett asked.

"They are dead."

"On this world, that goes without saying. But we seem to
have a live one." Payr commented dryly.

"No." The Technician struggled to make herself
understood.

"They are dead humans. Some humans die, and then return to life as Vampires, and prey on the truly living. That's why it revived on the table, not truly alive, it hadn't really died, the cold had only suspended it. It was dormant."

Payr sighed. What a pity he thought, so young and promising, and completely mad.

"There are many things strange about this world," Payr admonished the technician, "But one of the things they shared with us is that when the body dies it stays dead. Their representational culture contains strong beliefs in some sort of after death existence, but even they admitted that it was unverified or unverifiable."

The technician refused to back down.

"I think that it is actually a viral robot."

"What is that?" Trett asked.

Another technician in Molecular Technology stepped in.

"A viral robot is a theoretical construct. A sort of naturally occurring nanomachine. It postulates under certain circumstances a virus, or complex of viruses, may take over and maintain cellular activity and cellular functions. You would have an apparent biological unit, an animal say, whose activities were directed by viruses, and not natural life processes."

"Exactly. Viruses mutate extremely rapidly. There was a vacant ecological niche that the Virus was able to fill: A human specific predator. In the long term it probably wasn't very efficient, but it had no biological rivals to compete with."

"Human culture would not have had any concept of a viral robot complex activating a dead body. They simply called it a vampire and recorded its properties."

Something was killing their people.

"What are its properties?" Trett asked.

The technician clacked its beak nervously. Having at least partly convinced them, it was now hesitant to proceed further.

"It appeared to be nocturnal, I suspect that exposure to direct sunlight or heat caused the viral complexes to deteriorate."

Now, far beyond the orbit of Pluto it no longer needed to worry about the sun coming up.

"I must make the point that a viral robot is not necessarily an automaton. The viral complexes mimic cell functions, even nerve or brain cells. Vampires in representational cultures have the power of speech, wear clothes, use artifacts, and demonstrate planned and strategic behaviour. They have an aversion to religious culture artifacts, which I assume to be psychological. One might infer that there is a human mind functioning in through the new structure."

"That," said Trett carefully, "Leaves me with uncertain sentiments about this creature. I think I might prefer it as an automaton. What properties does this viral robot possess that might allow us to predict and capture it, or if necessary, kill it?"

"As I've said, sunlight was reported to be lethal. So is fire, and extreme physical mutilation like impalement or beheading. Traditionally, it was dormant during the daylight hours, but that doesn't apply."

"What else."

"It had numerous other liabilities. An aversion to religious culture artifacts, though that was believed to be as much due to the power of belief of the wielders. I don't know how or if it would work for us."

"It will work for me," chirped Joach, a Physical Structures Analyst, who had converted to Christianity. Everyone thought he carried things a bit far, the robes were all right, but the fake long flowing beard and the tablets of commandments were too much.

"Garlic, whatever that is, was supposed to ward them. They have an aversion to running water. And mirrors."

"Why mirrors?" asked Payr.

"They cast no reflection."

A number of people laughed.

"Obviously a cultural misconception," Trett said, "What else?"

"They are thought to be stronger and faster. They may exercise some form of mind control." the technician chuttered nervously, "They can turn into bats."

There was a moment of silence.

"What are bats?" someone asked.

"Small winged mammals, less than a hundredth weight of humans."

This was received with an embarrassed silence.

"Well," said Trett, "it could have been worse. We might have resurrected a used car salesman."

"One more thing..." the Technician spoke, "given that certain identified types may reactivate if disturbed..."

"Yes," Payr invited.

"When we excavate Japan, we should watch out for Godzilla."

* * *

"I'm nervous." said Trett.

Payr had left his James Dean sunglasses behind, but he'd kept his synthetic leather jacket. It was buckled tightly around him for whatever psychological protection it offered. He clicked his beak a couple of times in agreement.

Even without the human (he still found himself thinking of it as human, not a vampire, not a viral robot, but human) prowling around, they had enough to worry about with the fire rods.

As they proceeded down the lonely corridor, they passed a blood bucket, now stale and vaguely sour. The latest signs hung above it.

"Blood Brother." the sign read, "You cannot use our body fluids. We can help you. Make peace. We will help you. We understand."

In an attempt to stop the creatures futile predations, a task force in Molecular Analysis had attempted to synthesize terrestrial blood substitutes. Perhaps they had not succeeded. The creature showed no interest in it.

In the end, what had worked was organization. The Gerven had evolved without predators on an isolated land mass. Security was foreign, but faced with a crisis, they could reason things out.

They had determined group sizes and concentrations that the creature would not attack, then they organized people into these groups.

They had identified how the creature travelled, and then they had set about sealing it in. First it was excluded from half the base. Then its range was halved, and halved, and halved yet again. It was forced into ever tighter confines, until now it ranged through a tight area comprising less than a tenth of the bases territory.

The fire rods had only been the latest innovation. Primitive pipes that would funnel a sustained pressurised spray of incendiary droplets. Accidents in developing and using the devices had claimed nearly as many casualties as the creature itself.

Payr hoped that it would work on the human.

They proceeded carefully down the empty corridor, about thirty paces apart, clumsily covering each other.

Payr inspected a status display on a storeroom. Sealed and empty.

"Perhaps some other group has it trapped," he commented.

He turned. It had come out of nowhere and was almost on top of Trett. Payr skreeled, but it was too late. It fell on Trett.

Afraid to use the fire rod with his friend before him, Payr charged. Trett whirred with terror. Payr smashed the human across the back with the fire rod, a false discharge of incandescent particles spurted.

The human looked at him. It had burning red eyes. He felt some rational part of himself mentally dictating a memo to the Image Reconstructionists in Cultural: Red eyes, not blue, not green, not even brown. Red.

Then it hit him. He didn't even feel the blow. Suddenly he was flying down the corridor.

The human was on top of him. It was tearing at the buckles of his jacket. Its strength was immense. With a sudden moment of clarity, Payr realized that he was going to die. He desperately wanted to live.

Suddenly the creature was bathed in a halo of flame. It screamed and reared off of him. Desperately, Payr scrambled away. The flame was on him too, but his jacket continued to protect him. He rolled to put it out, then dove for his fire rod.

The monster was still moving as Trett, yellow blood dripping down his left side, fired another discharge at it. Payr added his own blast. They kept firing long after it had stopped moving. Long after it had ceased to be a recognisable shape.

* * *

Payr opened the door to his quarters to find Trett there waiting.

"I thought I'd walk with you to the departure point." Trett said.

"My friend," Payr answered simply.

They walked together, quietly down the corridors.

"This will be the first ship to take as many people back as it brought in." Trett volunteered.

Payr clicked noncommittally. He did not nod. He'd made an effort to excise all such influences from his mannerisms.

"I regret you're leaving. You were a superb Director, I won't be able to do half as well as yourself."

"Do not underestimate yourself." Payr answered, "It is only thanks to you that I live to return at all."

"But why?" Trett asked passionately, "When there is so much more to learn, so much more to discover, why leave now?"

Payr stopped abruptly, he turned to face his friend.

Drunk Slutty Elf and Zombies / Page 28

"Do you know what I saw when I looked into its eyes?" Payr asked.

He went on.

"Nothing. There was nothing there at all."

"It was like the mind of a frog. Do you remember that animal behaviour text we translated. The frog had a brain that was wired to recognize flying insects as prey, and to ignore everything else. The frog could starve to death, surrounded by edible food, because its brain had no wiring for any potential food that was not a flying insect."

"That's what it was. The mind of a frog. It wasn't conscious like you or me. It had no awareness. If it used language, it was without understanding, it was only to entice prey. That's why it never responded to our messages. That's why it ignored the blood buckets, it didn't have the wiring to understand. That's why it kept attacking us, kept drinking blood it couldn't keep down. It wasn't able to learn."

He started walking again.

Trett shuffled to keep up with him.

"But you can't generalize from that creature to them. The humans were thinking, feeling beings. Like us."

Payr slowed to allow his friend to catch up.

"No," he answered, "They weren't like us."

He paused to collect his thoughts.

"James Dean died," said Payr, "that's what made him who he was. That's what made them all. They were a race obsessed with mortality, with death. Their whole existence, for each one of them, was a struggle with death."

"It made them build pyramids, mausoleums, necropolises. Death was the force behind all their monuments. They were fascinated by death. Obsessed. Their own deaths, others deaths, inflicted deaths, and accidental deaths."

"The creature was just a biological curiosity. It was a peripheral entity. In the wild, viral robots couldn't compete with natural predators. They existed on the margins if at all. Among humans it shouldn't have lasted past the discovery of fire. It existed because they made a place for it, they needed or wanted it, it was part of their romance with oblivion.”

“I don’t know that any good can come of contact with such a culture. Even its remnants. I’ve taken a hard look at how it’s affected us, I’m not sure I like it.”

“The death star gave them exactly what they sought.” Payr said, “They died young. They made a good looking corpse.”

They waddled along for a while, the corridors were very quiet.

“I think you are being too hard on them. Their death was all they had to leave us. I think that there was a lot to them, and they would have been worth knowing. I want to get to know them. But all we have to work with is their remains.” Trett said.

They arrived at the airlock. Payr turned to his friend one last time.

“But that’s it, you see. When I was facing it, I stared at life and death. I chose life. I don’t want to live on a tomb working with dead things. I want to live.”

Trett nodded, but somehow, on him it seemed fitting.

“I do see,” he said.

They stood there for another moment, then Trett abruptly reached out and hugged his friend. A human gesture, but somehow it had become Gerven.

“What will you do?” Trett asked.

“I’m going back to my old hatching grounds, I’m going to bond with as many yearlings as I can find, and I’m going to raise a great big happy family.”

He stepped through the airlock.

* * *

Much later, deep in interstellar space, Payr’s comm bleeped.

It indicated a visitor. He started towards the door, keying it open at the same time. He stopped, shocked. Cirit was standing there, one of the missing victims whose body had never been recovered.

Cirit stepped inside, pushing Payr with inhuman strength. Its eyes were glowing red. Payr felt a tearing sensation on his chest, just above his major artery. He realised that Cirit had bitten him, the sharp points of Cirit's parrotlike beak had excised a neat wedge of flesh.

Dreamlike he watched in horror as the beak gaped, and the tongue, rolled into a tubelike structure, extruded itself into the wound and began to siphon.

Payr was unable to resist. The virus, he thought. Of course the virus would mutate quickly, it had had to in the first place to find a viable niche on earth. Humanity was gone, but it was just a matter of time and opportunity for it to mutate into something that could survive in the new host.

Payr wondered if that had been the Vampires original purpose all along, to give the infection an opportunity to find a new host.

With mounting despair, Payr felt his thoughts going dim. A deep sorrow overcame him as he realized that he would never walk on the welcoming soil of his homeland. Or at least, he would not do it alive.

The ship plunged through the void on its preprogrammed course to the homeworld, bringing with it a final legacy of the human race, the gift of night.

The End

The Cosmetic Session

"Ms Lamont is here to see you now," the intercom rasped. Tollard jumped slightly.

"Send her right in," he keyed. With practiced motions he swept the magazine into the waiting desk drawer and straightened his tie. He stepped towards the door.

The door swung inwards, as Katie, his secretary, ushered in a chunky young woman. She appeared to be in her twenties, with dark brown hair, and wore a shapeless business suit.

"Ms Lamont, I presume." Tollard gave her his most ingratiating smile, and seized her hand.

Huge breasts, he thought to himself. Natural too, he could tell by the way her body moved. She wasn't really chunky, he decided on second thought, the impression was more in the way she presented than in her form.

She briefly met his eyes, shrugging almost deferentially. Her handshake was loose and wary.

"I'm Doctor Ransom," he led her to one of the chairs facing his desk, "right this way."

As she walked, he noticed that she took moderate, almost hesitant steps. She's never taken a stride in her life, he thought.

When she had settled into the chair, he crossed around behind the desk and took his own seat. He ostentatiously glanced down at the file on his desk.

"May I call you Mae," he beamed at her. She blushed. Her full name was Mabel, but only a dedicated masochist would want to be called that.

"Uh sure," she replied.

He waited silently for a moment, just long enough for her to become uncomfortable and fidget nervously in her chair. Not well equipped for informal conversations he decided. She didn't go to parties much, and when she did, she probably stayed in the background, smiling nervously, nursing a pina colada because she'd heard of it in a song. She would probably sit there not knowing what to say when people spoke to her, being left alone to wonder why everyone but her was enjoying themselves, until finally late in the night, some drunk too foolish to notice her lack of subliminal responses would make a pass at her.

Did she ever get lucky? He wondered. He allowed himself a glance at her breasts, straining the fabric of her blouse and heaved a mental sigh. Potentially magnificent, he decided, and probably wasted.

"Um..." she said. Good beginning, he thought. "I'm supposed to see you for counselling..."

Tollard nodded. "That's right, you've been recommended by Doctor Livingston."

She shook her head dumbly.

"Well Mae, I don't really know much. You see, medical practitioners have an oath of confidentiality. Doctor Livingston couldn't tell me about your problem. That has to be between me and you." Mike Livingston was a plastic surgeon, and occasional squash partner.

She wrung her hands in confusion. "I, uh...I thought he would have told you. I want an operation."

Of course she did, he thought. All Mike's clients wanted an operation. That's what plastic surgery was all about.

"Elective surgery?" he asked, raising an eyebrow.

She nodded with relief.

"What sort of operation are you contemplating?" he asked gently. Breast reduction, he thought to himself.

"Breast reduction," she said, blushing slightly.

Of course, he thought, why not go all the way. Remove all distinguishing features. Become a complete non-entity.

Drunk Slutty Elf and Zombies / Page 2

"Well Mae, surgery is a big step, and you realize that it's also a potential threat to life and health," he explained in a reassuring voice. "When people opt for elective surgeries like your own, Doctors usually ask them to see a counsellor, just to make sure that it's what they really want."

Actually, it was the malpractice insurance companies that had required it. There had been too many lawsuits from too many dissatisfied customers.

"I really want this," she told him. It was the first forceful thing she'd said. He made a little check mark on the page.

"Then we won't really have a problem here, will we?" Tollard said warmly, "I just have to ask a few questions. How long have you wanted this?"

Probably since puberty, he thought cynically, as she began to talk. She spoke hesitantly at first, so he asked easy factual questions. Where do you live? Nice place? Live alone? Any pets? Simple basic questions anyone could ask and anyone could answer.

He doodled as he talked with her, anything relevant Michael had already told him, anything new he could file away in his memory and absorb later.

He practiced making doubleyou's, nice big looping ones.

As she answered more and more questions correctly, she began to relax, to feel confident. It was a common interviewing technique. He smiled warmly at her, and allowed the questions to open a little more. What's your favourite television show? How do you feel about your neighbours?

Tollard was an old hand at this. He'd conducted so many interviews it was almost routine. He put the pencil down and made a steeple of his fingers. It was remarkable how little the interviewer had to involve himself.

"I see, how did that make you feel?"

He remembered reading once about a simple computer program called ELIZA. ELIZA had been programmed to converse with people by spouting a simple set series of open ended comments and questions based on key words. As artificial intelligence, it had been a complete sham, but people, psychologists even, had sworn to its insight.

"Well, I..."

Mae spoke freely now, almost relaxed in the chair. Tollard had only to jog the conversation this way and that, towards areas of deeper and deeper insecurity and fear. He wouldn't get to any big fears of course, that was more effort than he cared to make. But he was content to have her wallow in the petty stews of her own perceived inadequacy and mundane self-loathing.

He listened with half an ear, studying her. Average looks, generally underused, so that her appearance was decidedly unattractive. The nose was too big, eyebrows two thick, could lose a few pounds. Overall, nothing major, but he had a clear sense of features perceived as flaws and shortcomings.

Lustrous hair, trapped in an indifferent hairdo, denoting neither courage nor commitment. Her clothes were conservative, dark suit and skirt, plain cream blouse buttoned up to the top, but not particularly flattering. She seemed to select without perception.

Take the jacket, he thought, it has shoulder pads. But she doesn't need them. She has good strong shoulders. She doesn't realize that. She bought the jacket off a rack, because it looked nice on the hanger, and she hasn't taken the pads out. It made her look like a linebacker.

Overall, Tollard decided, she looked awkward and ungainly. She picked clothes because she needed to wear something, and didn't seem comfortable in them. He imagined her without them; she still struck him as uncomfortable.

She was talking about her family now. Domineering mother, too many restrictions. She had fled to a job in another city to escape. But she had remained domineered, fully bent into the shape of a flat little wallflower. A retiring non-entity.

He leaned back in his chair. He had set her chair a few feet back from his desk to reinforce his authority behind the massive desk, and to emphasize her isolation and vulnerability. Also, from this angle, he could often see up women's dresses. Her skirt was too long to offer much. Pity.

Now she was tediously relating her school years. The avalanche of unwanted boy's attention and girl's hostility that accompanied her development, making an awkward shy child into a virtual recluse. He could hardly wait, he thought, for the shapeless trauma of her High School Prom.

Tollard straightened up and put a look of rapt attention on his face. Picking up his pencil, he began drawing little circles inside the doubleyou's.

"But that was all right, I remember I was the Valedictorian that year. My picture was in the town newspaper..."

"How did your fellow students react to that? Especially..."

Mae had a tendency to veer into her academic achievements, and Tollard several times had to lead her back towards raw adolescent wounds. Nobody needed a counsellor to come to terms with their triumphs, Tollard reflected, you had to marry them to their weaknesses. Besides, he thought, it was only when they lacked faith in themselves that you could tell them what to do.

He wondered if her nipples were pink. Brown, he decided, given her complexion. Probably medium sized, small for her breasts. Tollard wondered how her breasts would handle.

Now she was on work. Tollard had pegged her as a librarian and he hadn't been that far off. Mae was a records clerk, first class. Modestly well paying, reasonably tedious, fundamentally unsatisfying, demanding a capacity for organization and detail but requiring no particular social aptitude.

He watched her small movements in the chair. It was hard to tell with the bra on, but he judged that they were remarkably buoyant.

Good genes, he thought. Wasted on her.

She dreamed of moving up to supervisor, but he knew it wasn't going to happen.

"Mae," he said suddenly, "take my hand." He leaned forward slightly in his chair, and stretched his hand across his desk.

She couldn't reach him from where she sat, she half got out of her chair, then, changing her mind, dragged it towards the desk until she could rest her suddenly sweating fingers in his palm.

"I think we've reached a point," he told her, "where we can be really honest, so I want you to tell me what you really want."

He allowed her to stammer for a few minutes about adolescent trauma's and taking control of her own life.

"So you're telling me, Mae," he interrupted her, "that you are a plain, dumpy, colourless, unhappy woman with large breasts."

He paused for a second.

"And you want to be a plain, dumpy, colourless, unhappy woman with small breasts."

Tollard almost laughed at the look on her face. She reminded him of a deer caught in automobile headlights. Her hand jerked feebly in his grip. He put his most sympathetic expression on, and reached out with his other hand.

He held her trembling hand firmly between his. Her palm was sweating, he noticed. He looked into her eyes.

"Mae, it's not your breasts you really want to change, it's your life..."

An hour later, when he finally led her towards the door, her cheeks were flushed from crying, but she smiled nervously.

"Thank you, Doctor Ransom," she said, "I never really looked at it that way before."

"That's not really true," Tollard told her, "you knew you had to change something, you were just mistaken about what."

"You've got to learn to relate to your weaknesses and your strengths." Tollard caught himself from using the word 'assets' as he reached up to unbutton the top of her blouse. "You should be proud of your breasts; they're one of your best features."

Tollard could just see a flush of nervousness spreading down from her neck as his fingers brushed the bare skin. "You should use them."

With a tentative motion of her hand, she pushed his fingers away, covering her neck. But not, he noticed, buttoning the blouse again. He was pretty sure her nipples were hard.

"Thank you so very much," she whispered as he opened the door, "you've been a great help."

"I just helped you realize what you really wanted," he said, "that's all."

After she left, Tollard returned to his desk. Thumbing his mail order diploma certificate for good luck, as he passed it.

Breast reduction, he reflected, was a relatively cheap procedure. Not really worth the time. Pulling a calculator from under the pornographic magazines in his desk drawer, he began to make notes, itemizing a nose job, cheekbone shaving, liposuction, depilation and a handful of other minor but costly surgical procedures. He paused for a second, and then jotted down "health club membership."

Whistling tunelessly, he began to add up his commissions.

The End

About Gerrold

You're probably going to ask me, what kind of a man was Gerrold?

Everybody does, you know. They get that look in their eye, and before their mouth flaps open, like it always does, I know what's going to come out.

What kind of a man was Gerrold?

I'll tell you the same thing I tell everyone else...

Gerrold: Every morning, he'd get up at exactly six fifteen, and he'd polish his change.

Hey now, I see that look on your face, just like that look on every other face. That look that says you think I'm saying he'd be whacking it off? Palm action? Is that right? You thought I'd come up with a new phrase for the old five fingered flagpole salute?

And you wondered, just for a second, how I'd know about a thing like that. Is that right?

Hey! I was just his roommate, that's all.

Don't worry about it, it's okay. Frankly, just between you and me, I don't think that Gerrold ever had an erection in his life, or maybe that he was ever limp in his life. One or the other, Gerrold was that kind of guy, and it wasn't something I was ever going to check out.

This is a guy, after all, who ironed his socks and sweaters. Got good creases too. Who shaved his head because he couldn't stand the thought of a stray hair.

But anyway, you probably noticed that I was getting away from myself there.

Like I was saying, every morning at six fifteen precisely, he'd polish his change. Just like that.

He'd lay them all out on a white cloth he kept for that purpose. Dimes, nickels, quarters, even a smattering of pennies. He'd use turtle wax or something, I don't know. All I know is that he'd shine them til they glistened, until they'd catch any old ray of light and throw it back at you like you were looking right into the sun.

He'd just go through the day after that, handing out to beggars, giving exact change for newspapers and candy bars. Crap like that.

I mean, you look like a reasonable man, I gotta ask you, what's the point of that? Who was he trying to impress?

A few street beggars? Paperboys? A check out girl or two? What was in it for him?

Sometimes I'd see one of them, you know? One of his coins, glistening in the till, making all the other coins look like dull rocks. Especially the pennies.

I'd see them and I'd think to myself, "Gerrold's been through."

Every now and then I'd come across a vendor, just behind him. He'd just be turning the corner. Dropping out of sight, like he always did. I'd watch, as the vendor would reach into his register, fishing for the coins.

The vendor would always pull out Gerrold's coins. Hold them in his hands. Just stare at them shining in his palms.

They'd get this look on their faces. Like they'd been touched by God.

Maybe that was why Gerrold did it. But he never stuck around long enough to see that look.

So go figure.

The End

The Hoary Ghost

The ghost looked surprised at first, and then confused. It straightened up and delicately placed its hands over its genitals.

"Oh. Hello," It said. "I didn't notice you standing there."

"I can see right through your hands," she told it.

The ghost looked down at itself, shrugged in an embarrassed way, and let its hands hang at its sides.

The ghost was male, but not imposingly so. Standing in the pentagram she'd used to trap it, it resembled a nude man in middle ages, pot belly, sagging flesh, receding hair, an unsightly thinness of limb and thickness of waist. He was a picture of late middle age, gone to seed, the body of a man who'd chosen beer and Netflix over the gym, a body he clearly no longer cared about, because no one else cared about it either.

Maybe that was why he'd died.

His body had simply surrendered to lack of interest.

It was appallingly mundane, but for the fact that you could see right through it. He was like, she decided, a fading afterimage. She kept expecting him to be a trick of the light, not there at all.

"I thought something was haunting my bedroom," she swore softly, "but I guess I never really believed, until now."

Looking at it, she reflected that most people wore clothes for good reasons.

"I've heard of these things," it said, running its hand up and down the unseen cage created by the pentagram. "I never thought I'd come across one."

She watched as it tested the invisible walls of its trap.

"I got it out of a book of magic, The Arcana Gramarye," she told it proudly, "its major purpose is summoning."

The ghost looked alarmed. "You aren't thinking of summoning something in here with me, are you? There are some things that are awfully hard to get rid of, once they come up."

"No," she reassured it, "the book said that it could be used to trap a wandering spirit, if the general location of the spirit was known."

"Your bedroom," the spirit muttered wearily.

"My bedroom," she repeated.

The ghost had the decency to look embarrassed.

"So uhm...what are you planning to do?" the spirit asked.

"I'll try and exorcise you."

The ghost looked momentarily confused, "thanks, but I get plenty."

"Not exercise," she said emphatically, "I'm going to try and help you find your rest," she said. She tried to sound reassuring.

The ghost looked surprised, "I'm dead, that's about as rested as you can get."

"You know what I mean," she said, "you've died, but you haven't moved on, you have to go into the afterlife, into the light."

"What light?"

"You know," she prompted, "when you die, there's a light that you move into."

"No," the ghost said. "Where'd you get that from?"

"It's been reported."

"By who?"

"Well...people who have had near death experiences."

"Oh right," the spirit shrugged in exasperation, "experts. That's like looking at a picture of an airplane and deciding that you could fly one. Next time, check with real dead people."

"Wait a second, are you saying that there is no light? There's no heaven?"

"Not so far as I've noticed. We don't go anywhere, being dead is pretty much the same as being alive. Except for boredom and the clothes business."

"There's no God?" she asked.

"Of course there's a God," the ghost snapped, "nothing makes a believer out of someone, as much as dying. I've never met her but I sincerely believe that she's just swell."

"She?"

"Well there's a no telling about something like that," the ghost explained, "I mean, if you were to meet the great being, you probably wouldn't get away with looking under the robes to check the equipment out."

"Oh."

"So anyway, why not let me out of this thing, and we'll forget this ever happened."

"No!"

"Why not?"

"You're scaring my cat."

"Cats are skittish, it probably wasn't me, it was probably just some demon or bacteria."

"Sure," she replied sarcastically, "scary stuff, those bacteria."

"You should get a dog," it suggested gravely, "dogs are very easy going. Now, let's just call it a day and let me out."

"Why are you haunting this place?" she asked it.

It threw up its hands in horror.

"Me! Haunting you! I've never haunted anyone in my life. I'm appalled at the thought."

A look of confusion crossed her face.

"Are you haunting this place?"

"That's really a terrible thing to ask, I am just aghast."

"Are you haunting this place?" she demanded.

The ghost stared at the floor as it shuffled its feet. It looked up briefly.

"Well...maybe just a little. Now and then. On off days."

"Why?"

"Excuse me?"

"Why are you haunting this place? Did you die tragically here?"

"No, I died in St. Mary's Hospital."

"Did you live here?"

"Over on the west side."

"How did you die?" she glanced at her paperback, 'Get to Know Your Ghost.' This wasn't going well at all.

"Prostate cancer."

She frowned, "that's not tragic."

"Excuse me," the ghost looked offended, "I thought it was very tragic."

"No. What I mean is: struck down in the prime of life, to have existence cruelly stolen away from you. To be cheated of your natural span. To die unfulfilled, with things left to be done. That's tragic."

"So," the ghost retorted, "I was in the middle of a very promising career as a photomat manager. I was going to go fishing next Thursday. Prostate cancer is very unfulfilling."

Regain control of the conversation, she commanded herself.

"All right, this place had nothing to do with your life."

The ghost nodded.

"And it had nothing to do with your death."

It nodded again.

"So?"

The ghost looked puzzled.

"Why are you here?" she demanded.

The ghost looked embarrassed. If it were not translucent, she would have sworn that it blushed. Delicately, it covered itself with one hand, though, as she had earlier observed, she could see right through it, and the ghostly genitals.

"I like to watch," it told her.

"What?" she snapped, shocked.

"I like to watch," the spirit repeated. "It's boring being dead, there's nothing to do. Everyone is always talking about religion, you get bored to death."

"You've been watching me have sex?" She felt herself flushing hotly in a mixture of embarrassment and mounting horror. "All this time?"

"Well..." the ghost shuffled with embarrassment, like a child with his hand wedged irretrievably into the cooky jar, "it's not always me. Not all the time. Sometimes it's others."

"Aaagh," she said, and tried to jam both fists into her mouth.

"Not that many, usually, it's only around the weekend that we really get a crowd in."

"A crowd!"

"Usually, just the regulars."

"I have regulars!"

"Of course there was that time a few months back when you brought that guy home," the ghost reminisced.

"Trevor! A crowd of ghosts watched me with Trevor!"

"Standing room only, you were terrific, unanimous ovation."

"Oh my God," she whispered in horror.

"Please," said the ghost, "religious dead people are tedious enough."

"You're being awfully familiar," she tried to rally.

"Hey," shrugged the ghost, "when you've watched someone pick their nose on the toilet, you get to feel like you know them."

"You watch me on the toilet?" she was outraged.

Being spied on in bed was one thing, you could get used to it. After all, you had to have at least one other person in there with you to really get into the swing of things.

On the other hand, going to the bathroom was a completely solitary act. It was the most private act of modern civilisation.

Bowel movements were practically sacred.

"You always start with the left nostril," the ghost mused, "never fails."

Suddenly, she saw what was coming, "don't say it."

"Then you stick the finger in your mouth."

"Ick," it was the sound of complete mortification. The sound that came from the sudden knowledge that every tiny, unthinking, private gesture, no matter how intimate or disgusting, has actually been on public display.

"It's great," said the spirit, "I win the bet every time."

"You bet on it," she whispered. In her mind she suddenly visualized a racetrack crowd cheering her on as she sat on the toilet, her index finger automatically following the unthinking ritual - left nostril, right nostril, lips.

The ghost took no notice of her discomfiture. In fact, it seemed to have grown increasingly relaxed.

"We bet on all sorts of things," she was told, "for instance, we bet on whether Trevor would tell you about his rash."

Her heart jolted physically in her chest. "Trevor had a rash???"

The sense of acute exposure was quickly washed away by a surge of venereal terror. Suddenly all she could think about was gynaecologists and clinics, and what a blood test might reveal.

"Oh yes, quite a rash it was down there. Trevor was quite worried about it, although," the ghost eyed her, "not worried enough, in your case."

"WHAT DID YOU MEAN BY THAT?" Abruptly she was right up against the edge of the pentagram, screaming. The impending sensation that she might wind up on the other side, the out side, looking in, shredded her last vestige of control.

The energy of her rage seemed to wither the phantom; it cowered back against the opposite side of the pentagram.

"If he was worried, he should have told you," the ghost whimpered. "It was just a mild allergy. That's all. Nothing serious. His skin reacts badly to watermelon."

"Oh," she said, feeling her panic deflate. She carefully backed away, opening the door behind her. "I'll be right back."

"I'm not going anywhere," the ghost said ruefully, leaning against the invisible walls of the pentagram.

She quietly walked down the stairs, and wandered into the kitchen. Too much, she thought, way too much. She felt like a yo-yo, every other thing it had said had shattered some corner of her beliefs. She made herself a cup of tea, relaxing into the brisk ritual. She was careful not to note that her hands were shaking.

She sat at the kitchen table, sipping it slowly. It was, she reflected, a nice house. She'd really liked it. Until now.

She'd worked hard to be able to afford it, to put up the down payment. She couldn't just walk away.

Besides, she reflected, if what that thing says is true, it wouldn't help to go anywhere else. They're all over the place.

Did it really make a difference? If they've been watching her from the beginning, the only thing changed now was that she knew. If everything was the same, what did it matter to her?

Or to other people?

Abruptly, a stray thought slipped unannounced into her mind. What had Trevor been doing with that watermelon that he would have developed a severe skin rash there?

Involuntarily, the corners of her mouth turned up slightly.

And did he know that he'd been working to a crowd?

The more she thought of it, the funnier it became.

Soon she was laughing out loud.

Later, after the laughter, and after three more cups of tea, and after a short trip to the bathroom; where she picked her nose defiantly; but, self-consciously, did not slip her finger into her mouth; she decided to go back upstairs.

The ghost, true to its words, hadn't gone anywhere. It was still standing in the middle of the pentagram, trapped and waiting to see what would happen next.

She pulled a chair up to within a couple of feet of the pentagram, and straddled it.

At length, she asked "why me?"

"Because you're fun to watch," the ghost told her, "you have very good sex."

"What about other people? Do you watch them too?"

The ghost stared at the ceiling, "talking about God for eternity gets pretty boring."

"So, between the bunch of you, you know who's athletic and who's not."

The ghost nodded.

She went on, "Who's straight, who's gay, who's nice, and who's a complete jerk. Who's safe, who's a loser and who's got prospects..."

The ghost nodded again, this time strongly, as it began to catch the direction of her thoughts. It smiled at her, she grinned right back.

"You know," said the phantom, "this could be the beginning of a beautiful friendship."

"Provided you stay out of the bathroom," she told it.

The End

Training Day

"Gorgomak is rising in Sydney Harbour!" Channing yelled.

I was already on the move, bursting out of the mess and sprinting along the ring, knocking pedestrians and tourists out of the way, as I made for the drop chutes.

Gorgomak was over a hundred and fifty meters tall, over five hundred meters of charcoal black, spikey reptilian fury, a nightmare of glowing spines, secondary claws and jaws erupting like tumours, at one end the blazing maw of oblivion, at the other the scorpion tale of destruction.

Sydney didn't have a chance. The creature could level it in minutes.

I reached the drop chute, and leaped in head first, just the way they said to do it in the textbooks. There are all kinds of safeties that are supposed to get you to where you need to be intact, but you can't help but hear the stories of unlucky pilots who got turned inside out because they engaged wrong. Soon, I was whistling down the winding tube, micro-manipulators pulling my clothes away, tiny explosive bolts in the thread undoing the seams.

How had it gotten so close without being detected? The Satellites should have been tracking it from its first move.

I remembered to exhale just before the gel hit, fighting the feeling of drowning as I inhaled the complex oxygenated fluid that would keep me alive, even as it surrounded me, cushioning the shocks.

An instant later, I dropped into the pilot's pod. It always felt like a physical jerk, although by that time, I could no longer feel physical movement. Nanoprobes came at me from all directions, snaking into my cerebrum and neural system.

I gritted my teeth; this was going to be a bad one.

"Orbital Drop!" I confirmed, speaking out loud. I did that as a habit in the gel, you can make sounds, though it comes out muddy. The real commands were transmitted directly from the speech centers of my brain. But I'm old fashioned.

"Roger," Channing replied, "cycling through protocols, Orbital drop in forty seconds, counting down."

"Screw that," I yelled, my voice bubbling. "Emergency Jettison, let's go. Dropping now!"

High up in geosynchronous orbit, Conquistador and I broke away from the ring, magnetic bolts decoupling even as my literal thrusters turned them white hot. I stretched, Conquistador's humanoid frame arching, legs bending. As the magnetic bolts retracted, I leaped, 150,000 tons of mass and metal breaking free of the station.

Physics is physics, the equal and opposite reaction of my launch would shake the whole ring. It was dinner time on the station, I imagined a whole lot of meals getting ruined, drinks being spilled, even a few nasty tumbles. There'd be a lot of complaints when I got back.

If I got back.

Gorgomak was a tough customer.

No time for that.

In free fall, I plotted drop vectors. I was up around twenty-two thousand miles and change. Sidney was around nine thousand miles, south by southwest. That's a lot of miles to eat. In front of me, an illusion from the visual centers of my brain fountained with a dozen accelerated drop paths, all designed to take me into stratosphere thirty miles over Sydney, before reverse breaking and dropping on top of what I hoped would be one surprised. I waved at the most optimum one, get me there fast enough, but hopefully wouldn't break every window in Sydney.

Conquistador's iron thrusters in its legs and torso flared ultraviolet so hard you could see the purple discharge.

I stretched out Conquistador's right arm, and tucked the left close to my body. What can I say; I'm a kid at heart.

The acceleration would have ruptured me down to cellular level, but for the Gel. I didn't feel a thing, going from zero to 328,000 miles an hour.

I wished I could have a cigarette, that would be cool. You can't smoke in gel though.

Who knows?

Maybe I should ask the brain boys about that. They'd probably like a challenge like that.

Course was pre-set; I had a couple of minutes to myself. I checked vitals. Heart, lungs, lymphs, all the intricate squishy complexity of human mechanics, and the arcane chemical interactions that make us what we are.

It's all supposed to be automatic, no monitoring required. But you hear stuff now and then skeletons turned to powder, or neural nets unravelled like a wool sweater. I like to look in on my body from time to time. Everything looked fine.

I switched to an external feed, zeroing in on the ring stations, that silver necklace that safeguarded what was left of earth. I couldn't spot any launches.

"Hey Channing," I called. "Anyone coming down with me to fight this thing."

"Sorry Max," Channing sounded almost apologetic. "You're the only active unit in range. If you wait an hour, we can have Juggernaut and Shakazulu–"

"Sydney's not going to last that long," I snapped. So just me then.

That was fine with me, I like to work alone.

Cigarette? No. Cigar. I wanted to grip a big fat stogie between my teeth as I dropped down out of orbit like hell incarnate. Gorgomak, I thought, I got someone to meet you, compressing the knuckles of Conquistador's right hand. Call him Mister Fister.

It's going to be a big surprise.

We were sweeping across the arc of the world, descending fast. I could clearly make out the great Pacific Ocean scars.

Goddamned aliens.

How many dimensions are there? We thought three. Four including time. Turns out there's a lot more, even by the 20th century, physicists had figured out that our universe's math didn't work right unless you posited 18 dimensions.

We figured when the big bang formed the universe, the main dimensions just sort of took over, and all those extra dimensions withered and became vestigial, like the row of nipples on a male dog, unimportant, except to make the math balance.

Turns out we were wrong. Those hyperdimensions produced their own pseudo-matter, bent pseudo-energy, stuff that could be detected, exploited, even mined. And it turns out we were unlucky to have a lot of that hyperdimensional pseudomatter. We didn't even know it. The aliens did though, and they didn't mind taking it.

One day, they just showed up in their big refinery ships, and in a year, half the human race was dead.

They didn't even say hello.

Was it just Gorgomak? I did a positional scan of the world's Kaiju, trying to see where everyone was. Gorgomak was bad enough, I didn't need a twofer. Off in the English countryside, Big Ben was shaking down with Paiute and Cobragon; the great British mech looked like he was getting the worst of it. I didn't particularly like his pilot; let someone else ride to the rescue. I was going to have my hands full.

Everyone else was where they should be, except the ones who weren't. The Kaiju were getting sneakier, evading our sensors. But I did a backscan and came up with a 90% probability that there was nobody in the neighbourhood.

One on one fight then. Just the way I liked it.

Where was I? The Goddamned aliens. They didn't say hello. They just did their thing. Ignored our desperate attempts to communicate, our even more desperate attempts to fight them. Then they left, not even a kiss goodbye. They just took what they wanted, and buggered off.

Of course, they left their garbage behind, immense piles of technology and technological artifacts that Earth's survivors repurposed. We built mecha, space stations, Moon bases, a Mars colony, cities at the bottom of the sea and under Antarctic ice. It was almost payment for what we'd suffered. What they'd done to us.

No. Not even close.

And they left their waste. I don't know what you'd call it. Mine tailings. Industrial by-product. Refinery leftovers. Distorted, post-processed, hyperdimensional pseudostuff, piles of it, unnatural concentrations, mountains of cosmic toxic waste.

And that had produced the Kaiju. Earth's newest dominant life form.

Let me tell you, they were a surprise.

Graphic display threw up an image of the Sydney topography, the terrain, the buildings, the skyscrapers, and in the middle of it, like a big charcoal gray scar, was Gorgomak. Even a hundred miles out, on a holographic readout, the big bastard sent chills down my spine. You could even make out his glowing tips, coruscating with the radiation of hyperdimensional cosmic toxins.

Conquistador bottomed out a few miles above the troposphere, now merely travelling at supersonic speeds.

Hey, I noticed from the graphic image, the Sydney Opera House was still standing!

What do you know!

I calculated an approach vector. Hopefully, the sonic booms wouldn't shatter too many windows. We were going so much faster than sound, that even on a curving vector, he wouldn't hear me coming.

A bare couple of thousand feet above ground now, the landscape rushing past displays, in real time, real dimensions all around me, magnifying projections erupting everywhere like soap bubbles, demanding my hyper-acute attention.

I ignored all of it. I was coming up on the great charcoal gray shape ahead of me.

It was turning to face me.

How the hell had it sensed me coming.

No time to wonder. Conquistador slammed, into Gorgomak's side, a hundred thousand tons of supertech mech robot, colliding with three hundred thousand tons of reptilian hyperdimensional sludge, at three times the speed of sound. I just had time to calculate the kinetic force involved, in newton tonnes. I watched the rows of numbers adding up. Let me tell you, it was satisfying.

"Ow!" I screamed aloud. You're not supposed to feel anything in the gel. But an impact that monstrous? I guarantee, you feel it. Fire and feedback goes screaming down the nanoconnections, your entire nervous system lights up and your body spasms, you see sounds, taste colour, your mind explodes in a thousand directions at once, and the pain is like an orgasm. It's great.

For picoseconds, all the systems go offline at once, and then instantly reboot, surge protectors kicking in and shutting down instantly, kinetic energy absorbers blowing past their limits, systems cascading back and forth, error messages screaming from a molecular level on up.

But somewhere, there's a monstrous grunt of pain as a behemoth goes flying, and even as Conquistador flounders out of control into its own free fall crash landing, bouncing and tearing through entire neighbourhoods, I hear it.

And it's satisfying.

Conquistador is still bouncing, but I bring on the ion drives to control spin, kick in the boot thrusters, and swing out a giant metal arm for balance, you're not supposed to do that, but hey, it works. Somehow, I stabilize the giant mecha, on one knee, fist planting in the ground, demolishing an empty apartment block.

My imagers are scrambled, infra-red, ultra violet, telescopic, three D, flickering in and out, the AI manager so rattled it can't figure out what to present. For just an instant, my vision is filled with a Eucalyptus tree a hundred and fifty miles away, with a koala mother in it, baby on its back, chewing a leaf. It's looking out towards the source of the dull boom that marked our impact.

It's so pristine, so beautiful, so crystal clear, that I reach out to touch them.

I briefly spot my hand reaching through the gel.

There are red spots floating in the gel all around me. Blood?

By sheer force of will, I clear the displays, pulling up a positional map. Sydney's a ghost city all around me, the buildings and structures translucent. I don't care about that. Where is Gorgomak? Responding to half verbalized commands, to my focussed will, the map shudders and tilts, colours washing in and out.

And there it is, at the end of a wake of debris, writhing and floundering, its great legs kicking at the air as it struggles to get its feet under it.

I reach for the Omni-cannon. Off line. Electro-sword? Off line too. Boot thrusters, to fly over there and kick the bastard. All I get are error messages, diagnostic and self-repair stats. Railgun? Gattler? Turbo pulse? No. No. And no.

Fine, let's do this the hard way. Conquistador rises to its feet, the hydraulics of its left leg blowing out in a daisy chain, but I've already compensated for that, and as the systems kick out, the back-ups kick in. Conquistador raises its arms and slaps a fist into a palm.

In the gel, I grin, lips pulling back, exposing my teeth.

I like doing it the hard way.

Conquistador begins to charge. Massive ten thousand ton boots making earthquakes with each step, thrusters going off intermittently, boosting the acceleration, a hundred and fifty meters of mighty mech juggernaut, pounding across the countryside, faster and faster. There's something delirious about physically running, charging across the landscape.

Ahead of me, Gorgomak struggles. How can it even be moving after that blow? But damnably, the monster is already climbing to its feet. If I can just get to it in time, hit it with hammer blows from ten thousand ton fists, I can knock it back down, and keep it down.

But no, it's spotted me. Even before the warning protocols blare red across the visuals the signage flickering in and out, I know it. I can see the shift in body language, the sense of awareness. It's on to me.

Triple hinged jaws unfold, and a beam of pure hyperdimensional energy, half fire, half lightning, pours out, twisting and arcing. I'm already throwing Conquistador out of the way, ignoring the alerts and evasive manoeuver flashes, all of them a day late and a dollar short. That's why AI don't pilot the big mechs, there's nothing like accelerated human reaction and intuition.

The beam arcs past, just barely missing Conquistador's armour, as I knew it would. Conquistador's built to take a shot like that full on, my mech is tough. But not that many shots, if you know what I mean.

As Gorgomak's bolt goes wild, scorching a residential district to oblivion and taking out the side of a hill, I pull Conquistador into a massive tuck and roll, darting behind some massive apartment complexes. Another bolt punches through a building, and it begins to collapse, but I've already moved past without giving it a thought, concealing myself among the tallest buildings of Sydney's downtown core, using the smoke and debris of collapsing buildings to conceal myself.

The death toll would be incalculable, if there was anyone left in Sydney. But everyone here died, the day the aliens came. London, Leningrad, Lagos, Perth, city after city, just emptied out, no rhyme or reason to the ones where everyone died, or where everyone was spared

The aliens left earth full of empty cities.

Topographic mapping shows Gorgomak on the move, following me, looking for payback. The monster's sensor array isn't as refined as my own, and even on foot, my mech is faster.

Before the creature knows what's happening, I'm stepping out of nowhere, slamming a rocket powered fist into the side of its head. It looses a hyperplasma bolt, but the energy blast merely sheers off the top of an office building.

I've got him now. Conquistador throws an arm around the monster's neck, immobilizing it in a headlock, and with my free hand, I rain blow after blow down on the creatures head, punishing it with everything I've got. Taser knuckles come back on line, and I throw them in, my fist blazing a white smoking trail as I punch Gorgomak with everything I've got.

More bolts of hyperdimensional lightning fire spurt from its jaws, erupting harmlessly into the sky or into empty building. I'm in control, hammering away. It's scorpion tail lashes forward at Conquistador like a pile driver, setting off cascades of impact damage warnings, but I barely pay attention. I've got it where I want it. Do you feel that? Payback's a bitch.

For good measure, I activate the forearm thrusters, punching so hard Conquistador's structural monitors protest, kinetic absorption pads literally exploding as they come online, sequence of auto-repair flicker on and off as the steel-titanium super-structure literally bends and folds with the intensity of my blows. I'm vaguely aware of feedback something close to pain, and blood spurting into the gel from my knuckles as sympathetic parallel response, shatters the bone. But I don't care, because I'm hitting Gorgomak with everything I've got, and however it hurts me, it's hurting worse, the monster is screaming, screaming frantically.

With main effort it pulls, lifting Conquistador up off its feet. I engage the gravity locks, planting us back down. But Gorgomak just pulls again, hyperdimensional sludge muscles straining for all their worth, and as my gravity locks whine and protest, I feel my Conquistador's feet once again leaving the ground, as the monster heaves a hundred thousand tons of protesting super-mech hardware up into the air like an adult playing with a toddler.

But I've got tricks up my sleeve and just before the gravity locks blow out, I cut them and engage the boot thrusters hard for orbital burn.

Gorgomak can't compensate fast enough for the kinetic shifts, it's claws and secondary claws are biting into the armour, it won't let go, but it's off balance now the scorpion tale flailing wildly, missing Conquistador completely. Or a second, we dance crazily together, like some mad tango dancers, me in the air, thrusters blasting away, and the monster underneath, hanging around, twirling madly, neither us of us willing to let go. My railguns are back on, so I rain hot flensing metal down on him. It doesn't do more than make him blink, but while he's blinking I drench him with a rocket barrage, bathing the titan in white hot napalm.

The creature slips, our grips loosen, and we roll away from each other, the kinetic energy of our battle sending us careening in opposite directions. Gorgomak falls into the harbour, his crash raising a tidal wave that almost swamps the Sidney Opera house. I land among the petrified animals at the zoo. I've got the high ground.

As the monster struggles to return, I'm already bearing down, briefly taking flight and landing in front of it. My Omni Cannon discharges from my chest, the intensity of the energy blast so powerful that I have to brace Conquistador against the thrust. Leg servos whine and pop. But I only laugh. Take that, a white hot blast of the Omni Cannon's energy hits Gorgomak full on, and the monster bellows in pain, its feet digging trenches as it's forced backwards.

As the energy dissipates, Gorgomak breathes heavily and stomps forward, eyes blazing and incandescent, triple hinged jaws opening to let loose its own hyperdimensional blast.

And I hit it with the Omni Cannon again, this time
knocking it clear off its feet.

Take that!

Gorgomak wasn't expecting that. Its hide is singed and
smoking and I can tell it's almost disoriented.

I force Conquistador forward two more steps, closing the
gauntlets into fists. The Omni Cannon is only to be used in
direst emergencies, it's a massive strain on the systems, and
protocol dictates you only use it maybe twice in a full day.

I discharge the Omni Cannon again, for the third time in
as many minutes, hitting the creature with full force. The
intensity is so great that both Gorgomak and Conquistador
are driven back, I was unable to properly brace the mech in
time.

Suddenly a long scrolling document appears in my visual
array, superimposing itself on the scene. In a picosecond it
scrolls through. Oh no, it seems I've voided my insurance. So
much for manufacturer's warranty.

I laugh and brace Conquistador, and let loose with the
Omni Cannon's fourth blast, everything is going into redline,
circuits are physically melting. What the hell, why not, I
double the power output, giving the Omni Cannon
everything I've got, bathing the monster in apocalyptic fury.

And it hunkers down, bracing itself, and taking it, taking
every bit of it.

Abruptly, the Omni Cannon in Conquistador's chest
flickers and shuts off. I try to call up status reports, indices,
readouts, nothing. The whole unit is melted to slag. I hope
they don't bill me.

Gorgomak is standing there. Wisps of smoke are feeling
off him. One of its secondary claws brushes away once or
twice at its hide.

It looks mad.

That's probably not good.

In the few heartbeats I have left, I do a systems diagnostic; pulling up everything I've got left. Tasers, gattlers, rockets, laser eyes, cosmic sword.

Then it charges, roaring.

Conquistador is silent, and even though Gorgomak can't hear me, I scream inside the gel, responding with my own war cry. Conquistador lunges forward, cosmic sword protruding from left forearm, sliding into fist, unearthly hyper-lightning crackling down its lengths.

We meet with a thunderous crash like two titans of old. I swing the cosmic sword in a broad stroke, but it blocks me with the scorpion tale. But that only opens it up, and I lift Conquistador's leg and kick hard in its abdomen, activating thrusters to give it some extra punch. Distracted, the monster doesn't see my haymaker coming at its head until it makes contact, knocking a few teeth loose.

Take that.

But then before I can follow up, the scorpion tail comes punching, caving in Conquistador's shoulder section. For a moment, the arm is paralysed. I grab the creature's forearm with my free hand, and trigger the exploding bolts on the impacted amour plates, blowing them free and restoring my mobility. With the freed hand, I try to rake the Monster's eyes, but it turns its head and the gauntlet slides down its muzzle, catching its lower jaw. For a moment, the jaw drops in surprise, and before it can snap shut, I trigger the Tasers, sending enough current in a circuit between my grips to blow out the circuits of half the orbital stations. I'm rewarded with another cry of pain.

The jaw snaps shut, and Conquistador loses the tips of several fingers, Gorgomak pushes us away. Conquistador staggers, which is a bad sign, since the gyros should stabilise us automatically. My mech doesn't have much life in it, I check the diagnostics, but then shut them off. I don't need to read them to tell me I need to win this one fast.

I trigger the gattlers lighting up its hide with sparkles. There's a stray random thought that this is pretty. I catch myself; I'm in as bad a shape as Conquistador. Then I follow with a rocket barrage, until the launchers are empty. It's not going to do much but it'll at least distract the monster, as I come in with my real attack.

Conquistador lunges forward, swinging the cosmic sword in a mighty chop. Gorgomak's scorpion tale punches forward, crashing against the sword, which whistles through empty air.

But I'm not done. I take Conquistador's momentum, bringing it forward, lunging and swinging down. Gorgomak is forced to turn to the side, defending itself with the tale. I swing and thrust again, and again, timing rockets and thrusters, mech and monster duelling with their armaments, until a lucky counter thrust sends the ball at the end of the tail bracing down against Conquistador's wrist, the sword forced into the earth and shattering.

Despite the loss of my last great weapon, I see an opportunity. The monster is close, in striking distance, and so I aim a powerhouse punch at the side of its head, hoping to stun it. Not quite, it's too quick, and it moves, taking the blow at my shoulder. Warped metal and blown pistons, already far past manufacturer's specifications finally give up. Conquistador's left gauntlet practically explodes, metal bracing, hydraulics, electric cables flying apart.

That's not good.

The monster attacks. I step Conquistador back hastily, assessing the damage. The rail gun in the forearm is still intact, so I deploy that, trying to blind it. My screens are full of error and failure warnings, and I'm scrambling through it with diagnostics, trying to coax more life out of collapsing systems.

Abruptly, Gorgomak is on me, on Conquistador, the two hulks bumping against each other, as the Monster drives us backwards. Gorgomak's reptilian face is filling all my screens, the blazing eyes and buzz saw teeth overriding even the error messages. I command Conquistador's failing servos to brace its legs, bring the left arm around for a roundhouse punch.

But Gorgomak's flaws have already wrapped around Conquistador's head. Suddenly, I hear a tortured shrieking of metal, real auditory, not through a feed. Gorgomak twists, and then tears off Conquistador's head.

Sparks and fluids are fountaining from severed connections in the neck. The escape tube flops wildly and goes inert. The laser eyes flicker rapidly. Gorgomak tosses the head aside, and it tumbles through the air, crushing stands of trees as it rolls to a stop. Buried safe in the torso, I watch Conquistador's head turn end over end, its telemetry a garbled mess. The diagnostics all go dark. That contained was my escape module. A stray thought suggests maybe that wasn't the best engineering choice.

It occurs to me, finally, that I'm not going to win this one.

Gorgomak's reptilian eyes are blazing and luminous, smoky light is pouring from its jaws, and it's raining titan blows down on what's left of Conquistador as I desperately try to keep the mech staggering backwards.

I'm piloting eighty five thousand tons of scrap metal.

A blow, I think from the scorpion tail strikes the now unarmoured shoulder section, crushing a whole sequence of machinery. Just like that, the readouts up and down the left side all go dark. I try to orient the Gyros manually, using brute force commands. But another blow sends Conquistador reeling back. I try for thrusters, but there's nothing there.

Instead, Conquistador falls flat on its back, crushing a fleet of school buses, and some large metal sheds.

For a moment, everything goes black.

Then emergency reserve power kicks in. I run the systems check, but there's nothing to work with. Sensor suites are mostly functional. I send a tight beam data feed to the orbiting satellites. Orbital command should at least have a record.

I do a terrain sweep. Sydney Opera House is still standing. For some reason, that feels right.

There's Gorgomak, towering above me, hyperdimensional fumes coming off him, light streaming from between his jaws, a dark and angry god. He's just looking down at the ruins of Conquistador.

"All right, you bastard," I say out loud, the words bubbling in the gel, "you win this one."

Gorgomak cocks its head, as if it heard me.

Then, carefully, it advances on the ruins of Conquistador, looming over the inert shell I'm hiding in, bends forward, and pries the armoured chest plates apart.

There are a lot of innards in the chest cavity of a former hundred thousand ton mech. Fusion plants, ion drives, launch racks, servos, you name it. But it ignores all of that, digging through the scrapped metal.

I know what it's looking for.

Me.

It finds the command module, an octahedron of glass and steel, with me floating in golden gel, at the center of a complex of useless wires, now helpless with only life support and sensor systems functioning.

Almost gently, it reaches in, its claws wrapping around the module, and lifting it from the ruined innards of Conquistador.

Then, ponderously, it turns away from its defeated enemy, and carrying the module, begins to make its way into the Australian interior.

There isn't much for me to do but wait. Nanodocs repair bodily damage, burned nerves, broken bones and exploded blood vessels. I watch my physiological readouts until I'm completely bored. Oddly, there's a sense of motion that makes it through the gel as Gorgomak carries me along.

Finally, after a day or so, we arrive at Australia Earth Defence Base Twelve. There's a welcoming crew waiting for us as we approach. I call them up on the screens. They're all laughing and cheering, whooping and hollering. Some are dancing. They've set up a fireworks display.

There are a couple of Kaiju. Dreamsnake, who's technically more a centipede with tentacles, and Arthopodon, an insectoid. They're just slackers, hanging around the base.

Carefully, Gorgomak lowers my module into the center of them, and I'm decanted, which involves a lot of undignified spitting, coughing and puking goo from every orifice. But they're not bothered. They've decanted a lot of trainers.

A woman named Casey takes my hand, her eyes sparkling.

"That was a hell of a training bout," she says. "He really kicked your ass!"

Some people would be embarrassed by that. But both Gorgomak and I know it was a real fight, not a rollover.

"He surely did," I agree.

"Well," she said, "if you're up for it, we've got an orgy scheduled for tonight. I like your spirit. I've got some spare ova, not spoken for. Want to join up, do a vitro. I think we could decant a pretty capable offspring."

I smile. When you're a combat training officer, you get a lot of offers like that.

"Sure," I said. "To both. But excuse me, there's something I need to do."

I turn around. My skin is cold and the ultraviolet is harsh, I could use some coveralls. It's painful to walk; gel is hell on muscle tissue. But there's a ceremony to these things. I walk away from the group a hundred yards or so, until I'm looking up at Gorgomak, perched delicately on his haunches.

The monster looks down at me.

I look up at it.

I extend my arm, thrusting a fist upwards.

Down, down it reaches; extending a claw so monstrous that it could balance an elephant on its tip, until it just barely touches my extended fist.

We tap together, then lift side, right side, top and bottom, my fist and the claw tip describe delicate little arcs counter clockwise to each other, then bump. It's our secret handshake.

"That was a hell of a fight," I call up to it. "I wasn't holding anything back. You've come a long way. You did good out there."

The massive head doesn't move, but the glowing eyes blink. I can feel its pleasure radiating down towards me.

"I'm proud of you," I call to it. "We all are."

The head inclines in a nod, the sense of pleasure redoubles.

Oh just wait till they show up again, the thought which isn't mine rolls through my head.

I nod.

"Well," I said, "they're throwing us a party. Should we get back to it?"

Again, a thought that isn't mine rumbles assent.

I turn to being the arduous walk back. When you come out of the gel, your muscles are pretty strained.

But something stops me, and I look back up to the Kaiju, one of the beings that we share the earth with as willing partners.

Gorgomak's claw descends turning palm up till it touches the earth. There's a notch at the tip of the claw, just the right size and shape for a person to sit in. We've been friends a long time, and he knows me. With a sigh, I sit back, and he carries us back to the party.

Someday, we both know, the aliens will be back.

They're not finished raping our planet. We've decoded that much of their language to learn that at least.

When they do, Humanity and our new brothers, the Kaiju, are going to be waiting for them. We're getting ready.

Let me tell you, this time, there's going to be a conversation.

And we're going to make sure that they don't enjoy it.

The End

Consumer Reports: Monsters

People used to worry about simple things like death, taxes, inflation, getting a job and getting laid. Nowadays, its monsters.

Fear of monsters, is now a growth industry, with everything from the Black and Decker vampire slayers kit, to the silver bullet lobby (guaranteed to kill pretty much anything), to sleazeballs trying to sell you insurance policies against Godzilla.

We hear at consumer protection research have taken it upon ourselves to answer common questions about monsters, and show you how you, the ordinary citizen, can defend yourself against most monsters with ordinary household materials, and most importantly, at practically no cost.

Here are some common complaints:

Dear Consumers: I am an agnostic, which of course poses some problems when confronted by vampires. Is there any way to stop an attacking vampire without resorting to crucifixes or holy water? Archbishop Menendez.

Yes there is.

If confronted by a vampire, the best way to escape is to throw a handful of poppy seeds or rice on the ground. The vampire will be compelled to stop and count every single seed before continuing its attack. With enough poppy seeds, the

Vampire can be kept counting until the sun comes up. Why? Who knows, it's one of those vampire things.

Also note that vampires cannot cross running water. This is due to the electromagnetic effects of running water, which can be sensed by dowsers, rather than any fear of getting their feet wet. Vampires cannot cross over underground streams or over bridges. This means that if you're living in a community with water and sewer services, or living in a house with indoor plumbing, Mr. Vampire is going to have problems.

With all the recent Asian immigration into my neighbourhood and a spate of dogs and cats going missing, I'm starting to wonder if they've brought their monsters with them. Will the normal precautions work against Chinese vampires? If not, what do you do, and how do you tell which is which?

Reminder that this is the 21st century and this sort of attitude is not acceptable. We would caution you against racist attitudes. All restaurants serve pets, and why not? Pet cats and dogs are generally well fed, well cared for, in excellent physical condition, and free of parasites or awkward medical conditions. When you consider the appalling conditions on factory farms, you can understand why any good restaurant puts a premium on your Fido and kitty.

The best way to make sure that your darling doesn't end up on the menu is to teach your cat or puppy to make a sickly hacking cough, use eye drops to make their eyes watery, shave random patches of fur off, paint sores on exposed skin, have them tie one of their limbs to simulate a limp, a small amount of poison can induce random vomiting with no long term effects. No gourmet will want an animal in that condition. Restaurants don't want unhealthy diseased pets, and bonus, it keeps touchy feeling strangers from patting them.

Not all restaurants engage in the covert pet-napping and serving trade. High end restaurants are well known for serving human flesh. They fall into two categories – elitist restaurants that serve poor people to rich people; and postmodern counterculture restaurants that covertly serve rich people to other rich people.

Remember if there's a pet disappearance problem in your neighbourhood, your most likely suspects are not Asians, but any kind of new restaurant. Or maybe just a local Satanic cult, although mostly cults shop at pet stores.

Getting back to your actual (racist) question: Chinese vampires aren't bothered by crucifixes, holy water or garlic, which makes it important to be able to tell the difference. However, this is easy to do, since Chinese vampires hop around like bunny rabbits. Nobody's really sure why, but it makes them easy to pick out of a crowd.

Theoretically, there's nothing to stop a western vampire from hopping as well. But we haven't heard of any so far. Western vampires are apparently much too concerned with their dignity to hop. We think they should loosen up and give it a try though.

Anyway, although immune to most conventional responses, Chinese vampires can be paralysed by simply pasting a note to their forehead. For best effect, it should be a Chinese blessing. But in a pinch, you can try anything, a grocery list, an old lottery ticket, an overdue bill, a little yellow post-it note. After that, stick it in a corner, make sure the note never falls off, and forget about it.

Consumer Protection: I have a tremendous fear of being eaten by zombies, is there anything I can do? Steve Romero.

Your answer is common ordinary table salt. Sprinkle a little on the reanimated corpse, and it will suddenly realize its dead and go looking for a nice place to lay down.

And further: Will that work for all of the undead? What about Vampires and Mummies? Steve, again.

No. Vampires are their own topic. They're bothered by garlic, not salt.

Also, the salt trick will not work on mummies, which are basically dehydrated corpses, heavily salted to begin with.

Mummies are among the less terrifying monsters. When confronted by a mummy, it is important to take the proper life preserving actions: Turn around and walk briskly away in the opposite direction. Let's face it, they aren't very fast. Do not get into a car, however, for some reason; cars have trouble starting when Mummies are in the vicinity.

A similar effect is observed with UFOs, which may mean that UFOs are actually piloted by Mummies. This is considered to be corroboration of the ancient astronaut theory.

If you do get into a car, at least roll up the window. Forty five per cent of all people killed by Mummies died trying to start their car, while forgetting to roll up the windows.

As for more permanent solutions, Mummies are among the most resilient of monsters. Crosses and silver bullets will not bother them. Pretty much no form of injury will stop them. However, being desiccated corpses, excessive humidity can eventually destroy it. Most mummies in the past have been disposed of by luring them into swamps. Also moths will eventually do the trick. However, there are no fast solutions.

So remember, just walk away.

Dear Consumer Protection: I recently purchased a US Army surplus reusable LAWS rocket launcher with a six missile load. They guaranteed that it would shave the pubic hairs off any terrestrial non-blob attacker up to thirty tons. It also said keep out of the reach of children, but that's neither here nor there.

Here's my problem, I've recently booked a trip to England and I hear that their customs office is pretty strict about things like this. What if I'm attacked by the Loch Ness monster? A man has a god given right to defend his family. Is there any way to make the English listen to reason? A Real American (anonymous).

Actually, this is one of these product cases that really gets our goat down at Consumer reports. Just listen to the guarantee: Not effective against blobs, extraterrestrials, or monsters over thirty tons. So just what is your rocket launcher good for? Giant ants, and that's about it.

You'd have done well to check our 1994 Product effectiveness report which found that such devices compared poorly to the De-Luxe portable electrocution device, with accessory plates and cables included. A bargain at forty-five thousand dollars, fits into a U-Haul, no customs problems whatsoever, and is proof against the widest variety of supernatural, extraterrestrial and gigantic menaces known.

In any event, we're going to have to go with the British on this one. Leave the rocket launcher alone.

The Loch Ness monster, like its American counterpart, the Bigfoot, is a notoriously shy monster. Your best defence in the event of an attack is to try and photograph it. If you don't have a camera with you, take out your wallet, or any similar sized rectangular object, hold it up to your face in the requisite position, and pretend to be adjusting the focus. The monster, with its poor vision will not be able to tell the difference, and will immediately disappear.

Dear Consumer Protection: I think my next door neighbour is a werewolf. How can I protect myself and kill him without seeming rude? Sally Jesse Talbot.

All out of wolfsbane? Not to worry, horse radish makes a perfectly good substitute. It seems that the active ingredient in wolfsbane, aconite is also found in horseradish. So just remember, full moons are salad nights.

Dear Consumer Protection: I think too many people are spending too much time worrying about inconsequential things like vampires and werewolves, and ignoring the real threats to our standard of living, like inflation, the crime rate, the rising federal debt and killer robots and cyborgs. What can we do? George Jetson.

Well, sticking to killer bots and terminator cyborgs, everyone knows that these menaces are engineered to be practically indestructible. The off switch is invariably inconveniently placed, the batteries are always Duracell, in short, you have a problem.

Luckily, they have a secret weakness. You see, your basic terminator is just a weapons platform, passive in itself, operated by a sophisticated computer, using electronic storage for complex information processing and retrieval.

Electrical systems like this, are vulnerable to even weak magnetic fields which can also damage videocassettes, computer disks, and your credit card. Powerful electromagnets, such as used in car crushing operations should do the trick, but in a pinch, even throwing fridge magnets should slow it down and mess up that delicate programming.

Ladies, keep those fridge magnets handy!

Consumer Protection Persons: I am from the old country, and we don't take much stock in these new things. In my opinion, the real danger comes from traditional menaces, like the evil eye. Are there any economical defences against wicked witches? Bela.

We're glad you specified wicked witches there, because we wouldn't want to offend all the good witches protecting our neighbourhoods.

If you remember that classic movie, "The Wizard of Oz," you'll notice that Dorothy, surely the McCauley Culkin of her day, managed to off, not one, but two wicked witches. She dropped a house on one, and soaked the other with water causing her to melt. I'd have to say we should look to Dorothy's example.

No, not dropping houses on them, unless you have a tornado handy. Even then, just forget about your insurance.

Tap water is your answer. That's it, just simple ordinary H2O administered in any number of ways will solve all your wicked witch problems. Consumer reports recommends the use of a garden sprinkler for best effect, and it's good for your lawn too!

Water seems to be pretty effective as an all-purpose monster repellent. For instance, in "Neon Maniacs," the seventies disco group "The Village People" turned into killer zombies (or maybe they always were) and were vanquished by squirt guns.

As well, salt water can be used to defeat man eating plants called Triffids.

Holy Water is effective against a wide range of supernatural entities, such as Vampires and demons. As a general rule, monsters tend to be pretty gullible, so if you're stuck in a hard place: Lie, squirt, and run like hell, while they're rolling around screaming and not realizing that they aren't melting yet.

Even for monsters not vulnerable to water, it can be a great distraction allowing an opportunity to escape. Or making them angry enough to kill you quickly. Either way, win win.

Dear C.P's: We think that our daughter is possessed. She stays out late, spends hours on the phone, uses language we don't understand and dresses like a prostitute. Is there an economical alternative to exorcism? Bob and Ruth, Amityville.

First, are you sure your daughter is really possessed. Perhaps she's just going through puberty.

The simple way to tell, is also your economical alternative to exorcism: Television.

Just put her down in front of it, turn on the tube and surf for old classic television. Look for The Brady Bunch, Oprah, Ricky Lake, Gilligan's Island, Dukes of Hazzard or just about anything with Scott Baio or Tony Danza in it.

If there really is a demon in her, it'll soon be begging for mercy. Be strict. Hold out until it agrees to mow the lawn.

If nothing happens, then it means she's not possessed, she's just a teenager. Be patient. It will clear up in five to ten years.

Dear Consumers: Are there any effective defences against serial killers? Yours, Hannibal.

This is a tough one. There really is no foolproof defence against the dedicated serial killer. But just remember this: Your basic serial killer doesn't just want to kill you. He wants to enjoy it.

If you can ruin the aesthetic of his experience, you stand a good chance of surviving. If he doesn't kill you in disgust.

Try picking your nose in public. If that doesn't have enough impact, try eating it. Sure to turn the hardest stomachs.

Of course, there is no way to tell who is a serial killer, so you'll have to do this with everyone you meet. Ah well, no protection without a price.

Dear Consumers: Should we be worried about aliens? My girlfriend says that aliens are older wiser beings here to help us, or just stopping by to use the phone. What's the story here? Elliot.

Many people think visitors from outer space are mysterious benevolent beings. Unfortunately, forty years of cinema have shown us that that concept is generally false.

People who have actually been abducted by aliens have learned to their horror that they have just one thing on their minds: Probes.

Your best defence is the chastity belt. Wear it at all times, as you never know when they'll beam you up. Keep the key locked in a safety deposit box where they can't get at it.

Also, never eat eggs offered by aliens. They are often quite hard to swallow and may well continue to incubate after

ingestion. No one wants a chestburster, the dry cleaning alone
is horrendous.

Finally, as a public service, we'd like to say a few words
about alien invasions.

When you see a full scale alien invasion: Report it to the
authorities. Do not try to deal with it yourself. If nothing else,
the government likes to keep accurate records of these things.

No one knows why aliens invade; it's just one of those
things. From what we've seen, however, they don't appear to
be that smart. For instance, a frequently cited cause of
invasion is lack of water in their home systems, which poses a
quandary as water is one of the most common substances
around. They must have bypassed trillions of tons of the stuff
just getting here.

Possibly it's a marketing thing for them. "Why bother
drinking sterile pristine water from an Oort Cloud, when you
could be drinking amoeba laden Earth water, swimming with
bacteria, microorganisms, microplastics and all kinds of
pollutants. Drink the water that Earth fish pee in, and that
humans use to make their sewage go away." We imagine it's a
specialty taste.

Fortunately, they don't appear to be very good at invading
Earth. They are often disabled by computer viruses, the
common cold, strong light, sonic rays, magnetism or even
small children and their dogs.

A common tactic of alien invaders is to take over peoples
bodies. Again, we have no idea why they do this. It might be
their idea of a vacation. You know, for us it's two weeks in
Aspen, for them it's two weeks as Madonna, or as Bob the
Mailman.

Nevertheless, they are easy to spot while invading human
form. Look out for tentacles or things waving out their ears.
Look for changes in behaviour, walking in a zombielike
shuffle, staring into the sun, speaking in monotones, referring
to friends as "stupid stupid earthlings." Are your parents or
friends dressing badly? Have they lost the ability to operate a

blender or tie their own shoelaces? It could be that they've
been taken over by Aliens, or perhaps they've just become
chartered accountants.

Once again, in either case, report it to the government.
That's what they are there for.

*Dear Costumers Protekshun: I think monsters are really
getting a bad break. A giant crocodile ate Billy Momson
who was always beating me up and stealing my lunch
money. People should be nicer to them. Billy, age 9.*

Well, there wasn't actually a question there. But we'd just
like to agree with Billy that monsters can sometimes provide a
valuable contribution. Godzilla for instance, when not acting
as a major tourist attraction, has proven to be quite a boon
for the Tokyo construction industry.

Actually, monsters from our extensive experience in books
and movies are actually quite delicate. Their apparent
invulnerability nearly always conceals obvious and usually
fatal flaws.

In many states, monsters are considered an endangered
species, and it is illegal to blow one up without a permit.

Always, when considering how to deal with your particular
spawn of hell, it is a good idea to check municipal and state
regulations. Or for further information, please consult
Consumer Protection services.

The End

The Troll's Trap

The trap sprung suddenly as the net coiled about the hero, lashing him tightly and hauling him into the Trees where he hung suspended and helpless. The sages and storytellers have often argued about the exact combination of circumstances that lead Blogg the Barbarian into the Troll's trap.

The Thespians of Sircassa Tra hold that he was in headlong flight from the vengeance of the Priests of Anon Baa, for despoiling their annual sacrifice of virgins.

In contrast the dancing Bubbaloonians, a wandering sect, hold that he most likely blundered into the trap due to sheer exhaustion. This being due to the fact that on the night prior to the sacrifice, the thirty scheduled virgins had reconsidered the career opportunities flowing from having their hearts cut out and waylaid the first man they could find, this being Blogg who wandered into their quarters searching for a vacant privy.

The Bubbaloonians claim support for their theory in the resemblance of many of the modern day inhabitants of that region to Blogg. The steely grey eyes, the lionlike manes of tawny hair, the rippling thews, and the sharply sloping foreheads all recall the ancient adventurer and suggest that many results flowed from that heroic night.

The Philogians of Sarda San across the shining sea, do not speak to the circumstances of the capture at all but rather point out that Blogg was almost certainly named after the sound his putative mother (for she always denied parentage) made after a long night of carousing as she worshipped at the porcelain altar.

This they say set the meter for the life and defined the pivotal qualities of the Barbarian.

What they mean by this is uncertain, as the Philogians are masters of obscurity. However, it is well known that they absolutely deny any trace of the hero's bloodline in their own parentage.

In any case, all agree that Blogg well and truly stepped into it, and hung dangling, twelve feet above the forest floor. He could only glare as the Troll stepped into view. It was a fearsome monster basically human in shape, some eleven feet tall, covered with dirt and curly black hair which it scratched frequently. Its heavy pot belly hung over its rotting loincloth. It gnashed its yellowing tusks and glared at him with fierce red eyes. It lifted one beetled brow, as if in surprise.

"Surprised, Monster," Blogg snarled "surprised to find a real man in your fiendish device?"

The breath of the Troll was so redolent with corruption he would have blanched, were it not for all the blood in his body being forced into his head from hanging upside down. The Trolls reply, however, was surprisingly cultured.

"Frankly yes." responded the Troll. "This is a woodland sheep snare, but lately they have been too clever for it."

"You'll find I'm no sheep."

"I hadn't finished concealing it."

"I have no stomach for deception."

"It was right there, and you walked into it."

"Free me," Blogg commanded.

"I should probably let you down and reset the snare."

"Give me back my weapons, and then we will see about woodland sheep you loathsome mound of pus." Blogg blustered, "I'll gut you like a rotting artichoke."

Diplomacy was ever his strong suite. But maybe it was just all the blood rushing to his head.

As if somehow offended by those words the Troll rapped him sharply on the head with a wooden cudgel it had been carrying and then he knew no more.

When he regained consciousness, he found himself in an iron cage. Betraying not a sound to warn his captor of his return to wakefulness he surveyed his surroundings through slit eyelids.

As wary and acute as a tiger with a splitting headache.

He was in the heart of the Troll's lair, near the doorway a few sheep and deer stood tethered, their odour adding to the stench of the huge cooking pot which bubbled in a most unwholesome manner. Across the lair, on the other side of the pot, the Troll bustled, doubtless with diabolical purpose.

Instantly, Blogg formed his plan, moving with feline stealth his arms reached out to grasp two of the bars close to the base. If he could just bend the bars enough to slip out he could surprise his nemesis. As his hands wrapped around the iron bars of his cage, his mighty thews and biceps began to strain. His face grew red and the tendons of his neck stood out as he exerted all his heroic strength to bend the bars. Sweat glistened on his brow and ran from his smooth tanned body in rivulets, his very eyes crossed and still he strained. Every fibre of his powerful frame was devoted to the herculean task before him. The irresistible force of his sweating, trembling muscles struggled against the iron stolidity of the bars.

He grunted.

The Troll stopped and lifted its head.

Quickly, noiselessly, with unnerving speed and catlike stealth Blogg slid back down in his cage until he was sprawled sitting up against the bars. Although his head was lowered, his eyes were slits, allowing him to watch everything around him. He issued a snore.

Across the lair the Troll stood up and scratched its bottom. The vile creature wandered over to Blogg's cage, seeming to stare intently. As the hero continued to feign sleep, it locked the door to his cage and then wandered back to whatever it had been doing.

Blogg cursed.

The bars were unbendable and as the Troll seemed satisfied to have him expend his energies in the attempt, Blogg soon gave up. He sat back in the cage, glaring at the Troll.

He had to think. It was another humiliation that he swore he would pay the Troll back, for Blogg thought only when absolutely necessary, and often, not even then. For in his experience, both in battle and the boudoir hard muscle and bulging thews invariably overcame the more cerebral men and women, that and a five foot broadsword.

A five foot broadsword and the element of surprise.

Many of Blogg's mightiest duels were fought with enemies who had been looking the other way. Who hadn't seen him coming. Whose backs were turned. Who hadn't even known he was in the room. Or who'd made the mistake of letting their guards down and doing everyday activities like sleeping.

A five foot broadsword, the element of surprise and several doughty allies. That was all he needed.

After all, what was the heroism of manly one on one combat unless there was someone there weren't friends and allies to witness it. Or to help out if you got in trouble. Or to just plain help out and kill the bastard. As far as Blogg was concerned, the best thing to bring to one on one combat was an army.

Which might have defeated the whole point of one on one combat. But then again, when your hated rival was hacked to bits, and you and your friends were celebrating your bravery and might over beer, no one brought up details like that.

Such trifles only mattered to the losers, who were dead anyway, so who cared.

He clenched his tongue firmly between his teeth as he tried to marshal what he knew of Troll lore. Let's see. Trolls were solitary creatures, patrolling large territories through traplines and making their homes near crossroads and streams where prey was easily caught. They preferred entrails and rotting meat for their diet, and avoided most plants.

Trolls, while avoiding companionship, were not automatically hostile to visitors. True they were dangerous and unpredictable, but the wise traveller could usually bribe or bargain for safe passage through a Trolls territory. Sometimes a silver tongue was all that was necessary, as Trolls were great lovers of word play. Stories, riddles, clever jokes, even music could sooth the savage monsters to let a traveller pass unmolested.

Blogg recalled his friend Endel telling him that if ever he was caught in a Trolls snare, he should courteously and politely request to be released. When Blogg had asked why, Endel had replied that there was always a chance that the Troll would grant a friendly request. Under no circumstances should he curse the fiend as they would, for some reason known only to Trolls, take offence.

Blogg cursed Endel for his foolish advice, and more importantly for Endel's not having Blogg remember it at the right moment.

But then the Barbarian replayed the initial conversation with the Troll. He could find no fault with his words. Endel had clearly been mistaken.

"Hey, Loathsome gut swallower." Blogg called.

The Troll ceased butchering a boar and came over. "What do you want?" It asked.

"Let me out of this cage." Blogg ordered.

"Why?" asked the Troll.

Blogg was stuck for an answer. He wasn't used to people questioning him. Usually people did what he told them or he struck them with whatever was handy and sharp. His mind raced as he tried to think of a reason for the Troll to let him out.

So he could cut off the Trolls head, spread its entrails around, wreck the lair and make off with the treasure? In a rare moment of insight he realized the Troll probably wouldn't go for that.

He tried to think of something else.

After waiting patiently for a few minutes the Troll told him "I'll let you out when it's time to eat you."

Then it wandered back to its butchering.

For the rest of the day Blogg formulated plans for escape. Most of them involved getting out of the cage somehow and overpowering the Troll. Aside from the fact that the Troll was nearly twice his height, four times his weight, and could easily bite off his whole head he considered it the easier part. How could he get out of the cage? He recalled that monkeys were good at getting out of cages; he briefly wished that he was a monkey.

He decided he would have to appeal to the Trolls better nature.

Which would be difficult as Blogg had no better nature himself, and therefore nothing to appeal with.

"Hey Troll," he called "did you hear the one about the travelling priest and the concubine?"

"Is it the one with the wolf?"

"Yes."

"Heard it."

"Oh....want to hear it again?"

As the night wore on, Blogg discovered that he didn't actually know that many jokes and stories. Truth to tell, it took a serious concussion to reach the state of mind necessary to appreciate Blogg's jokes. In the past this hadn't been a problem, most of his friends laboured under extensive brain damage, and he had always been willing to bestow that condition on the unappreciative.

The next day he decided to give up with jokes and riddles which made his head hurt. He began to sing his favourite drinking sounds. He quickly discovered that he didn't actually remember the songs; he was usually too drunk to remember anything on those past occasions when he usually sang. Further at that state of intoxication he was usually too incoherent to pronounce actual words. Still, he gave it a

credible try, tunelessly bawling incoherent sounds until the
Troll dumped a bucket of water on him for the third time.

Finally, late in the day, he hit upon his favourite subject.
Himself. He began to tell the Troll of his many adventures.
He told of his battles, of his duels, of his tavern brawls. Of
the time he accidentally beheaded King Ranulph and was for
that reason cheated of a week's pay. Of his time as an Officer,
and how he unjustly lost that post when he accidentally
directed thirty men over a cliff. Of how he had duelled Borg
the Terrible to the death under the impression he was actually
fighting Dink, lover of little boys.

He talked of his many conquests, and his insatiable
appetites. He lovingly described the princesses and virgins he
had deflowered. Or at least they had told him they were
princesses and virgins; they had certainly charged enough,
especially the ones without teeth. He told of the time he had
slipped into the royal harem, and in the dark accidentally
wound up in the goats milking enclosure, not that it had
made much of a difference. The goats had been appreciative,
or so he assumed. It was always best to never ask for notes
on your performance.

He talked of his youth as a shepherd and commented that
in some ways women were very like sheep.

Wisely, the Troll did not ask him to elaborate on this.

He talked often about getting very drunk as regularly as
possible.

And about the terrible hangovers in the morning.

He went on at length about his rippling muscles; he
lovingly described each bicep in exquisite detail. He
discoursed upon his bronze tan. He dwelled at length on the
subject of his sweat. He spent hours rhapsodising his thews
and their quality.

Indeed, Blogg was astonished at how much there was to
talk about now that he had found a subject that interested
him. The Troll continued about its lair, doing its various
tasks, and pretending to ignore him. But Blogg could tell that

Drunk Slutty Elf and Zombies / Page 35

it listened avidly by the sound of its teeth grinding whenever he went on about a particularly good part.

Blogg quite forgot about the Troll and continued his one-sided conversation even when the Troll left the lair. Which it seemed to do more and more as the days wore on.

Blogg, for once considerate of others, made sure to bring it up to date on the revelations that had occurred in its absence.

Finally, near the end of the fifth day Blogg was startled from a fascinating rumination on the nature and diversity of his intestinal noises when the Troll threw open the cage door and threw him into a sack.

The hero cursed and struggled as he was rudely bounced around in the sack for what seemed like hours. Then suddenly, the sack dropped, opened and he tumbled out.

"Go forth," the Troll loomed over him, "and have many, many children."

Blogg hurriedly grabbed up his weapons and gear and scurried off. He did not hear the Trolls parting words, for it mumbled them to itself as it stalked away in the opposite direction.

"Sometimes," it murmured "you should throw the really stupid ones back."

Of course, some tale tellers deny the Troll said any such thing. However, all sages agree that Blogg went on to have many more adventures, and many, many more children

The End

Assembly Instructions

August 20, 1993, Milwaukee, United States.

"Do you think that's really possible?" Louisa May asked the red haired young man.

"Huh?" Barry Dunver grunted. He'd been sipping his milk shake, and trying not to be obvious about staring at Louisa May's cleavage.

He'd been trying not to be obvious at it all night. Louisa had shown up for their date in a form fitting dress with plunging neckline. It had been distracting from the first moment, and it had been distracting all the way through the dinosaur movie based on the Crichton novel. It hadn't helped that Louisa May had gasped at each reveal of the dinosaurs, had squeezed his hand each time the T-Rex had menaced the characters.

It had certainly made the night unforgettable. Barry didn't go out on many dates. He was working hard on his physics degree and hoped to go into advanced studies. But somehow, Louisa and he had connected and he'd been thrilled when she agreed to a date. So far the night had gone perfectly.

He just hoped Louisa hadn't noticed his distraction.

Louisa had in fact noticed. And through the night, she'd gotten progressively more tired of noticing. The dress had definitely been a bad idea, and Barry was clearly rather less mature than she'd expected.

Still, the movie had been terrific, the CGI dinosaurs were utterly stunning, the entire runtime had seethed with family-friendly tension. She was in a good mood. Which meant she was willing to give Barry a chance and give conversation a try. He was a science guy after all.

"The amber thing," she said. "You know: Getting dinosaur DNA from ground up amber and bringing them back."

"Oh that." Barry ran his fingers through his shock of red hair. Louisa liked redheads. It was the reason she had agreed to go out with him. On some level, Barry had picked up on that, and so he tended to unconsciously call attention to his hair.

He was being careful to make eye contact as he was speaking to her. She appreciated it.

"Technically," Barry said, losing points, "what they were doing was extracting insects from amber, and these insects had fed on dinosaur blood, so they had bits of dinosaur DNA in them."

"So dinosaur DNA from amber," Louisa repeated, with just the slightest trace of irritation. The term 'mansplaining' had not been invented yet. "Do you think that's possible?"

Barry shrugged.

"Um...." unconsciously he ran his fingers through his red hair again, "I suppose it's remotely possible..."

He thought about it a little more.

"I don't know if it's plausible though. I mean, it's not like every piece of amber has a mosquito in it. You'd need hundreds of tons of amber, maybe thousands, millions... more amber than is on Earth."

"And I don't know that amber would really preserve stuff on that molecular level? That feels far-fetched to me."

"Oh," Louisa replied. She laid her elbow on the table and propped her fingers under her chin. She didn't actually care that much about amber, or dinosaurs. But she'd wanted the conversation to go somewhere, to open up about possibilities, speculations, musing. She'd hoped to have the chance to evolve into a real talk about themselves and their lives.

Instead, Mr. Science had shut it down with a clinical 'No.'

Barry was just perceptive enough to know that he'd made a misstep. Not enough to know what it was or why. But he was smart, and he could tell he'd stepped wrong. He desperately needed a way to recover.

"But I think," he said suddenly, "you could do it with viruses."

Her eyes widened slightly.

"Viruses?" she asked.

"Yes," he said quickly. He could tell she was interested. "Viruses. You know, it's a little known fact, but viruses aren't alive at all."

She raised an eyebrow, not sure where he was going with this. But at least he seemed enthusiastic. She knew what viruses were, but decided to play long.

"They aren't. They're inert, they're just bits of protein, there's no cells, no cell structure, they don't reproduce or have biological function. They're just... molecules."

He continued, warming to the subject.

"They reproduce by invading a cell, and taking it over, reprogramming it to make copies of itself. That's how it works. The infected cell becomes a virus factory, turning out copies of the virus until it collapses, and then those viruses take over other cells and convert them, and so on..."

He was genuinely making eye contact with her, not simply obviously looking at her eyes to avoid looking at her breasts, and while his conversation was abstract, there was at least some feeling to it. She rewarded him with a slight smile.

"Until everything is overrun," Louisa replied, "like in zombie movies."

"Yes," he said, failing to pick up the gambit to open up the conversation. "Like that. Now, here's the interesting thing with viruses. They're coded for different species. Each virus is like a key shaped to fit a particular kind of lock. So that's why humans don't get tobacco mosaic virus... plant viruses. Or insect viruses. That's why only cats get feline leukemia virus, and only dogs get distemper virus. Each species has its own set of viruses, and they're designed... not designed... evolved to match that species DNA."

"So what about rabies?" she said. "That goes from animals to humans. Or Swine flu. There are cross-species viruses."

His eyebrows lifted, half irritated with the distraction, half excited by her interest.

"Yes. Because viruses mutate to jump species. And because some of them are fitted to common parts of the DNA that are the same in similar animals."

She nodded.

"But here's the thing," he said. "They're shaped to fit the code. Like a lock and key, or two interlocking parts."

He held up his hand, and laced his fingers together.

"Yin and yang," he told her. "So if you've got a virus, you can tell by looking at it, the shape, the structure, of the DNA it was designed to interlock with."

"Okay."

"Including extinct species!" he said brightly.

"Okay?"

"So there you go," he said. "Viruses aren't alive, so they don't die. They're just inert. Which means that if there's no species to infect, they just lay there. The ocean sediments, they're probably packed with inert viruses for all kinds of extinct species, dinosaurs and everything else. All these keys, shaped to fit locks. But the locks are all gone, so they're useless."

"But!" he held up his hand, "but the keys are still there, and with the keys, you can figure out the shape of the locks. So if you could find enough viruses, enough kinds of virus for a species, you could figure out its genetic code."

"You could bring dinosaurs back!" he said. "Not with amber, but by decoding and reverse engineering their DNA from the viruses of extinct animals."

Barry was pleased with his display of intelligence and perception. He'd really thought on his feet, and hit it out of the park coming up with that on the fly. He wasn't at all sure if it was plausible or not. Certainly it wasn't with today's technology. But it had worked. He was back in the game.

"Uh huh," Louisa said, waiting for him to take the conversation somewhere interesting. He was smart, that was for sure, and she liked intelligence in a man. But he didn't really seem to know how to talk to people, rather than talk at them. She wasn't particularly interested in a crashing bore.

But then, he'd been enthusiastic, and there was a genuineness to that. He'd talked about something, rather than simply being self-absorbed and going on about himself. Why not.

"Agreeing," she said, that "viruses aren't alive, I don't think that means that they'd be immortal. Lots of substances degrade because of heat or fire, oxygen, water, and so on. If they're complicated molecules, wouldn't they tend to break down over time."

As he smiled at her, she noticed he wasn't trying not to look at her cleavage, wasn't being shallow and self-conscious. He was simply looking at her, smiling, making eye contact. She smiled back, and laid her hand on his.

"I guess you're right," he said. Point for him, she thought. She hated guys who had to win every argument no matter what. "Still, they might preserve longer, and in the right conditions, possibly a very long time. Anyway, it's cool to think that there might be a way to bring dinosaurs back."

"It is a cool thought," she said. "Romantic even."

Maybe there was something here to work with, after all. Perhaps a future, which inspired a thought...

"Do you think we'll make it out there, out to the stars?"

Barry sparkled.

There would be a second date.

And so it goes.

***

And so it went.

Humanity never actually made it to the stars. It had a pretty good run, all things considered, and after about fifteen million years, give or take, the last specimen that could be called human, or at least hominid, toddled off into extinction.

After about five hundred million years of geological processes steadily sequestering carbon from the atmosphere and locking it in increasingly inaccessible rock formations, animal life on earth became extinct. It wasn't sudden, just a gradual thinning away, until one day, there was nobody around.

Within another hundred million years, most varieties of plant life vanished, leaving only a few thin and hardy lineages of vegetation, perpetuating themselves on the barest slivers of atmospheric carbon.

But in another hundred million years, they too were gone.

The Earth returned to its original masters, the prokaryotes, bacteria and single celled organisms, floating in the briny vanishing seas, buried in the soils, hanging on as a thin scattering of extremophile life at the fringes of the planet.

As it happens, life is rare in the universe, but not unheard of. The universe is unimaginably vast, and in a cosmos which tries to give infinity a run for its money, the rare can become commonplace.

But most life that emerges prokaryotic, and goes no further. Prokaryotes lack a sufficiently distinct nucleus, no mitochondria, no cell membranes or organelles to build energy and take chemical and biological processes to the next level, to make complex eukaryotic life possible. Throughout the universe, life is to be found. But on world after world after world, it never reaches much past matts of slime molds, if that.

Eukaryotic life, on the other hand, is even more rare. By comparison, the empty universe is exploding with prokaryotics.

But eukaryotics, they're the precious diamonds in the vast abyss. They're vanishingly rare. Their events are widely scattered, separated by hundreds of millions of light years and hundreds of millions of temporal years.

Earth had begun with prokaryotics for billions of years, and after a mere billion year experiment with eukaryotics, had returned to its roots and would remain there for the remainder of the history of life on this planet.

***

Imagine if you will, an empty, desert windswept world of dust and gravel and sluggish muddy seas. That's Earth for the rest of time, or at least until the sun grows large and eats it.

But wait! Look closer! Something moves across the empty skies. A star where no star should be, tracking across the frozen firmament, a thing in motion.

A starship.

Another world has produced eukaryotic life! And more than that, these eukaryotes have created multi-cellular life forms, have evolved photo-synthesis and chemo-synthesis, have diversified into multitudes of forms, the forms compete and cooperate, building ever more complexity, until finally culminating in a tool using species calling themselves the Valach, which looks out over a sky full of stars... and wonders.

And eventually the Valach build starships, in which they discover near infinite numbers of sterile worlds, and handfuls of worlds of teeming single celled organisms, and finally Earth, a mere billion years after the last eukaryotes of have passed away.

In cosmic terms, the coincidence is astounding. To have two eukaryotic biologies producing intelligent species emerge so impossibly close to each other in space and time, well, it's nothing short of miraculous. Humanity and the Valach were literally born practically on top of each other.

The Valach had never found Eukaryotic life before, no surprise given its rarity. They've never even found remains of Eukaryotic life before.

But on earth, there are remains. There are fossils, treasure troves of them. The bones and scraps of entire ecologies, multitudes of species, piled atop each other in layers. There had even a civilization on earth, leaving traces everywhere, beings just like the Valach, although these earthlings never made it past its own solar system.

The Valach are fascinated. They've missed us by a cosmic heartbeat.

Fascinated?

Hell, they're obsessed.

They also find, buried in sedimentary layers, buried at the bottoms of oceans, and in sterile ice caps, buried in tombs and necropolises, inert viruses.

Unassuming, inoffensive little molecular sculptures, shaped by evolution to infect species long extinct, preserved by flukes of circumstance, now laying there without purpose. Never alive, therefore never dead, simply… inert.

The technology of the Valach is so much more advanced than Earth's ever was. Their curiosity is utterly insatiable. Like everything else in Earth's cobwebbed history, the viruses are identified, classified and matched to various extinct species.

And inevitably, someone has the idea.

***

N'rkkik rubbed his manipulators nervously and cycled moisture through his feeding filters as he watched the throng assemble. The great auditorium was filling, preparing to witness what he considered the greatest moment in the history of the Valach race.

Over a thousand Valach were filing in, taking their mounting positions. The Valach were practically human looking - sensory clusters on an elevated anatomical structure, manipulator limbs, a columnar torso and mobility limbs at the bottom. Considering the infinite diversity of options, this was yet another astonishing coincidence.

There are utterly alien beings out in distant reaches of the universe who, if given the opportunity, could not have distinguished the two races to save what passed for their lives.

He stepped up and ritually tapped the microphone, chugging with his respirator to gain attention.

"Greetings, Fellow Valach," he announced. "I'm proud to be here this day, addressing this August assembly of castes and caste-mates, for this momentous announcement. As you know, we have spent long centuries reconstructing the human race from the signatures of viral remnants..."

At which point, he ventured into an extended technical discourse on the mechanics of reconstructing bits of human genetic code from the molecular shapes of inert viruses which had originally shaped themselves to infiltrate that code.

From there, a vast armada of scientists had painstakingly assembled the reconstructed bits into a coherent genome, fudging a bit here, and using reconstructed genetic bits from other closely related life forms, or in a pinch, simply making educated guesses with the help of planet-sized super-computers.

They had then inserted that genome into exquisitely reconstructed cells, based on the chemistry of Earth's remaining prokaryotes and fossil traces, and then carefully cultured those cells into an actual motile life form.

It was an astonishing accomplishment really.

And they'd done it again, and again, building up specimen after specimen, extending out to species after species, recreating an entire, albeit simplified ecology to sustain this cultivated human race.

Most of the audience knew all of this, of course. But it was still thrilling to hear the process described. By dint of sheer will and immense intellectual processing power, the Valach had managed to reach through space and time to resurrect their sibling civilization.

N'rkkik felt spasms of pleasure at the rapturous applause. Although he'd seen and interacted with the humans himself, that had been work. This was something different. This was a coming out, a ceremony, a presentation to shift the universe on its axis. After this day, the Valach would no longer be alone.

"But of course," N'rkkik continued after a sufficient pause, calculated for just the slightest shade of discourtesy, "without the cooperation and dedicated efforts of many other castes, these accomplishments would be little more than a biological curiosity."

"We must acknowledge the painstaking labours of Archeology-cast, in excavating and reconstructing human culture. Not for them, the tribulations of carefully assembling molecules. But instead, the retrieval of billion year old remains, traces, even records. Every facet of human history and culture was minutely sifted."

Privately, N'rkkik considered the entire Archeology-caste a pack of whiners and blowhards, and he half suspected them of simply fabricating their data. They'd been formed as an awkward fusion of assorted science castes, geology, chemistry, neurology, bio-mechanics and wildly intuitive artistic castes, along with a few social-science castes.

Even the formation of the Archeology-caste had been a challenge, as there had never been the remains of another civilization to study. The Valach had always been tidy and meticulous that way, they'd documented their own rise to civilization quite thoroughly as they were coming up. The result had been the only true caste created specifically for the problem of humanity.

It gave them a bit of an attitude really. Endlessly quibbling about this or that, always challenging, always complaining, an endless stream of memos, disputing every little thing.

It was like the old saying, 'soft-caste soft carapace.'

Although he'd never admit it publicly, N'rkkik was actually looking forward to the dissolution of the caste. Now that humanity was about to be up and running and a self-sustaining, going concern, they would no longer be necessary. If humans were interested in archeology, they'd be able to do it themselves, likely with far more insight.

Still, you had to hand it to them. They'd re-created human language, human clothing, culture, things as subtle as hair styles and jewelry, cultural elements so exquisite and so ephemeral that it was almost beyond the capacity of the Valach mind to comprehend. They'd done it whining every step of the way, but they'd done it.

"... and through their unyielding efforts, the biological humans have been raised and refined within a reconstruction of their original culture, adapted and implemented, through successive generations, until finally, we have achieved the human experiment."

"We are no longer alone in the Universe, the human race, steps through the archives of time to join us, to stand with us side by side as we look upon the infinite abyss."

He paused.

"Caste and Caste-mates," he trilled. "I present to you, the first human: Barry Dunver (V.2), the first of the new race of humanity, representative of his species!"

The audience exploded into a frenzy, respirators were purged noisily, mandibles clattered like a rattle of thunder, there were hoots and stompings. Every Valach there was overcome by the awesomeness of their presence at this historic moment.

Barry Dunver (V.2) strode out onto the stage, waving at the cheering audience and wearing his best 'aw shucks' grin. He walked up to stand beside N'rkkik, and adopted a casual stance, self-consciously running his fingers through his shock of red hair, a nervous habit he'd picked up somewhere. He leaned forward to speak into the microphone.

When the applause died down, he finally spoke. The first words to the crowd by a real live human, a being extinct for a billion years.

"Thank you," Barry (V.2) said, "thank you. I really mean that. It's good to be back."

He grinned at this sly joke.

There was another thunderous burst of applause, while Barry (V.2) smiled and fidgeted.

The alien looked up at Barry (V.2), towering over him, and felt a moment of doubt. Had humans really been twenty feet tall? The bio-science caste acknowledged that possibly a few errors had crept into the reconstruction, but nothing that would make a substantial difference. He shook his head, dismissing the thought.

"Barry (V.2)," he said, "it must feel remarkable to know that your species has been brought back from extinction."

"It does," Barry (V.2) replied. "We feel lucky and honoured, and we certainly appreciate it."

"Well, what do you–"

He never had the chance to finish the question. Barry (V.2)'s feeding tentacles whipped out with blinding speed and grabbed the startled alien, snapping it in half and catapulting the creature into his ingesting pouch. N'rkkik's last thought was to wonder if, maybe they'd gotten the reconstruction slightly wrong after all. What if those asses in the Archeology-caste had been right, and they'd bunged up the assembly? And then the ingesting pouch teeth crunched, and he knew nothing more.

For an instant, the audience was startled into silence by the awesome sight of the twenty-foot tall human, and its assembly of limbs and tentacles. Atop his ring of eye stalks, Barry (V.2)'s blue eyes winked.

He leaned into the microphone. The alien throng hesitated, caught between panic and uncertainty.

"Oh don't worry, folks," Barry (V.2) said. "We were just having a little fun. No harm done. But while he's being digested, I'd like to bring out the rest of us. Say hello to the new human race."

From the sides of the stage, a succession of monstrosities lumbered out, resplendent in their blue jeans, checkered shirts and cowboy hats - all absolutely authentic human-style clothing, or so Archeology-Caste asserted, although the need to make adjustments for these titanic frames undermined their claims.

"This is Louisa May (V.2)," Barry (V.2) announced. "My girl!"

A twenty-five foot leviathan lumbered out on her three legs, her eye stalks blinking, grinning shyly and blinking a little. She tossed her blonde hair coquettishly, and waved to the crowd, unfolding her long saber claws.

"Isn't she just the greatest!" Barry (V.2) called.

Louisa May (V.2) spied a precocious little alien child in the front rows. Cooing with delight, she bent down and dismembered the entire family with clean swipes of her scythes. She picked up the child, and gently bit its head off, drawing the internal organs up through the torso with it, streaming from the head like steaming wet, brightly coloured confetti.

And that's when the audience really started to panic, screaming and climbing over each other in a desperate rush to the exits... where more humans were waiting.

Louisa May (V.2) moved over to stand next to Barry (V.2), beaming happily out at the terrified surging mass. He hugged her tenderly, their maws kissed, sabre teeth briefly interlocking as the chelae clicked together, and turned her to face the shrieking audience.

"We've been keeping it a secret," Barry (V.2) announced into the microphone, he placed a gladule palp over her rounded throbbing abdomen, "but I guess now is as good a time as any to make it official. Louisa May (V.2) is in the family way."

"That is," Barry (V.2) couldn't keep the sheer happiness from his voice, "she's with child... Or children... A quarter million by our reckoning."

Shyly, Louisa May (V.2) distended her ovipositor and began spraying the shrieking crowd with her parasitic eggs. No sooner did one touch a horrified audience member than it would burrow into their flesh, sending out cancer tendrils to eat the host alive from the inside.

"Spray and pray, my girl!" Barry (V.2) screamed cheerfully. "Spray and pray!"

As his fellow humans lumbered out, tearing the screaming members of the throng to shreds, Barry (V.2), ran his fingers through his shock of red hair and grinned.

It was a beautiful day. The human race had been given a second chance, and he was going to make sure they made the most of it.

The End

Usher of the Falling House

They say that eventually everything under the sun and moon passes through a crosstown but nothing stays ever there.

Stavra and I had been kicking our heels at the Warriors hall for the better part of a month so perhaps the aphorism didn't to apply to Trolls and mercenaries. But this was the height of the caravan seasons so I assumed something would turn up.

In fact, that very day something did turn up. Particularly its nose, which was turned up very high indeed.

"Greetings fair ladies, Allow me to introduce myself. I am Pyotay R'dunner, the renowned Artificer Extraordinaire" and gave an elaborate bow.

He was tall, thin, and pale with that particular facial cast found only in the Inner Families. He was dressed in luxurious shimmering robes, now tattered around the edges, but his hands were soft. I assumed that whatever hard times he had fallen upon were not especially hard.

He was doubtless the product of centuries of careful breeding by a decadent and incestuous aristocracy. I doubted that he would ever father a child unless some putative mother happened to bear an astonishing resemblance to a pubescent boy in the dark.

I liked him immediately.

"We've never heard of you," I told him.

The Troll yawned, displaying large numbers of very prominent teeth. "What's an Artificer?" she asked.

She stood around nine feet tall, which is average for a Troll, was covered with shaggy mats of hair on her shoulders and back and boasted prodigious and appalling tastes. She was far stronger than any Troll had a right to be and relentlessly loyal. One morning after I woke up from a fierce bout of drinking and there she was. I had no idea where she came from. I had moderated my drinking since then.

I tended to think of her less as a friend or companion than as a nine foot tall wart that I couldn't get rid of.

"Artifice is the highest of art forms," he began; he looked like he would be going on for some time. "It is a wonder. It is a dream. It is a thing to raise the lowest high, and bring the highest low..."

"I am familiar with the Empires Arts, I never heard of Artificers," I told him.

He spat. "Rot the Empire; I am glad it's gone. They would not allow my Artifice. No tolerance."

I tried to imagine the magnitude of a perversion that the Empire would not tolerate. My mind boggled. If we took any money from this man it would have to be sterilised.

"Jealousy drove me out. Jealousy." he clutched at his heart in grief, "The Storytellers hated me because my art transcended their own." He looked like he would be going on for some time. I was losing patience.

"What is it? And what does it have to do with us?" I asked him. To make sure he didn't wander from the subject I pulled him close and stuck a knife into his nostril.

I wanted to be polite, so I used a small knife.

"It is a practise whereby artificers gather and perform a story. But where a storyteller merely tells a story, each artificer presents a part of a story which is realised through all of them working together." He explained.

"Ahhh," I said. I should have done this earlier. "And what do you want with us?"

"Ushers," he said.

I thought about that.

"What are ushers?" I asked him.

"Ushers lead the audience into the stadia, see that they are properly seated and lead them out again."

"Is that all?"

"Well sometime when we perform our audience tends to get a little ...enthusiastic. Ushers ensure that they do not...injure anything."

Watch guards. Basically, he wanted Watch guards to keep people under control and suppress riots and insurrections. We'd done that.

"We don't work on spec." I told him. To ensure a good impression I took the knife out of his nose. "What are you offering?"

"Two gold pieces each per night for five nights. Standard caravan rates to get us to the next town."

"We'll take it," said the Troll.

"Excellent!" he grinned "I have some errands to run. Meet me at the Falling House and I will explain your duties." and he swooped off, doubtless to price some little boys.

The Falling House was the local Stadia. It was so named because it had been built partially on a marsh. The western wall had a tendency to fall over, except when it was built of wood, then it had a tendency to burn down. As we left Stavra leaned down to whisper a question.

"What exactly is it, again?" She asked.

I thought for a moment.

"It's like storytelling," I told her, "Except that there is a bunch of them, and they take turns telling the story."

"Sounds like a long story."

I grunted. We arrived at the Falling House in short order and met the other prospective ushers. They were a couple of caravan drivers, an archer from the Southern Kingdom, and a burly fellow of indeterminate race. The west wall leaned dangerously, but so far the only effect had been to reduce the price of seats on that side.

The ushers struck me as odd, and it took me a moment to put my finger on it.

We were a good looking bunch. We were all relatively young, which is not uncommon among mercenaries. It's not a trade to get old in. But more than that, we all had most of our teeth, there were hardly any scars, and our skins were mostly fair and fresh, rather than the weather-beaten leathery flesh of the seasoned mercenary. It even smelled like most of us had bathed recently.

We had been chosen for our looks not our abilities. Knowing the unlamented Inner Nobility I was not surprised. But I didn't like the smell of it.

I had no time to express my misgivings as R'dunner flounced in drawing with him a small band of callow youths that I took to be the other Artificers. I noticed that none of them were women, which I took as further evidence of his character.

Another of the Ushers commented on this lack of female Artificers. R'dunner flushed and explained that thus far he had been unable to lure any women into the craft of Artifice.

He handed out our weapons, which he chose to call `Ushers Prompts.' I was appalled; it was a six foot stick of hardwood so swaddled in cloth that we would be lucky to raise a bruise.

"How can we kill anyone with this?" One of the Caravan drivers complained.

"No." R'dunner explained "This is Artifice. You aren't supposed to slay the audience."

"Well, I certainly can't do it with this stick." the Caravaner complained, "How are you supposed to keep order if you can't kill a few to make an example."

"My audience pays for the privilege of witnessing Artifice. You are not to kill them. Do you understand?" We all grumbled, he went on, "Should, among them, be some whose attention wanders...then you may chastise them with the prompt."

"We'll be beating people with these things all night." the Caravaner complained. I had to agree with him.

Our experience as City Watch made Stavra and I the natural leaders. My earlier misgivings faded as we got things underway. Luckily, less than half of the Falling House would be used, which made things easier. Quickly we quartered the seating area, setting out lines of command and communication. Then as night grew close and the Artificers prepared we began to seat the audience.

The first step of course, had been to disarm the audience before they came in. It had been simple to have Stavra glowering at them as they paid their silver and filed in. Trolls' tempers in general, and Stavra's strength in particular, were well known and served to convey our wishes in a convincing manner.

More difficult was managing the crowd once they got into the Stadia. Now the obvious thing to do would have been to let people sit where they may. But my experience with the City Watch had taught me not to let that happen. Trolls and Giants could not be allowed to sit near each other, likewise Frothinger barbarians sitting with their hereditary enemies the Moromen was a sure prescription for a race riot. Instead, Orcs must sit with Trolls, since only they could stand the smell.

However, as any Watch will tell you, the only thing more dangerous than allowing enemies to congregate is allowing friends to gather. Frothingers and Gallaci if together would ally and cause the rest of us no end of headaches. No, Gallaci had to mix with Moromen, who they coldly ignored.

I must confess, I quite enjoyed the work. Moving people from one place to another, and then moving them again as the stadia filled and the ethnic balance of the audience shifted.

"What is this, musical chairs?" one brawny oaf complained.

I knocked him unconscious. These sticks weren't half bad.

Suddenly, the incessant background rumble of the audience was hushed. Torches flared to life down around the broad platform designated as a stage.

A youth appeared on the stage. In a ringing voice he introduced himself as Morgip the Heir and began to tell the story. He was an unimpressive figure, scrawny and plain with an irritating squeak to his voice. The audience quieted down to listen.

The boy was awful. He seemed to lack even the most basic skills of a good storyteller. He did not look once at or attempt to capture the audience, ignoring them all through his monologue. His rhythm and cadence were atrocious. The audience began to sneer and hiss.

He introduced his fellow storytellers, or Artificers as they called themselves, but these sensed the mood of the crowd and quickly vanished or were booed off. Things were looking ugly; I wished that I'd gotten paid in advance.

Suddenly the entire crowd gasped. One of the other Artificers had leaped upon the stage and stabbed the first storyteller. He did not die well, but with a lot of fussing and gasping. There was much whispered discussion, but in general the audience seemed to feel that this was a good thing.

It put me in mind of some of the southern kings who if they were not sufficiently entertained by their fools would have them struck on the head with a mallet. The most civilised of them, like King Barris had replaced the mallet with a brass gong. It was said that he would go through several fools in a day; he loved the sound of their heads against brass so.

On stage the Artificers seemed to have completely forgotten their purpose. More astonishingly they seemed to have completely forgotten about the crowd. They just stood around wondering how to hide the body at the top of their lungs.

Members of the audience loudly voiced a few suggestions but the Artificers ignored it. Instead, they began to pick up where Morgip left off, making loud and on the whole poor speeches. Perhaps these would be assassinated as well.

Perhaps Artifice was a forum for the execution of inept storytellers. In that case, I was all for it. Storytelling is a high art, but every fool thinks they can master it simply because they can speak. It would be good to enforce some standards for the breed.

"He's still alive, you idiots," a voice caterwauled, dwarfish by the sound of it.

A handful of other voices joined in. "Finish the job, finish the job." and "Sloppy workmanship."

They were right. There on the stage the corpse lay, breathing shallowly and twitching occasionally. The rest of the Artificers marched about, shouting at each other as if they were deaf. They must have been, otherwise they would have heard the audience.

I sighed. I would probably have to go up there and finish the job for these idiots. It was going to cost them extra. But it would have to wait; we had our hands full with the audience.

There were angry murmurs from the few parts of the Audience whose sympathies had been with the not quite corpse. Snarls and shoves were exchanged.

The Troll and I waded into respective groups, hitting people at random until they lost interest in fighting each other.

What was needed, I thought to myself, were buckets of cold water.

There was a kind or rolling gasp from the Audience. I looked towards the stage. Some tavern tramp with the audacity to call herself Princess Mircalla was flouncing around. The other Artificers were after her, acting as if she hadn't been kicked in the face by a particularly ugly mule.

The audience was quieting down now. But there were a number of whispered conversations punctuated by frequent gestures toward the stage. Others were watching the Artificers with rapt and altogether unhealthy fascination.

Meanwhile, Good Prince Greywhip, who seemed to be the best of the fowl lot of conspirators who had done in Noble Morgip now had Princess Mircalla cornered. The rest of the conspirators had wandered offstage, presumably to give them some privacy in their courting.

They needn't have bothered. Mircalla and Greywhip were shouting romantic nonsense at each other at the top of their lungs. I bet that they could be heard clearly even at the back rows. I shuddered to think of what their lovemaking would sound like.

Speaking of which, the Goblins over in the front rows were becoming entirely too caught up in the spirit of things. We would have to do something about that before they got out of hand, and out of pants.

Where was Stavra? There she was, over to the left chatting up some beer swilling Troll while an orgy got into full swing, not a dozen paces from her.

I marched down to Stavra and her Troll.

"Excuse me." I said to them. With a clean swift motion I took the bucket of beer from his hands and threw it at the Goblins. I would have preferred cold water, but it did the trick.

The Troll snarled and snatched back his bucket. Which put the finishing touch on the rapidly deflating orgy and Stavra's budding romance.

Meanwhile, I chanced to glance towards the stage. My jaw dropped. I stared at Princess Mircalla in wonder. Beneath the wig and garish make up was Morgip in disguise!

My mind boggled at the incompetence of these assassins. Hadn't they even scratched him? Hadn't they noticed the body was missing?

What was Morgip playing at? He and the Prince were getting hot and heavy, when they were mercifully interrupted by the return of the conspirators.

Silence reigned as everyone listened to the conspirators hatch their plot to slay the king and divide the kingdom. It somewhat unwise to do so in a hall full of people, and in voices that could be heard a day's ride away, but they were all for it.

Then they each graphically described what they planned to do to the King and his family when they had them in their clutches. Some of the cruder types seemed to be taking copious notes. Here and there bands looked to be getting quite upset at the whole thing. The whispered conversations were rising again.

There was a large band of barbarians in the back row who seemed to be of too like a mind for my taste. Frothingers they looked like.

The Conspirators left the stage. Where were they all going? And what were they doing? I wondered. Maybe they were taking naps? I was certain that, given their conduct on stage, if they were at all active the entire audience could hear them, on stage or off.

Mircalla/Morgip entered the now dark and empty stage, looking nervous and uncomfortable. And well he should, flouncing around in that outfit.

A fistfight broke out in one of the middle rows. It didn't seem to be related to anything going on stage.

A chorus of "Cut that out, we can't see." and "Down in front." came from those seated behind the combatants.

I waded over and hit them both until they were unconscious. Gold changed hands over the number of strokes it took me to do it.

Hissing noises arose from the audience signalling the advent of Dark Lord Prosver. Mircalla/Morgip gasped. Prosver advanced on him. Apparently no better a judge of sex than Greywhip he was a good deal more aggressive.

Prosver chased the apparent princess about the stage, to yells of "Hump her, Hump her." and much giggling from the Audience. A few of the more kindly patrons yelled for Mircalla to escape by leaping from the stage and hiding among them, but these were drowned out by a flood of ribald jokes.

"Down in front." a voice yelled. As I turned to locate it a bucket bounced off my head. I felt that it would be an opportune time to fall down.

I landed in what is best described as a clutch of men. As my wits recovered I fought them off as best I could, but I had but two hands and they appeared to have a dozen each. Also my clothes didn't seem to be fastened nearly as tightly as I had thought.

I was saved suddenly by a huge hand that reached into the melee and pulled me to my feet, and then off my feet and three more feet into the air. Stavra the Troll looked at me with a knowing smile.

"You can do that after we get paid." she sniggered.

I felt a hand on my thigh and looked down. Attached to the hand was a handsome blue eyed barbarian looking up at me. Or should I say, looking up at parts of me.

For a moment I wished I was wearing hob-nailed boots, but the ones I wore worked just as well.

Greywhip had appeared, Mircalla/Morgip had finally found the wit to escape. Prosver and Greywhip were snarling at each other.

"Fight, Fight, Fight," the audience screamed in encouragement. For once the Artificers seemed to hear the crowd as Prosver leaped at Greywhip.

Bets were hastily laid as the two chased each other onstage and off. Steel clashed, along with shouted advice and commentaries on technique.

As I worked my way to the back near the Frothingers I heard boos and catcalls rising. Most of the action was taking place offstage.

"What goes, Brother?" I asked as I sat near a particularly intoxicated Frothinger.

He leaned towards me. His breath was strong enough to kill insects, which is as nothing for a person who has kept company with Trolls.

"We dono like theesh murferr...murgersh...killers. When they try to assash...asnisay...get the king we will rise and sweep down on them like a woof...wolf on sheets."

"Sheep." I corrected him.

"That too." he agreed. "For our heartsh are full of fire and our bellies full of beer." he struck his breast nobly, and passed out.

They were full of something else I thought. Likely something soft and brown.

I decided that the other Ushers had to be told about this.

The chorus of boos was rising to dangerous peaks. Apparently the fight had concluded offstage, with no clue as to the winner. This spoiled a great many bets.

The King stalked onto the stage. The crescendo of howls continued to mount.

A voice called out "Bring back the Princess." and was immediately answered by a chorus of "Humper! Humper!"

The King faced the crowd, glaring balefully from one end of it to the other. This was new. The other Artificers had ignored the Audience completely, which I considered a nearly impossible feat.

It settled under his eye. He cleared his throat.

"I've had just about enough of this." he roared.

A small flurry of cries to watch out for assassins erupted, but he silenced it with a fierce scowl. He gave no sign of having understood a word of it.

"You are going to sit down and pay attention." he told them.

"I am going to make a speech." he announced in a more pompous tone. "So behave yourselves."

There had been something familiar about his pompous manner. But I couldn't quite put my finger on it. It probably didn't matter. I took advantage of the lull to sidle up to a smaller group that seemed to be watching the Frothingers too closely.

"They plan on stopping the assassination." I whispered. I figured they knew it already. The Frothingers were only a little quieter than the Artificers up on the stage.

"Bugger that," he whispered back "the king is safe as a bird with those prancing posers. Remember Morgip."

There was a quiet murmur of assent around him.

"Once it starts we'll go down there and make sure it's done right. That way we can share in the spoils."

"Good plan," I whispered back to him. I got up, and headed down the aisle to notify the other ushers. On the way down I clubbed an Orc on general principles.

I noticed that many of the darker races seemed to be quite well behaved. Trolls, Ogres, Giants, even a few Vampires were all sitting quietly, watching the proceedings with calm attention. I guessed that being solitary creatures by nature, they were less likely to worked up over the scheming and plotting onstage. And being sneaky and untrustworthy, they were doubtless watching carefully for an opportunity to steal something.

As I passed my information on to Stavra and the other front Ushers I finally recognised the King. It was Pyotay R'dunner, a high born noble he might be, but I knew he was no king. It seemed to me as I made my way back to my post that this whole Artifice thing was just an elaborate sham.

I guess it was the bucket to the head that slowed my mind. Certainly my temples felt like they were throbbing in a manner I usually associated with parts of men's anatomy. But as the webs of deceit and intrigue coiled around the King I began to realize that King or faker, this was the man who was paying us. I could not allow him to be assassinated. I gripped my staff and headed down to the stage, intending to secure my livelihood and sort things out.

Half way down I heard a strange noise behind me that I hope never to hear again. It was as if a multitude had for an instant begun to breathe and move as one. I turned, and it was as if the entire back rows had decided en masse to rescue the King from the assassins.

I whirled my staff above my head and began my fiercest war cry. Halfway through it I went down under the charging feet of the host.

"Save the King!" they cried as they trampled me underfoot. I had never been trampled before; I found the experience distinctly unpleasant. At least with the grasping hands there was an appreciation of what they handled; here I was just a short stretch of uneven road. Also, the view left much to be desired.

The tramplers slowed, giving me a chance to struggle to my feet. Above me the second wave was rushing down.

"Death to the King!" they shouted.

This time I got out of the way. Standing to the side, I shoved my stick between the legs of the leaders. As they went down they slowed the horde behind, giving me a chance to get out there and start whacking them with the stick. Bellies, heads, groins, knees, it mattered not, there were too many to be selective, so I just swung away. I enjoyed every minute of it.

As I worked I noticed that large things seemed to be flying over my head. After a few moments of fierce swinging the crowd began to slowly abate and return to their seats. I was able to see that the flying objects were primarily barbarians, although increasingly Dwarves were taking to the air. I risked a glance backwards and saw that my friend Stavra had singlehandedly halted the advance by simply picking up one rioter after the other, and throwing them back the length of the aisle.

The second wave broke, and none too soon. As I turned back to the stage I saw that the Artificers had entirely forgotten about their plot, as had the audience, they watched riveted by Stavra's appalling display of strength. Even the giants were impressed. But I could see her strength was waning rapidly, the last dwarf had flown only half as far as those first barbarians.

In the back of the horde pressing on her I spotted a particularly noxious kilt that had passed over me. It was time to attack. With a war cry I spun and leaped.

A scream interrupted our work, and the attention of the audience was captured once again by the stage. I cursed. The scream could only mean that R'dunner had been killed. No matter. I would get my wages out of whichever of these mincing loons survived.

There was a scattering of cheers and "Pay up. He won the fight. You lost the bet." mixed with angry protests. Greywhip had appeared out of nowhere and foiled the assassination. In short order the King had dealt with the plotters.

I wasn't sure which side of the factions on stage I'd been supposed to be on, but as long as they paid me, I didn't really care who came out on top.

The rioters had taken their seats, so I hobbled back to my post, supporting myself with the staff. Greywhip explained, despite a remarkable lack of resemblance, that he was really the Kings lost son, which provoked some rude jokes to the effect that any king stupid enough to misplace a son would probably swallow a whopper like that. But it worked, which provoked several members of the audience to announce hopefully that they too were lost offspring of the King.

I waded in with my staff to quiet them.

The King made a speech about ungrateful children which provoked much discussion in the audience. Greywhip replied with yet another speech about how he had been loyal throughout, and had killed Prosver to guard his sister.

The nobility really are a different breed. I couldn't believe these people, airing all this out, in front of a crowd, acting for all the world like there was no one watching. It's one thing to argue or dally in front of servants, they're servants, you can cut their tongues out. But here? How could they be so oblivious?

At this there was much grumbling and passing of Gold. Greywhip had not been a heavy betting favourite.

Mircalla/Morgip sang a song about her love for Greywhip. It provoked general hysteria when she came to a verse about how he touched her womanly heart, which most of the audience heard as "womanly part."

The King made another speech about how Mircalla was not really his daughter. This to an avalanche of hooting agreement and "Look under her skirt." And giving Mircalla to Greywhip to wed and live happily ever after.

I didn't care, clearly they were all old nobility, and nothing old nobility does should surprise anyone. Why in the reign of King Polyp, one of his minister's, Amyl the One-Side-Bearded had married a family of goats, and eventually wed his daughter, Stamen, to a conglomeration of small furry animals he'd cunningly tied together in the shape of a man. Apparently, she'd found the arrangement satisfactory. This? This was nothing.

The King beamed as the loving couple clasped and the foolishness ended to a torrent of ribald jokes, shouted advice and warnings, and loud discussions as to exactly who would be walking funny after the wedding night. Down in the front rows the Goblins were at it again, I didn't care.

"Some fun." said Stavra to me, as the crowd filed out.

"Too much like work." I told her.

"And then we can ride around pretending to be women. It'll be great. They'll never suspect an ambush. Some of us can even pretend to be men."

"We are men...."

"Oh! Right! Totally, we're all men. I'm a man, definitely."

"Men… or whomever, I think we stand at the threshold of a glorious new age of warfare!"

I wandered away. I hoped that these were the barbarians who had landed headfirst when they had taken flight. But I doubted it.

Colour, plumage, silks and embroidery, fitted clothes, capes, stylish gowns, and fashion? Madness. These things had no place on a battlefield. Not even accessories. The Artificer was like a big wet stain, spreading inexorably, wetly corrupting and awkward. At least, I thought, this awful notion would take care of itself.

"Hi, remember me?"

It was the smiling handsome blue eyed barbarian who had so recently had his hand on my thigh, and now wore my bootprint on his face. I hit him again. He went down in a thoroughly satisfying way, and I enjoyed leaving another boot print lower down as he lay unconscious in the dirt. It would be something to remember me by.

"She threw them from the length of the aisle. I couldn't believe it. I had agreed to spend the night with her." this from a big Troll with an empty beer bucket.

"So are you going to meet her?" its companion, another Troll asked.

"Are you crazy? She'd break me in two."

As they passed I allowed myself a small smile. It was all I could manage. I had been groped, trampled, fought an entire rioting horde, been hit on the head, inhaled raw beer fumes, and walloped so many heads I could hardly lift my arm. I was sweating, tired, and covered with bruises. I wanted my money.

I understood why R'dunner had been unable to find any women to practice Artifice. Women were far too sensible to ever get involved in anything that lunatic. I was amazed that he had been able to get anyone at all to do it.

"Yes, but what does it all mean? What is the deeper metaphysical understanding that is revealed?" I stepped through a pack of arguing storytellers.

"Besides the fact that they were all idiots."

"Yes."

"They were all sexually perverse idiots. It's like the Empire never fell."

"Well, be fair, if this was Imperial days, there would have been a donkey up on stage."

"It might have given a better performance.

I groaned, four more days of this.

I found R'dunner with the Troll. I hobbled over. He grinned and waved at me.

"I was just telling your friend how pleased we are." he said "You did an excellent job. Why I remember when we played Forbane last year we had race riots."

He chuckled. I recalled that Forbane had been destroyed recently by civil war.

I collected the money. I was so tired I didn't even bother to have it sterilised.

"I am going to have company tonight," the Troll said in her smuggest way.

I chuckled.

"You know," said Stavra "I bet that if we set up a booth outside to sell beer and foodstuffs like live rats and rotten tomatoes we could make a lot of money."

I ignored that.

"There's real opportunities here," she said enthusiastically. "I think this is going to be big."

"Sure," I sighed. "Stavra, this is just an inferior kind of storytelling. But where storytelling is bounded only by the skill of the teller, and the imagination of the audience, this...artificing is restricted to the stage and the ability of the artificers. It rots and restricts the imagination and confines reason, reducing the complex subtlety of a story to its most basic outlines."

I paused to let that sink in. "Additionally, where any rich house or busy streetcorner can afford a storyteller, productions such as this can be supported only by a rich town or the wealthiest patrons. Artificing is just a passing fad."

The Troll seemed saddened. I leaned against her.

"You really think so." she asked.

"Trust me," I told her "it will never last."

The End

The Speed of Divine Regard

Tancred and Hetherfox were engaged in their usual midday game of chess in the staff lounge, when the damnable Godfrey, put his two cents in.

To be perfectly fair, it was not entirely Godrey's fault, for the two distinguished local theologians were engaged in their usual debate over the nature of the celestial being, and chose to invite the godless physicist into the discussion.

"What ho, Godfrey," Tancred had said, "Hetherfox is on about the photian schism again, what do your make of that?"

It must be said that neither expected much of an answer, as far as Godfrey was concerned, a photian schism sounded like some vain attempt to split the component particles in a beam of light.

Perhaps the blame should more properly be placed on the penurious institution which forces the humanities to share lounge space with the small rump of hard sciences, which the college regrettably supported.

"I'm sorry," Godfrey said apologetically, while polishing his glasses, "I wasn't listening."

The two old stalwarts smiled at each other.

"Don't worry about it, Godfrey," Hetherfox told him, "we can see that you share a diminishing attention span with your nominal students. Do not let my friend bait you into questions beyond your depth."

Now it might be that Godfrey, young though he was, and slender of form and firmament, may have considered that he had been insulted in some way, and therefore felt a need to rise to some imagined challenge.

For he said, "Well, if your talk was on the nature of the hypothetical heavenly entity, I must say that a diminishing attention span would put me in closer proximity to such a being than yourselves."

Hetherfox looked up from the chessboard, fixing his acerbic gaze upon Godfrey in a manner reminiscent of an eagle at five thousand feet altitude who has just noticed a tasty fieldmouse directly beneath it.

"Are you presuming to instruct us on a point of theology?" Hetherfox asked in a reasonable voice. The sort of reasonable voice that, had it been employed in select townships of the American west in the last century, would have cleared the streets admirably.

"Uhm," said Godfrey with great presence of mind. For such ambiguous utterances, far from being the bane of language as many parochial educators have held, have actually saved many a life and reputation by preserving one from the need for an actual word.

However, luck was not with Godfrey that day. For Tancred was sitting across the chess board from Hetherfox, fully prepared to pitch the damnable Godfrey straight from the skillet into the fires of, if not perdition, a reasonable academic facsimile.

"I think what our young colleague (and I use that term loosely) was saying is that he posits the admittedly perfect and omnipotent being as suffering from dwindling attentiveness."

As he said this, Tancred took full advantage of Hetherfox's fixation on Godfrey to rearrange some of the chess pieces to what he deemed a more aesthetically pleasing configuration.

"A sort of cosmic Alzheimers," he concluded.

Hetherfox raised one eyebrow at the hapless Godfrey. Although to describe the look merely as a raised eyebrow is to describe the great lightning strike of 1944 which exploded the

College tower, melted the great brass door, and incinerated the Dean and a pair of attentive young men all in a heap, while completely vaporising any trace of said trios clothes, a mere static build up.

To be quite frank, many supposedly primitive cultures would have considered a look such as Hetherfox bestowed upon the pitiable Godfrey to be immediately fatal.

It must be said, by way of explanation, that Hetherfox was quite sensitive to the word 'Alzheimer' due to his propensity, of late years for occasionally forgetting such commonplace trivialities as his wife's name, where he lived and the fact that he should take his pants down to perform bodily functions. As of the present, no one had felt the presence of mind to voice such concerns to the great man, for the feeling was that if in fact one raised eyebrow was likely not fatal, the both of them definitely were.

"Perhaps you could explain that," Hetherfox invited in a reasonable tone.

It is reliably reported by the learned historian Tacitus Vulvulus that the Roman Emperor Maximus Gluteous used just such a tone to inquire of the invading barbarian king, Gingivitis Huffalus, of the strength of his forces. The poor barbarian, unable to count past twenty-one, had chewed off his own arms and legs rather than respond.

Thus Godfrey, as any disinterested observer might divine, was in a tight spot indeed.

Tancred, who during the course of this initial dialogue had conceived a great affection for one of Hetherfox's rooks, quietly slipped it into his pocket.

"Well," said Godfrey, framing his words carefully before the two great men, "It would seem to me that while an infinite being would be fundamentally unknowable..."

Hetherfox and Tancred nodded in agreement at this. A simple problem, like how to build a brick wall was an afternoon's work for a craftsman, but the contemplation of unfathomable mystery translated directly into lifelong tenure.

"Still, it would seem to me that at least some elements of such a being's motives and nature could be extrapolated from its works..."

Hetherfox and Tancred glared suspiciously at this, but said nothing.

Emboldened, the hateful Godfrey proceeded, all tremulous and hesitating.

"...by which, I refer to the universe. Or the universe as we currently perceive and understand it.

"God, we will concede, created the universe."

The two learned men nodded carefully.

"Probably some forty billion years ago..."

Hetherfox coughed. Tancred took occasion to again rearrange the board into a more pleasing configuration, as his last aesthetic had been disturbed by the removal of the rook.

"...although estimates vary. It seems to me that as we look at the universe we are struck by ever diminishing time frames and scales, which may reflect god's attention."

In it now, Godfrey had no choice but to plow forward.

"Consider: God creates the Universe, clouds and galactic masses coalescing over cosmic scales. Great events happen, which take tens of billions of years to occur.

"These vast events give birth to stars and stellar cosmologies, which follow fascinating histories, of some few billions of years. Obviously, God has sped up the merry go round.

"Eventually bored with the pace, the Deity calls into being planets, small clumps of matter and atmosphere, whose geological processes flit by in hundreds of millions of years.

"Why just look at the diversity of planetary geologies in our own solar system. This new toy was not only faster, but offered infinitely more variety than the eventually repetitive stellar sequences.

"But I imagine even this must have grown boring, so the creator called life into being. Consider the riotous diversity, new species springing into existence in a few million years, ages and ecologies eclipsing one another in rapid succession.

"Eventually," Godfrey continued, "even this breakneck pace must have seemed slow and plodding, as the creator, like an addict becoming ever immune to greater dosages, strove to find an even more rapidly proceeding source of amusement.

"Us?"

Hetherfox gave him both eyebrows, but otherwise said nothing.

"A parade of diversity and adventure condensed into a few thousands of years. Whole new cultures being born and dying in just centuries."

"Why, we are but a moment in the history of life, a hiccup in geological time, a microsecond in stellar histories which stretch billions of years behind us.

"Frankly, to suggest any divine interest in us at all is to imply that the cosmic ruler suffers from a most colossally telescoping attention span.

"Why," and here Godfrey, as they say, went too far, "we may not even be the end of the process..."

The class bell rang, at that moment, startling the diminutive professor.

"My classes," Godfrey explained meekly, and gathering up his notes, scurried out from under the hot gazes of his elder colleagues.

Tancred and Hetherfox watched him go, and then turned back to their game. Tancred moved a pawn.

"Checkmate," he announced.

"I thought I'd just made the opening move," Hetherfox swore.

"They you should have been more careful about it."

"Hmmm."

"Odd duck, that Godfrey," Tancred volunteered, to move the conversation along.

"Hmmm." Hetherfox continued to stare at the chessboard.

"I wonder what he meant when he said we weren't the end of the process."

"Communist tripe, no doubt," commented Hetherfox, "if only this were the good old days, we could have him burned at the stake."

"Amen," chimed Tancred.

Meanwhile, throughout the college, and at colleges, in offices and homes across the continent, computer after computer manipulated millions and trillions of units of data through microseconds and milliseconds...

And in those trillions of bits, the name of Saint Godfrey the Prophet was carried on electronic whispers...

The End

The Sharebear Apocalypse

OPENING - A news desk with two local news casters, Tom Nabors and Merica Johnson, a regional news hour.

ZOOM IN on the male Newscaster in the center, middle aged, blandly handsome, carefully coiffed. Tom Nabors:

NABORS: ....And that's the news for Chicago. Turning now to the human interest side of life, we have Merica Johnson, who went into the field with this evening's in-depth feature about Chicago's newest invasive species, and for once, it's a welcome one. Chicago, say hello to the ... Sharebears.

CUT TO MERICA JOHNSON, blonde, perky, on a busy Chicago street. Beside her, holding her free hand, is a grinning Sharebear, and with it, a pair of smiling children and their mother.

MERICA - Thank you... Jim. Yes, Chicago has a new invasive species, and for once, Chicagoans couldn't be happier. The windy city is for once, opening its arms wide for a hug for the Sharebears..."

CUT TO montage of file footage clips, rats, pigeons, rabbits, raccoons, skunks. A shot of a coyote slinking down a street. Deer munching in peoples lawns.

MERICA (VOICE OVER) - the urban environment is home not just to people and their pets, but to a variety of ride along animals. Animals which have adapted to city life and people. We have rats and pigeons of course, but in the last few decades, skunks, raccoons and even deer have adapted to the urban and suburban way of life. Mostly, they just stay out of our way, or are considered pests and troublemakers. But not these little fellows.

MONTAGE SHIFT - shots of Sharebears and children playing in a park. A garbage man pausing on his rounds to hand out sandwiches to Sharebears. A busy executive pausing on his rounds to exchange a hug.

CUT TO INTERVIEW WITH GARBAGE MAN, standing next to his garbage truck

MERICA - do they ever cause trouble? Are they ever a nuisance?

GARBAGE MAN - well they tip over some trash now and then, you can understand they might get hungry. But no. They're not like rats or raccoons. It's nice having them around. We don't mind picking up after them now and then; it's just a little thing.

MERICA - what happened to your hand?

GARBAGE MAN - Oh this? (holds up a bandaged hand, missing fingers) Caught it in the machinery. It's a risky job sometimes. No big deal doesn't hurt at all.

MERICA - the Sharebears aren't a distraction.

GARBAGE MAN - (laughs) Not at all. It's nice having them around. It brightens up my day. My wife has taken to packing extra sandwiches for the little rascals.

CLOSE UP ON MERICA, addressing the camera.

So what exactly are Sharebears? Where do they come from? Why are they so gosh darned friendly and loveable? To find out, we went to the experts...

CUT TO MERICA in what looks like a laboratory office. Caption identifies the "Doctor Penfield Stangwill - Expert on Sharebears." Doctor Stangwill wears an eye patch and has heavy scarring down one side of his face, testament to a previous history of working with dangerous animals.

MERICA - Doctor Stangwill, are Sharebears actually bears?

STANGWILD - (laughs) Oh no, not at all. They're not related to the genus ursus. What they are is an offshoot of Mustelids, a Procyonidae - their closest relatives are raccoons and badgers, and of course, skunks (chuckles). The resemblance to bears is remarkable, but that's a result of parallel evolution - having much the same lifestyle and diet - on average, Sharebears are a tenth or less the size of real bears. And of course (chuckles) real bears are much more dangerous.

MERICA - You said similar lifestyle?

STANGWILD - Yes. Well, Sharebears are order carnivore, like dogs, felines and bears of course, but despite that, they're basically omnivores. Like bears, a large part of their diet comes from vegetation. Like Bears, they're basically forest dwellers, going through seasonal phases. I believe that they originated in the Pacific Northwest.

MERICA - (interrupting) I guess the question everyone wants to know is why they're so darned cute!

STANGWILD - Oh... Oh... Sorry. A lot of reasons, I think. They're plantigrades, partially bipedal, like Bears they can stand up on their hind legs and walk. They actually walk better and further than bears. Even more than apes at times. So there's a humanlike quality there that attracts people. Of course they're small, so harmless - an average Sharebear is around sixty pounds. And then there's the appearance - the whole 'Disney' thing - they have large eyes, short muzzles, rounded features. Their vocalisations sound a lot like happy children laughing or playing. And of course, there's the 'Sharebear Share' which is hard to resist (chuckles).

CLOSE UP ON MERICA - ADDRESSING CAMERA

MERICA - Whatever the reason, the Sharebears make friends no matter where they go.

INTERVIEW - KENNELS, mostly empty. Subtitle, 'Animal control.' A second subhead identifies the person Merica is talking to - Vic Wakin, Manager.

MERICA - So you're the head of the Chicago's animal control department?

WAKIN - that's right Ma'am, twenty years now.

MERICA - So you must have seen a lot of animal cases, not just stray dogs and cats.

WAKIN - Mostly dogs and cats, but just about everything. Lots of raccoons and skunks. Skunks are bad. Some coyotes. Deer even. There was a python once, someone abandoned in a hotel room. And then there was even one time a cougar wandered into the city. Vermin, hate em all.

MERICA - What about Sharebears.

WAKIN - (visibly lightening up and breaking into a grin) Well now that's a different thing. I remember the first time we saw one - had a call for a bear in a back yard. Figured it was a real bear. Those things are dangerous, you get a bear, it's a crisis. We were loaded up, tranquilizers, shotguns, a big bear trap... we get there, and it's just a little thing. At first I thought it was a cub or something. But then, damned if it didn't get up on its hind legs walk over and give me a hug. Everyone laughed! (Wakins smiles at the memory)

MERICA - Are Sharebears a problem?

WAKIN - No problem at all. They're as harmless as can be. Unless you don't like hugs.

MERICA - But don't they cause a nuisance? Dig up things, get into trash, make nests, poop?

WAKIN - Oh not so you'd notice, it's never anything to get all worked up over.

MERICA - So no one minds?

WAKIN - Well, I suppose some do, but you know, they're just Grumps. Grumps we like to call em down here. And the thing is, Sharebears, they do a lot of good.

MERICA - How so?

WAKIN - Well, they're just so darn adorable you know. But besides that, I can tell you that since the Sharebears started showing up, we hardly get any calls for raccoons or skunks, it's like they just take off. Hell, we pick up hardly any stray dogs even.

TRACKING SHOT OF LONG ROW OF EMPTY DOG POUND KENNELS

WAKIN - All I can say is that I'm all right with the Sharebears. I wish there were twice as many.

MERICA - Twice.

WAKIN - They just make you feel good, you know. You feel good having them around.

SCENES OF MOUNTAINS AND GREEN PACIFIC RAIN FORESTS

MERICA (VOICE OVER) - Originally, Sharebears were native to the American northwest. Their range was the hills and valleys of the Rockies, from British Colombia to as far south as Oregon, where they were beloved by the Native People.

CUT TO - A native American elder sitting in front of a Haida village, totem poles and longhouses, the Rockies rising majestically behind him. Close up on the Elder.

ELDER - The animals you call Sarh-beras, we knew them as Hahn-a Ber-Ber-Ah. They were a very spiritual animal. Very powerful magic. We were taught, you must always be respectful of the Hahn-a Ber-Ber-Ah. You could only approach them from behind. And if they saw you, you must run away as fast as you can. The lands of the Hahn-a were forbidden to men, we did not go into them.

CUT TO SHOT - MERICA in a laboratory setting. On the wall behind her are a series of larger than life diagrams of Sharebears and Sharebear anatomy. With her is a tall man in a white lab coat, balding. Zoom in.

MERICA - this is Doctor Stanton, an expert in biochemistry. Doctor Stanton, I understand that you're also an expert on Sharebears.

STANTON - In a manner of speaking.

MERICA - Doctor Stanton, we've heard a lot about the 'Sharebear Share' what can you tell us about that?

STANTON - Well, technically speaking, it's not a share at all. It's a chemical defense mechanism. Like a skunk.

MERICA - A skunk! Oh no!

STANTON - It's a defense mechanism, Merica. Like skunks, Sharebears don't have much in the way of teeth or claws; they're not very fast comparatively, so they need a way to defend themselves from attackers. Sharebears are related to skunks, and they've evolved a very similar defense mechanism. Skunks discharge a powerful noxious chemical from their anal glands.

MERICA - Can we say anal on the news?

STANTON - (ignoring her) As I said, SKUNKS discharge from ANAL glands. A lot of animals have ANAL glands. But Sharebears, instead of discharging from ANAL glands, discharge from a pair of modified NIPPLES on their upper torso. Skunks lift their tails, Sharebears rear up on their hind legs and spread their forelimbs wide (demonstrates).

MERICA - Now nipples. We may have to edit this.

STANTON - (irritably) yes, Merica. NIPPLES. The big difference between Sharebears and Skunks though, it's not just about NIPPLES and ANAL glands, is in the chemical nature of the discharge.

MERICA - and what is that? We all know skunks are pretty noxious.

STANTON - Correct, skunks are... as you say 'noxious.' The Sharebears chemical discharge, however, is a psychoactive.

MERICA - You mean like a perhomone.

STANTON - (sighs) No, not a pheromone. A psychoactive chemical, loosely related to opiates. The molecule is coupled to a neurotoxin, so it works either inhaled or through skin contact. It brings about a feeling of tranquility, wellbeing, passivity, aggression vanishes, and while it's not a full paralytic motor coordination declines.

MERICA - So skunks spray a terrible odor, and Sharebears spray a feel-good. Isn't that amazing? Sharebears defend themselves from attack by making their enemies feel good.

STANTON - It's not unlimited, each Sharebear has maybe a dozen or so shots, and then their bodies have to manufacture more. That's why Sharebears will often line up together to discharge, the more animals, the more intense the discharge, the less strain on each individual.

STANTON - Well, there's more to it than that. It's incredibly potent stuff; even a trace amount strongly affects behaviour. As I've said, it's linked to a neurotoxin for skin absorption, and it's surrounded with an oil base, so if it gets on you it clings, which extends the effect.

MERICA - Oh.

STANTON - That's why Sharebears like to hug. It's in the area of the oddly shaped patch of fur.

MERICA - The heart shape?

STANTON - In some, yes, it resembles a heart shape. Sometimes a triangle, or a starfish, or a cloud, it's actually just random. It's a specialized patch of hair follicles that hold the discharge, and are used to rub it into the subject.

MERICA - That's just amazing. Doctor Stanton, I want to thank you for your time. There you have it folks. Aren't the Sharebears just the most wonderful little things ever!

BACK TO NEWS DESK - MERICA AND NABORS

CLOSE UP ON NABORS, HE TURNS TO CAMERA

NABORS: The Pacific Northwest is a long way away from the Windy City. How did they get here? The answer is in the Sharers.

CUT TO: Exterior - windy day, overcast, the wind is making popping noises on the microphone. A Winnebago pulls up to a playground, riding over the parking dividers with a lurch before coming to a stop. A group of children cease playing, their mothers stepping forward protectively.

The Winnebago door opens, and a group of Sharebears file out. They mill around. Seeing the children, they open their arms wide for a hug. After hesitation, the children run to embrace the sharebears. Mothers beam happily.

VOICE OVER, CLOSE UP ON AN UNKEMPT BEARDED MIDDLE AGED MAN, SOMEWHAT EMACIATED, TALKING TO NABORS

NABORS (VO): This is Dave Mundy. Dave is part of a network of 'Sharer's men and women who have made it their life's work to bring the Sharebears to the world.

MUNDY: That's right, Tom. Me and the family, we've been bringing the good news, introducing these adorable creatures to the wide world.

NABORS: How long have you and your family been doing this?

MUNDY: Oh, I'd say going on twelve, fifteen years now. You lose track. I think we might be the first Sharers, me and Doris and the kids. (Looks vaguely off camera) I used to have a job, right. And a house. But you just get called right? You fill with purpose, and you go where the lord wants you to go. And the lord wants us to spread these little fellows around. There's not enough love in the world, and god sent them to redress that balance. And god sent us to help them get their message out there.

NABORS: How did you happen to do it?

MUNDY: Well we were on vacation, me and the family, in the Northwest, and we just came across these little fellas. We were pulled up, and having dinner? Out in the wild, you know? And I think... I think... I think... My daughter, Angie, she came back to camp, and she had one of the little guys with her. She said 'He's my new friend, he's hungry, can he have supper with us?' He looked like a bear cub; I was concerned there was a mother bear around. I shooed everyone in the trailer. I said, 'Angie, come away from that.' But she wouldn't, she just said over and over, 'He's my new friend.' Then the little fellow got right up on his hind legs, and walked right up to me and gave me a big hug. Suddenly, I knew it was all right. So I called the family out, and it was amazing, he gave each of us a hug, just like a person. I could tell he didn't mean no harm, so we treated him just like a human guess. And others came along, and soon we were feeding a pile of them. They just kept coming. And we kept staying, making new friends. Until the food ran out.

MUNDY'S SMILE IS BEATIFIC

MUNDY: So then Delores, that's... that was my wife, she said we had to go get food. But we didn' want to be away from them. So she said 'let's take them with us!' And off we went.

Everyone loved them, everyone we met, they loved them just like we did. A few got tired of travelling with us, they made so many new friends, I guess, they just wanted to stay. And we kept travelling... That's how it started.

NABORS: So you're not working?

MUNDY: No, not since we started sharing.

NABORS: How do you support yourself and your family now?

MUNDY (SMILING): When you share love, people give you what you need. I go into a gas station, a grocery store, and all of a sudden, there's so much love and goodwill, people give me money, food, I fill up the gas at the pump, and the clerk won't even take money for it. That's the effect these little guys have. It's as if Jesus himself was walking with us.

CUT TO: CCTV camera showing a gas bar lot, featuring rows of pumps, as the Winnebago pulls up. The Winnebago door flies open. A man staggers out, followed by a small horde of sharebears scampering about. Cars pull away, or swerve to avoid entering the lot. A pair of sharebears run up to a man pumping gas in his car, pulling him down. The gas nozzle falls to the pavement, still pumping away, as the man frolics with the two sharebears. His shirt begins to stain red, but he is not bothered. Some of the bears on all fours race into the gas bar's convenience store.

CUT TO: CCTV interior of the convenience store, the bears are scampering up and down the aisles pulling products from the shelves and scattering them about, tearing open packages. One of them manages to open the cooler section. Bottles and cartons are flung about, until it finds its way to the ice cream. The humans in the store watch without any signs of terror or distress, as the animals run riot.

NABORS: Can they be destructive?

MUNDY: They're high spirited, I'll admit that, but they don't mean no harm.

NABORS: What about your family? Where are they? Do they still ride along with you?

MUNDY'S SMILE FLICKERS - for the first time, he looks uncertain. He tries to focus, his brow furrowing. And then it fades.

MUNDY: They're not around any more...

SLOWLY, MUNDY'S PLACID EXPRESSION RETURNS, HE STOPS THINKING ABOUT THEM.

CUT BACK TO NEWS DESK - MERICA BEAMS AT TOM.

MERICA: Well, from the gas station footage, it seems like they sure can be a handful, those frisky camps.

NABORS: Yes indeed, but you can tell from the footage, and I can verify from talking to people, that no one seems to mind.

MERICA: What's a little mess, after all, right?

NABORS: Exactly, what's a little mess?

MERICA: It can always be cleaned up. No big deal. And it's a small price to pay for these adorable visitors.

NABORS: That's right Merica.

MERICA: Chicago's got quite a population of these friendly critters now, would you say?

NABORS: Well, we couldn't get a hard answer from anyone, but the consensus seems to be that there aren't enough of them yet. They haven't worn out their welcome in Chicago. And I don't think they will for some time to come.

MERICA: Chicago's welcomed them with open arms. Even into people's homes.

CUT TO: ESTABLISHING SHOT IN A ROW OF TOWNHOUSES.

CUT TO: INTERIOR IN A RESIDENTIAL LIVING ROOM, ESTABLISHING SHOT, MERICA SITTING IN AN OVERSTUFFED CHAIR, WITH A MIDDLE AGED MARRIED COUPLE, LEANING FORWARD OVER COFFEE.

MERICA: I just want to say, this is good coffee!

MAN: Thank you, Merica. (Caption identifies him as Sydney Blasco)

A GOLD FURRED SHAREBEAR WALKS UP TO MERICA ON ALL FOURS, YEARS AND GIVES HER A HUG. MERICA MAKES A SURPRISED NOISE. THE SHAREBEAR'S CLAWS DRAG ALONG HER SHOULDER, TEARING HER JACKET AND BLOUSE. FOR A MOMENT, A BREAST IS EXPOSED, NIPPLE PROMINENT, BUT ALWAYS PROFESSONAL, SHE COVERS IT. THE CLAWS LEAVE RED WOUNDS DOWN HER SHOULDER, BUT SHE DOESN'T SEEM TO NOTICE.

MERICA: (Laughs) That was surprising! I guess this is the newest member of the family?

WOMAN: We call him Jake. (Caption identifies her as Marion Blasco) Actually, our son Anton named him. Brought him home one day. Just like that. He was so friendly, he was like family right away. He was just like a person. We brought him a chair; he sat right at the dinner table with us. He slept in Anton's room that night; it was as if they'd been best friends their whole lives.

SYDNEY: We weren't sure what to do. I mean, it is a wild animal, right?

MARION SLAPS HIS KNEE REPROACHFULLY

SYDNEY: But winter is coming, and it's getting pretty cold out there. We were worried that the little guy might have a tough time of it.

MARION: Anton insisted that he stay with us, just for the winter. So he'd be safe.

SYDNEY: Well, that's a little unusual, sheltering a wild anim– anim– .... But hey, we had plenty of room, right.

CAMERA PANS ACROSS THE ROOM - THERE ARE VISIBLE CLAW MARKS ON THE WALLS, THE FURNITURE IS TORN, WITH STUFFING RIPPED OUT, THERE ARE FAECES ON THE FLOOR ALONG THE WALLS. WHEN SYDNEY SCRATCHES HIS LEG, HIS PANTS LEG LIFTS, SHOWING A HEAVY BANDAGE JUST ABOVE THE ANKLE.

THE SHAREBEAR MOVES TOWARDS THE CAMERA, WHICH SHAKES SUDDENLY. THE WORDS 'GET AWAY' CAN BE HEARD FROM THE NEWS CAMERA. THE SHAREBEAR VEERS AWAY.

MARION, SYDNEY AND MERICA LOOK TOWARDS THE CAMERA. SHE LOOKS CONCERNED.

MERICA: Are you okay, Billy? You didn't kick it? Did you?

BILLY (VO): No, no. It just surprised me, that's all.

MARION: (laughs) That's Jake. I swear he's the friendliest thing you ever saw.

BILLY (VO): (interrupting) Merica, are you okay.

MERICA'S SCRATCHES ARE BLEEDING, SHE HASN'T NOTICED. HER HAND IS STILL COVERING HER EXPOSED BREAST. SHE LOOKS IRRITATED AT THE INTERRUPTION. SHE RETURNS TO THE INTERVIEW.

MERICA: I'm fine Billy. Now, Marion...

BILLY (VO): (interrupting) Merica, I think you're bleeding.

MERICA LOOKS IRRITATED AGAIN.

MARION: (seeming to notice) Oh dear! How did that happen! Let me get something to put on that for you.

MARION GETS UP AND LEAVES FOR THE KITCHEN. CAMERA WATCHES HER GO. SHE LIMPS A LITTLE. JAKE FOLLOWS HER INTO THE KITCHEN.

MERICA: Now where were we? Yes, I can certainly see that Jake is friendly.

SYDNEY: (Continuing) Loves people. Loves animals. He's just best friends with our little dog Perkins.

BILLY (VO): (interrupting) I haven't seen a dog around here.

SYDNEY: Oh he's around here somewhere. He just loves Jake. We all love Jake. Why, he could be my own son... if my son was hairy and went around on all fours sometime.

BILLY (VO): Anton, that's your son right. Where is he right now?

SYDNEY: At school, I guess. That boy studies hard.

BILLY (VO): It's Saturday.

SYDNEY LOOKS BLANK.

BILLY (VO): It's Saturday, there's no school on Saturday. Sydney.... listen carefully to me. Where's Anton?

SYDNEY SEEMS TO THINK, CONCENTRATING.

SYDNEY: I guess... I guess... He must be... (brightens) He's up in his room!

MARION: (Returning, with a white towel and some medical tape on a tray.) What?

JAKE FOLLOWS HER FROM THE KITCHEN.

SYDNEY: Anton, he's up in his room.

MARION: (Smiling, as if having been reminded) Oh... that's where he is. Such a good boy. He brought Jake into our family. Did you know that? Walked right through that door with him.

BILLY (VO): If I went to Anton's room... what would I find?

MARION AND SYDNEY LOOK BLANK. MERICA IS PRESSING THE WHITE CLOTH TO HER SHOULDER, SHE'S LOOKING INCREASINGLY UNCOMFORTABLE.

SYDNEY: (Hesitating) Anton's up in his room.

BILLY (VO): I'm going up to Anton's room.

MERICA: Billy! Enough!

PATTING MARION'S KNEE, LEANING FORWARD TO THE TWO OF THEM.

MERICA: I'm so sorry. I promise, we'll edit this part out.

CUT BACK TO STUDIO, MERICA AND NABORS AT THEIR NEWS DESK.

NABORS: Well, it seems that Chicagoans are opening their homes as well as their hearts. It's a beautiful thing.

MERICA: That's right, Tom. The Sharebears are here to stay. There may be some downsides, but I can tell you, their greatest gift is to bring out the best in people!

NABORS: And that's our show.

MERICA: (laughs) Not quite Tom, to bring things to a close, we have a surprise special guest to say hello.

NABORS: (laughing) Oh that's right. Bring him out!

FROM OFF CAMERA, ACCOMPANIED BY A HANDLER WHO IS NOMINALLY HOLDING A LEASH, A SHAREBEAR, LIGHT BROWN IN COLOUR,

COMES WADDLING OUT IN A FOUR LEGGED
GAIT. IT SEEMS CONFUSED BY THE LIGHTS,
REARING UP ON TWO LEGS AND DROPPING BACK
TO FOUR FEET, AGAIN AND AGAIN. FINALLY, IT
TURNS TOWARDS THE CAMERA, REARS UP, AND
SPREADS IT'S ARMS WIDE FOR A HUG.

***

TWO YEARS LATER

**YOUTUBE - VIDEO - NINE MINUTES LONG
POSTED BY BRONWIN**

The video shows a mother pushing a baby carriage out for a
stroll in the park. A Sharebear walks up to her. She stops to
pet it, kneeling down.

"Hello fella, how are you?"

It licks her face and she laughs. As she tries to stand, it wraps
its arms around her in a hug. She pauses a second and then
disengages herself, standing upright. The Sharebear rubs itself
against her leg like a cat, and pushes at her hand with its
muzzle.

"You sure are friendly," she says. "Do you want a treat? I'm
sorry, I don't have anything. I'm sorry."

The Sharebear licks her hand. Nuzzling it. The baby cries.
Another Sharebear approaches.

"I'm sorry; I don't have anything to feed you..."

She pets the second Sharebear, as it sniffs around, its nose
poking at her knees, at the other bear, at the carriage. The two
sharebears touch noses.

"You guys are so hungry! That's awful! I wish I had
something... Wait, I know."

The mother pulls a baby bottle from the carriage.

"Here, I have something. Here you go!"

She squirts milk at the first bear, wetting its muzzle. It licks its muzzle and opens its mouth wide. She squirts milk into its mouth, and then into the open mouth of the second bear.

"Here you go, here you go, here for each of you, you babies like that. Yes you do. You like that."

Two more Sharebears are approaching. The mother doesn't pay attention, instead focusing on squirting milk into their open mouths, and cooing and laughing.

"That's it babies, drink up. That's it. You like that. I know you do! This is the good stuff. It's not formula. It's straight from mommy herself. I pumped this morning. Oh yes yes yes, you love it! I know you do."

The other two sharebears have arrived, she squirts milk into their mouths, alternating among the four of them, and laughing. One of them grabs at her hand with its forepaws, wrestling the baby bottle away from her. It takes several comical steps away, holding the bottle in its forepaws, and then rolls onto its back to suckle from the bottle.

The baby is crying. The camera returns to the carriage. One of the sharebears is hugging the mother, who is returning the hug, bending forward, wrapping her arms around the creature. Another rears up, and she hugs it. The third Sharebear is becoming interested in the carriage, poking its nose. The baby cries louder.

"What's that," the mother says, "what's that."

The hugs are over. Now two sharebears are rearing up to poke their noses into the carriage. The third is examining the wheels of the carriage.

"Oh you guys! You've never seen a baby! Want to see? Want to see?"

She takes the baby out of the carriage and bends down, holding it out for the Sharebears to see. They all rear up on their hind legs. Two of them reach out with forepaws. One of them pulls the baby from her, holding it in its forelimbs.

"Oopsy!" The mother says. "You want to hold him. You hold him. That's a good boy. You're holding him just like mommy."

The Sharebear turns to walk away, not hurried this time, but clumsily walking upright carrying the baby. The other three sharebears, including the one that was sucking on the bottle, follow after, together with the mother, still making cooing noises.

"We're all going for a walk together," she says. "Yes we are. Yes we are."

The five of them amble on out of camera range.

VO - "What the hell?"

COMMENTS

Jess Morrow - I can't believe she handed her baby over to those things to eat.

Amatagat - Jesus Christ, Jess, you're a cynical bitch. Seek psychological help.

***

SHARECROWS NEST - A MESSAGE BOARD, THREE YEARS LATER

ELIAN - It's not just a North American problem. They're in Brazil.

ROBIN- What? How the hell did they get down there? Ship?

ELIAN - No, flew down. Apparently, one of these Sharers bought three of them tickets as children. They walked right through the terminal, right through security, no one did anything. On the plane, they freaked out and ate a stewardess and nobody was the least bit bothered.

MIKE - God dammed Sharer!

SANDIP - That shit goes way beyond pheromones, or neurotoxins or whatever. I swear those things have some kind of psychic power.

NIGEL - Nope, all chemistry. They're just animals. They're not even any smarter than raccoons or apes or creatures like that.

ELIAN - Yeah, so there's a colony of them in Brazil, ended up in the Barrios, where the poor people just love them. Government tried to eradicate them, riots went on for three days.

NIGEL - I've heard of colonies in Europe. They're in London, France, Berlin. Apparently, in Berlin, they were in a zoo, that didn't turn out so good. Even Moscow. I heard that they were doing biological research.

ELIAN - These things are just getting everywhere. I tell you, we need to be worried.

SANDIP - I don't think they'll show up in places like Calcutta or Lagos, they'd just eat them there. Riyadh's too hot for them.

NIGEL - You ever look at the growth projections. Active predator, high reproduction rate, no enemies. Hell, we end up protecting them. There's no limit.

MOD - I've warned you about fearmongering.

***

SHARECROWS NEST - A MESSAGE BOARD, FIVE YEARS LATER

THOMAS - Hey, anyone seen that video of a mother handing her baby over to those things?

WIN - It's ancient. What is it, ten years old?

CAREGIRL - It's fake.

THOMAS - You don't know that.

CAREGIRL - It's been debunked. No one could find the mother or the baby. It's a hoax. All these videos popping up of Sharebears attacking humans, I'm not saying it doesn't happen. But most of these clips are faked, fake blood, edits, if you watch, it's all play behaviour that people are misrepresenting.

THOMAS - Some of this looks pretty real.

WIN - I'm not denying that it's possible to get hurt. They're carnivores, they have teeth and claws, it's easy to get scratched or bitten by accident, if you're not careful, and most people aren't careful.

THOMAS - Accident, uh?

WIN - Accident.

THOMAS - What about that woman in Detroit, they found her half eaten in her own home, the Sharebears were still chowing down when they found them. Human remains in their stomachs. Open and shut case.

CAREGIRL - Heart attack, the bears were stuck in there with her, the dead body was the only food source. There was no sign of a struggle or attack. We see dogs and cats doing the same thing when their shut in owner dies.

THOMAS - Bull.

CAREGIRL - There are very very few cases of Sharebears deliberately attacking or injuring a human being, almost none.

WIN - Because they 'love' us.

CAREGIRL - Yeah, they're friendly and affectionate, and they get along with people. But that's not it. If you can set aside your kneejerk hysteria, I'll explain it.

WIN - Explain away, professor.

CAREGIRL - It's very simple: We feed them. We feed them constantly, so they're never hungry around us. It's that hormonal thing they do, yes, it makes us like them and makes us want to feed them. As long as we keep shoving food at them, they're not interested in eating, or even attacking humans. It just doesn't happen.

THOMAS - Unless they feel like it.

CAREGIRL - Come on, this is just anthropomorphising. They're not from outer space. They're not secret geniuses. They're not plotting together. They're just animals. They're just a version of skunks, but instead of a stinky toxic spray, they evolved a euphoric that didn't work particularly well in nature, so they evolved social behaviour to compensate, and these traits just happens to serve them very well in human society. It's not magic.

THOMAS - Tell it to the cats and dogs.

WIN - What?

THOMAS - Where they start showing up, cat and dog populations start to drop.

CAREGIRL - Boo hoo, people are finding a better, more emotionally rewarding pet. That's competition in the marketplace. That's capitalism, boys.

THOMAS - Feral cats and dogs, and urban wildlife, raccoons, rats, you name it.

WIN - Anything that makes the rat population drop is a good thing.

THOMAS - You're pretty glib.

CAREGIRL - And you're over-reacting. I bet you haven't even met these things up close.

THOMAS - I don't want to be any closer than a snipers rifle.

WIN - Amen!

CAREGIRL - Like that guy in Tucson? He shot a civilian, you know.

THOMAS - The civilian jumped in the way.

CAREGIRL - Like in the movies? Yeah, that's not how it works. In real life, bullets go really fast. He was a psycho, and he didn't care if he killed a few people.

THOMAS - Still...

CAREGIRL - I've seen them up close. They're not big deal. You can get a little goofy at first, but that's all. It's not like they're mind controlling you. Hell, I spent eight hours on a train with some. No ill effects.

THOMAS - Jesus. You mean to tell me you're a Sharer.

CAREGIRL - We don't like that word. We're not fanatics.

WIN - What the hell.

CAREGIRL - Look the ecology is out of whack, species everywhere are out of balance, there's no more natural order left. You act like it's a crime to reintroduce, or introduce species into a damaged ecosystem.

THOMAS - I can't believe this.

CAREGIRL - Yeah, well, if we don't do something pro-active, there isn't going to be an ecosystem left. Then what are you paranoid conspiracy theorists going to do.

***

SHARECROWS NEST - A MESSAGE BOARD, TEN YEARS LATER

AL - There was another plane crash.

JEN - Oh cripes, not this again.

MOD- Al, is this another conspiracy theory? Because this is your third warning. Your privileges are about to be revoked.

AL - Haven't you noticed the last ten years, more plane crashes every year, more accidents, more malfunctions?

JEN - Here it comes. Goodbye Al, it was nice knowing you.

AL - At the same time, their population has skyrocketed. They're everywhere now. They're all over the place. Remember when we used to argue about whether they would attack a person. Now, its official, they eat winos.

KEVIN - Who cares about winos? Remember when everyone was always pissing about the homeless. Remember the crime that came with the homeless. The losers, the addicts, the bunch of them. They don't bother people that can look after themselves. It's just nature, man, and you can't blame them for being natural.

JEN – Nature's law trumps man's law.

AL - And there's cases documented where they'll go into an only child household, and kill the child, and the family just starts to revolve around them.

JEN - Yeah, that's ugly, and we should watch out for that. We should be making sure that the kid can co-exist, that he's not a threat.

AL - No, that's not acceptable. Ten years ago, fifteen, people would have been freaking out about this, people would have been going nuts. Now it's 'who cares about winos' and 'too bad about the kids.'

JEN - That was offensive. I didn't say 'too bad about the kids.' You're not being fair.

AL - Things are changing, and we don't even notice. It's like we're frogs in water that's slowly being brought to a boil, and we just keep sitting there.

JEN - I disagree.

AL - There's studies linking their euphorics with long term cognitive breakdown, permanent neurological changes, and no one is paying attention.

KEVIN - A lot of those studies are exaggerated.

AL - There's more of them around in urban centers than ever before, and they've been around for a long time now. There's evidence their euphorics persist in the environment. No one knows what those concentrations are doing. And we've got planes dropping out of the sky.

KEVIN - I'm not following you. Are you saying that it's causing airplanes to fall apart.

AL - No, I'm saying that euphorics are in the environment, and people aren't as careful, error rates go up, planes fall out of the sky, surgeons make mistakes, mechanics make mistakes, drivers... people are dying.

KEVIN - You're saying that because of Sharebears, people are on the whole happier, and that's a bad thing? Geez, you're delusional on so many levels.

AL - We used to be afraid of sharks. Leopards. Lions. Tigers. Wolves. Saber Tooth tigers. In the end, we beat them all. Nothing could touch us. We were the dominant species. But I think we've found a predator that figured out a way to use us against ourselves, and we have no defence. Their weapon wasn't teeth or claws, it was love and hugs, and we fall for it. We can't stop ourselves from falling for it.

MOD - Final warning, Al.

AL - What happens to prey, when there's a predator that it has no defence against? A predator that we can't kill, because it makes us want to protect it. Everywhere I look, the world is falling apart around me, and no one seems to care. It's not that the evidence isn't there, the studies the predictions, the graphs. No one cares. What's the world going to be like in another ten years? Or five?

MOD - Banned from the list, conspiracy theory and negativity. Goodbye Al. Have a nice life. And for god's sakes, hug a bear, maybe you'll be able to stand yourself.'

The End

A Note and More Books by the Author

If you've skipped to the end, looking for an apology, well... Sorry? Also, no refunds.

Thank you for taking the time out to read my little book. If you've made it all the way here, then I'm just going to assume you liked it.

What else do I have to offer? Well, there's the first volume of this series, a collection imaginatively titled **Drunk Slutty Elf and Other Stories**, as well as a trilogy of collections of horror stories, another trilogy of collections of alternate history stories, another two part alternate history novel, a fantasy murder mystery. For non-fiction, I have three kick ass **Doctor Who Pirate Histories,** and **LEXX Unauthorized**, the chronicle of a cult sci fi series.

If you liked this, could I suggest you leave a review? Mention it on your blog? Or your Facebook? Say nice things. Just toss me a couple of stars? A little appreciation is a wonderful thing. But there's more: It's about trying to get out there. There are a lot of people writing a lot of books, and it can get hard to get noticed. Reviews help.

And speaking of writing more....'
Check out my Website,

denvaldron.com

Drunk Slutty Elf and Other Stories
Hilarious Science Fiction and Fantasy

The first volume of savage, satirical, subversive wicked, funny, frantic science fiction and fantasy. Demented ghost hunters, frustrated aliens, horny giants, drunken elves, sneaky ghosts, wayward barbarians and many more.

ALTERNATE REALITIES
A Trilogy or Strange New Worlds

The Dawn of Cthulhu - The Secret History of H.P.
Lovecraft's Cthulhu Cult; Lost Continents Found – real and
legendary; The Monsters of Sesame Street, is a light hearted
examination of Muppets as if they were actual animals.
The Fall of Atlantis – Retroverse, An Accidental Cinematic
Universe of 50's Sci Fi movies, Greenland Without the Ice,
Rome Crosses the Atlantic, and the Rise and Fall of Atlantis,
an ecological catastrophe.
**The Bear Cavalry, the True (Not!) History of the
Icelandic Bears**, an off the wall, short novel about the
Viking domestication of bears, their evolution into a medieval
cavalry Bonus novelette, The Sharebear Apocalypse.

HEARTS IN DARKNESS
A Trilogy of Horror Collections

Giant Monsters Sing Sad Songs – The connection between the author of the Necronomicon and a boy in Providence; a girl who meets the last Sasquatch, a poet who shares abandoned Tokyo with a Kaiju, and more…

What Devours Also Hungers – The unkillable killers in masks are recruited into the army, vampires and their hunters, clever   monsters, ghosts and more….

There Are No Doors in Dark Places – A childlike cancer that talks to its owner; A single mother drawn into dark magic; A man who turns into a different monster each night; a vampire that twists lives; a pregnant woman finding her body being stolen from her; and many more

AXIS OF ANDES
NEW WORLD WAR
A History of WWII in South America

Berlin, 1937, Adolph Hitler and his cabinet meet with a strange delegation from Ecuador. The delegates from the small South American nation beg for help, fearing an impending invasion from their rival, Peru. What happens at that meeting sets in motion a chain of events that lights the entire continent on fire. By the time it's done, millions are dead, nations are in ruins, and the map of Latin America will be changed beyond recognition.

The Pirate Histories!

What's a Pirate's History, you ask? It's the things they don't want you to know about, or that they don't care about, things that are great and marvellous and intriguing... but unapproved. It's a history of secret and forgotten corners of the Whoniverse. The first woman Doctor, the first black Doctor, animations, audios, the stage plays and fan films.

A Dark Fantasy of Murder and Redemption

There's a City where all the races come together uneasily, descending into civil war.

There's a Mermaid, murdered cruelly her people distraught and crying out for justice.

There's an Orc, the lowest and the worst, her mission: Solve the murder, before it all comes crashing down.

She finds something else... the world's first serial killer.

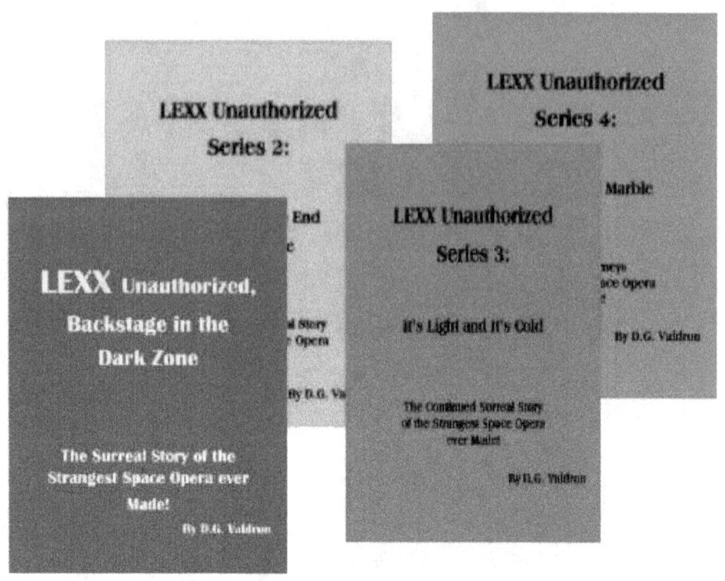

LEXX UNAUTHORIZED

LEXX Unauthorized about the making of a show about a giant space bug that blows up planets, the cowardly security guard who is its captain, and the undead assassin, runaway love slave, and robot head who form its crew.

Originally billed as 'Star Trek's Evil Twin,' the cultiest of cult sci fi, LEXX's forte was black humor, startling visuals, big ideas, and a sensibility that had more to do with surrealists like Jodorowsky or Bunuel than mainstream science fiction. And, as unconventional as it was onscreen, the story of how it came to be is even more bizarre.